BEHOLDEN TO YOU

Carlie Sexton

Cover Image by Najla Qamber Designs
http://najlaqamberdesigns.com/

Edited by Marion Archer
www.makingmanuscripts.com

The author acknowledges the copyrighted or trademarked status and trademark owners of the following wordmarks mentioned in this book of fiction:
Starbuck's, Victoria's Secret, The Blue Man Group, Jaws, Bellagio, ESPN, Hot Wok, Mama Mia's Big Bang Theory, Tiffany's Jeweler, Pehoe's Restaurant, Nordstrom, It's a Wonderful Life, Harry Connick Jr., It Had to be You, Michael Buble, The Man I love, At Last, 7 Up, The Princess Bride, Eyes Wide Open, Barbie.

DEDICATION

To my wonderful husband who has supported me throughout this amazing journey of becoming a writer. Your love means everything to me. Thank you for inspiring me to write such a loving man like Mac Carter.

ACKNOWLEDGEMENTS

When I began writing, my intention was to write one book, Fallen for You (The Killer Next Door.) My one book turned into a trilogy, much to my surprise. When I created a scene for Mac and Natalie in book 2, Taken by You, I realized I had a story to tell about them. Now they have a book of their very own and I am planning on spinning off some other characters as well. Neil and Kate will be in each of the spin offs as they are the reason I developed the secondary characters. I am blessed and grateful to be able to share my stories with you.

So many people have helped me, taught me, listened to me, advised me, and loved me through this incredible venture. Of course, none of this would have come to fruition if not for a dear friend at work Darren. Thanks Darren for not knowing the meaning of anonymous and sharing so much with me so I could realize this dream of being an author.

To my amazing friend Raine, you have inspired me and taught me more than I could ever imagine. Thank you for your support and love. You are a gift to everyone who knows you.

To my dear friend Jacelyn, writing books alongside of you has been more incredible than I could have imagined. Being able to talk to you every day about our characters, developing our stories, and fulfilling this dream has been extraordinary. I am so grateful to have you in my life.

To Najla Qamber, thanks for making a rockin' cover. Your patience paid off and it is perfect. Thank you for tweaking it just one more time.

To my spectacular editor Marion Archer. You have helped me in ways that are immeasurable. You have taken my words on the page and not just tidied them up, you have shown me how to breathe life into them. I'm so grateful for you.

To my street team. You share my books even when I am too tired to share. Thank you for you love and dedication to The Killer Next Door series and now to Beholden to You. You all are such a blessing to me.

Finally, to the bloggers who have read, reviewed, shared, supported, and become treasured new friends. Thank you for reading my work and posting on your phenomenal pages! Without you, I don't think anyone would know I'm alive!!

I love all of you so much!
xoxo~ Carlie

PROLOGUE: THANKSGIVING

I checked the bathroom, but Natalie wasn't there. Deciding to go outside, I found her sitting on the terrace, and sat beside her. Natalie was crying and had her head down, resting it on the back of the sofa. She barely noticed my presence.

"Are you doing okay?" I asked, taking her hand.

She looked up me with a trembling lip. "No, not really, Mac. It's only been a few years since my parents passed and just two weeks since my sister was killed in a car accident. It's hurting so much today. It was a mistake for me to come. When Mr. Statton prayed about being thankful, all I could think about was what I've lost. I feel so alone without my family."

I nodded and kept holding her hand. "I can understand, to a degree, how you feel. I felt the same way when my parents died, but for me it was many years ago. I miss them, but I don't feel like I'm grieving their loss anymore."

"When does the grief end? I just want it to go away."

"I hate to say it, but it's going to take time. Years probably. You'll think you're fine, and then something will hit you and you'll miss them with the same intensity as before. I'm not sure it ever completely goes away."

Natalie exhaled loudly. "I had finally felt okay with it being just Jessica and me. We had made it through the darkest part and were moving on. Now that she's gone, I feel like I have fallen down a deep well and there's no way out."

Tears continued streaming down Natalie's beautiful face. I wanted to kiss them away, make her forget everything, but I didn't.

"Come here," I said, pulling her closer. I put my arms around her and held her as she cried, her head resting on my chest. I didn't know why, but I felt strongly connected to Natalie. Perhaps it was our similar pasts—losing our loved ones. Unsure of where it came from, I felt a need to protect her and watch over her.

"Do you want me to take you home?" I asked.

She pulled away far enough to look me in the eyes. "Would you? I really want to go. I can't stay and do small talk."

I got up and held my hand out to her. She took it, and I escorted her back into the house.

"I'm going to take Natalie home. She's not feeling well," I announced. Just like that, Natalie Mason entered my life and nothing was ever going to be the same.

CHAPTER 1: NATALIE

Putting my hand to my head, I realized the many drinks I had consumed the night before were still leaving a lasting impression. People say the morning after is horrible. My eyes were open, but focusing on my surroundings was proving to be a challenge. Slowly rolling over in bed, I found an unfamiliar figure under the sheets. It was the first time I had found a man in my bed because I had promised my dying mother I would remain a virgin until I was married. So much for keeping promises. I thought it was my bed, but wasn't sure since I didn't actually know where I was at that moment. Looking around for anything familiar, I realized I must be in his hotel room. His back was to me, but I knew exactly who he was. I didn't speak at first, not knowing what to say. "Good morning" probably would suffice, but the words were stuck in my throat.

I covered my mouth in horror as the night before came crashing back to me. We had been drinking to celebrate the engagements of Kate and Neil and Charlie and Mitch, my dearest friends, who were both moving on with their lives, marrying the men of their dreams. And there I was in his bed, in his hotel room. I felt like I was waking up to a nightmare.

I've heard all the advertisements claiming that "what happens in Vegas stays in Vegas," but I wasn't sure how that was going to play out, especially since I had no idea if anyone saw us enter the room together. *Wait a minute*, Mac and I had left early. Oh, how my head hurt from my unwise decision to overindulge in libations that had obviously taken away all my inhibitions.

Even though I clearly had a great time with Mac the night before, feelings began to swirl around in my mind. Losing Jessica for one, welled up inside of me. My baby sister gone without warning. Mac had been so attentive that I had dropped my defenses and let him in. I hadn't done that since ...Ty. That got me thinking about Ty and how much I had wanted him, still wanted him. But, he was a million miles away and made it clear he'd moved on. I needed to move on too, but it had been easier to stay stuck in the past than risk being hurt again.

I lifted the sheets and found a small amount of blood. I could tell by the soreness between my legs that we'd had sex, and all those years being a good girl, and saving myself for my husband, were down the drain from one night of drunken stupor. *What was I thinking? Why had drowning my pain in alcohol seemed so appealing?* Someone once said there are no accidents. Maybe my actions were on purpose: my subconscious acting out because I was too chicken to take a chance with Mac when sober. *Would I be brave enough when he woke and I wasn't under the influence?* I got up to go to the bathroom, hoping a robe hung on the back of the door. I needed the feeling of cozy fluffiness to embrace my body. Maybe the robe could cover my body, but nothing was going to cover up what I had done with the man still sleeping. Fortunately, a fluffy chenille robe was waiting for me. *Thank* God.

As I washed my hands, I felt something unfamiliar on my left hand. *What the hell?* I don't remember having this ring. Why would I have a ring on my left hand? Oh, my head hurt. Gazing at the ring, it seemed impossible this was happening, that I'd be waking up to an alternate reality.

In a panic, I ran out of the bathroom to wake up my sleeping stranger. Well, he wasn't technically a stranger. I had met him once before, on Thanksgiving, at Neil's parent's home and we had been keeping in touch though texting. When he offered to drive me to Vegas I was elated, and jumped at the chance to spend some time with him, which was completely unlike me. I liked this man and probably ruined everything by sleeping with him on what I had considered our first date.

The drive had been so much fun and we talked nonstop about everything and nothing. I didn't even spend much time thinking about Jessica. It was a relief to say the least, and strangely, I felt relaxed with Mac. He seemed to understand me without explanation.

"Mac," I said, shaking his shoulder. "Wake up."

Mac began to stir, but he wasn't fully waking up. I went toward the drapes and pulled them open, inviting the bright sunshine to illuminate the room, but had to cover my eyes from the searing pain in my head, opening them had created.

"Oh, my head. Close the drapes...please," he murmured.

"I need you to wake up and tell me what happened last night, Mac."

"What do you mean, what happened last night?"

"I have a ring on my finger telling me something happened. A ring on my left hand ring finger. Did we do something crazy? Do you remember?"

Mac sat straight up in bed. The sheet pooled around his hips revealing his upper body. His bare chest looked like a work of art sculpted by Michael Angelo. I had thought he was good looking with his sandy brown hair, big blue eyes, Hollywood smile, and the slight beard framing his face, but I had no idea his clothes were hiding all that. Mac swung his legs out of bed and got up, revealing the whole package. Every part of him looked like it had been chiseled by a master. I tried to avert my eyes as he walked past me, but I couldn't tear them away. Mac was one magnificent man.

When he came out of the bathroom a few minutes later, he was wearing the other bathrobe, looked like he'd washed his face, and had a hand towel around his neck. He looked like he had taken a minute to regroup. I was a little disappointed he was covered up, as part of me would have liked another viewing of his muscled physique. I felt myself turning crimson at my own lustful thoughts of him.

"How about some water?" he asked, as he reached for an overpriced bottled water the hotel supplied. Obviously, for times like this.

"Thanks," I said, as he handed me a bottle.

We both took a moment, and I drank practically half of it in one long gulp.

I frowned at him and asked again, "Do you know what happened last night?"

"I think we got married last night."

"What?" I practically screamed at him.

"Take a look for yourself," he said, lifting a piece of paper toward me. I took the paper out of his hand and sat on the sofa next to him, staring at it, blinking my eyes, as if that was going to change what I was seeing. Sure enough, it had both of our signatures on it and indicated we were married.

"This can't be. We can't be married," I said, as I stared at the piece of paper that somehow had to be a joke.

"I'm afraid it can be. We got married last night."

"Do you think anybody knows? Do you remember any part of this?"

"I remember us drinking and making out. But as far as tying the knot, I don't know. I'm not sure how we went from partying with our friends to the here and now."

"Okay, let's just think for a minute," I said, getting up to pace the floors. "Maybe we can retrace our steps if we each talk about what we remember."

Mac nodded. "Do you want to go first?"

"Sure. We started out in the limo with Kate, Neil, Charlie, and Mitch. We all had champagne in our hands and we were toasting the happy couples."

"I remember that," Mac said nodding. "Continue."

"We arrived at the first place and we had shots of tequila. I know I had at least two shots. How many did you have?"

"I think I might have had three."

"After that, you and I danced for a while. A slow song came on and you pulled me close. It was nice," I said, a smile spreading across my face as I looked down at my fingers. It was a little unnerving discussing the details with him in his hotel room wearing bathrobes with nothing underneath.

Mac gave me a devilish smile. "Glad I could be of service," he said, waggling his eyebrows. He was such a guy.

I rolled my eyes and slightly shook my head. "Anyway, at the next place we had more shots. I think I was pretty much drunk by then. We danced some more and kissed during another slow song."

Mac rubbed his jaw with his fingers. "I most definitely recall kissing you. I think we decided we would catch a cab and come back to the hotel. You were feeling dizzy or something."

"Okay, well how did we go from getting a cab back here to getting married? That seems like quite the leap."

"Well, maybe you just found me irresistible," Mac said, with a lopsided grin that I was beginning to find *irresistible*. But I didn't want him to know that.

"I'm sure many women find you attractive, but I was waiting to give myself to the man I love, not some guy with an overinflated ego."

"What do you mean by waiting?" he asked, with a scrunched up face.

"What do you think I mean?" I practically barked back at him.

Mac sat there for a minute not saying anything. "I think we both need some aspirin and a drink. He got up and made his way to the mini fridge. Opening it, he found a beer, cracked it open and took a sip. He came toward me and handed me the bottle.

"A few sips will help you to feel better."

I took a few sips, mortified at what I had just admitted to him— that he had taken my virginity—that I had handed it to him on a silver platter. I gave the beer back to him after taking one last swig.

"So, we had…"

"Yes, we did."

"Are you sure?"

"Yes, I am."

"Did you have a good time?"

At that, I laughed, which hurt my head.

"I don't know. I don't remember."

"Then how do you know we did anything?"

I got up and lifted the covers on the bed. "Here's some evidence," I said pointing to the bed. "Also, I can just tell," I said, giving him a hard look.

"Okay," he said, nodding.

I sat there for a moment, an unreal moment. I couldn't believe what was happening to me. I stared off into the distance as if taking a mental vacation would somehow bring clarity to the situation.

"Can I ask you a question?" Mac inquired.

"Of course."

"Did you basically just tell me you were a virgin until last night? That you were waiting to have sex until you got married?"

Oh, he finally got it. I groaned quietly. "That would be correct. I had promised my mother on her death bed I would do things the right way in my life. Part of that promise was waiting until marriage to have sex. I just want her to be proud of me even if I can't hear her express the words."

Mac picked up the marriage license. "Well, it looks like you haven't disappointed her. We are married. I know it's not ideal, but you technically didn't break your word to your mom."

I took a moment to let his words sink in. "You're right. At least we are married. Thanks for pointing that out. But what are we going to do now?"

"I don't know. I haven't been in a situation like this before. What do you think we should do?"

"Well, for starters, I don't want to tell anyone. I don't want to steal the limelight from Kate or Charlie. They each deserve to be the center of attention. Plus, Kate has been going through so much lately, I don't want to add to her worries."

"I can agree with that. What else?"

I ran my hand through my hair. "Why don't we figure this out when we get back to San Diego."

"Okay. We can get an annulment if you want to," Mac said. He didn't look convinced about that. Odd.

"An annulment seems like the most logical thing to do," I said, looking around to find my purse and clothes. As I moved past the bed, I tripped on the bedspread and fell onto Mac. Fortunately, he broke my fall and there I was covering his body with mine. We were nose to nose for a minute and I couldn't help become dizzy by his heavenly manly scent. A flash of him kissing me blazed a trail through my mind, and how good it felt to have his lips on mine. Mac's eyes were locked with mine and I saw a fierce passion resonate in them. I quickly pushed myself up, using his shoulders to do it, not wanting to reveal my desire for him.

"Are you okay, Natalie?" Mac asked me, with concern on his handsome face.

"Yeah, I'm fine." All I wanted was to get dressed and run until my clumsy feet couldn't carry me anymore. I didn't need the complication of being attracted to Mac. He was a nice guy and all, but I had too much to deal with in the coming months.

"I'm going to get dressed in the bathroom," I said, as I picked up my clothes off the floor.

Getting out of his hotel room was my number one priority at that point. I locked the bathroom door behind me, not wanting any more surprises. Taking off the robe I slipped on my panties, then my bra. Finally, I stepped into my dress and zipped it up the side. All I needed were my shoes and I could go back to my room. I took a quick look in the mirror. My blonde locks were tussled and my mascara smudged. I rubbed away the mascara underneath my eyes and ran my fingers through my hair. I might be freaking out, but I wanted to have some semblance of being put together.

When I returned to the bedroom, I found Mac sitting and texting. I heard the familiar buzz on my phone, letting me know I had a text waiting for me. Mac looked up, his blue eyes captivating me. "Neil just sent me a reminder about meeting for breakfast in about forty minutes."

I picked up my phone to find a similar text from Kate. "Great, I'll see you down there. Let's just act like nothing happened."

He looked at me and smiled, saying, "Whatever you want to do is fine."

I could see myself falling for this man. He doesn't seemed freaked out at all. He's so calm. Is that how he really is?

I nodded and then turned toward the door. I was out of his room within seconds. Hopefully leaving his life would be just as easy, although somehow, I had a feeling it wouldn't. I pushed the button on the elevator. My room was two floors above Mac's and I needed to shower before going down to breakfast. At least I had enough time to get ready.

CHAPTER 2: MAC

What just happened? I looked at the marriage license again. For some reason, I wasn't as bothered about this as I should be. Cassie pushed marriage and I ended our relationship. I didn't want to marry her. But, Natalie was different somehow. She genuinely cared about other people, and the fact she didn't want to steal Kate or Charlie's thunder, said a lot about her character. Plus, she was so damn beautiful. I could very easily lose myself in her long blonde hair and curvy body. How was it she hadn't been with anyone before? I found that so hard to believe. Keeping a promise like that to her mother was unfathomable.

I wanted to stop her from leaving my room but she was like a scared rabbit, and I was afraid any big movements from me would cause her to run. But she ran, anyway.

I went into the bathroom and turned on the shower, which I desperately needed to deliver me from the alcohol-induced haze. My muscles welcomed the hot water cascading down my body. I wouldn't have minded if Natalie had been a different kind of girl and actually joined me for that shower. I'd love an instant replay of the night before, to be perfectly honest. But, part of me was glad she was a woman with convictions.

When Natalie had looked at me with her big blue eyes, there'd been too much pressure to be able to recall specific details from the night before. However, relaxed from the shower, it all came back to me. I was excited to have, what I presumed was, a date with Natalie. Our drive in from San Diego had felt effortless; she was so easy to talk to. Neil had said a lot of great things about her and suggested

I spend some time with her. So, I did just that. She didn't seem to mind my attention, either. After the two tequila shots, she and I were having fun, laughing and dancing. When we slow danced, I felt something. She tugged at my heart in a way no one else ever had before. Here was the gorgeous woman who had just suffered a tragic loss, and she had put her friends before herself, by coming out here to celebrate their lives. There was something incredibly alluring about that...about her.

When we had additional shots at the next club, we ended up making out in the booth while the others were out dancing. I remember suggesting we go back to my room. That's when she told me she was waiting for marriage. It was all slowly coming into focus. When I heard that, I think I suggested we get married! *Shit! What did I do?* I freaked her out, that's what I did. She probably thinks I just did whatever it took to get into her panties.

Okay, wait a minute. She had said yes. I know she was drunk, but she still said *yes* and married me. That must mean she was as interested in me as I am in her, even though she comes across so reserved. Being in bed with her was anything but. I put my hands on the shower wall. *Damn.* Making love to her was coming back to me—every moment was hot. When I closed my eyes I could feel Natalie's mouth on my body, her gorgeous breasts pressed against my chest and her tight spot that I had fit into so nicely. *Shit.* I opened my eyes with the realization I didn't want an annulment. I wanted to see where this took us even though we had done it backwards. Another man having her in his bed was out of the question. I wanted her to be mine. I shook my head as if cobwebs would fly out. *How could I be this irrational about a woman I hardly knew?*

I turned off the water, dried, and wondered how I was going to get to know the beautiful creature with golden hair, crystal blue eyes, and a heart that I wanted for mine. *How am I going to convince her to give us a try?* She was unlike any woman I had ever met and I didn't want to let her slip through my fingers.

CHAPTER 3: NATALIE

Closing the door behind me, I was grateful to be back in my own room. Peeling out of my clothes, I quickly got into the shower. It felt like an oasis, the water caressing my body. Thoughts of Mac and I in bed were coming back to me like rapid fire from a machine gun. These thoughts startled me as my body began to respond to the pictures in my mind. Mac knew his way around a female's body and it certainly felt as though he had pulled out all the stops with me. When I closed my eyes I could visualize his head between my legs. The memory of it made my insides clench down deep. Then I remembered the culmination of his efforts and my body's response in a tantalizing orgasm. It was unlike anything I had ever experienced before.

I had to push those thoughts out of my head because the whole situation was crazy. We got married, and he didn't seem to be taken aback by it. In fact, he was calm about the whole thing. Strange reaction for a guy. I felt kind of bad for running out of there like I did, but when I fell on him, things became real—too real. In that moment I began remembering our intimate interaction, and for a split second, I thought about surrendering to my desire for him. Again. Willingly. While sober. If I had, we'd be in bed together, and he'd be doing...

No, I wasn't going to torture myself. I needed to get ready for breakfast. Hopefully Kate and Charlie were so wrapped up with their men they wouldn't ask me too many questions about where Mac and I went.

I got out of the shower and began getting ready. Fifteen minutes later, I was out the door and making my way down to the restaurant. I wasn't the first one there, Mac was. He was drinking coffee at a table for six. Walking up to him, I felt butterflies in my stomach. He stood when I approached, the look on his gorgeous face penetrating my heart and making my insides melt. He pulled out a chair for me and motioned for me to sit.

"Natalie, let me just start by saying I'm sorry about last night. Obviously, neither of us were expecting to wake up married this morning."

I let out a sigh and watched Mac pour me a cup of coffee from the carafe. "Mac, this isn't your fault. You didn't force me to marry you. I did it of my own free will, even if my will was completely plastered."

Mac smiled. "What I'm about to say might scare you, and I hope it doesn't, but I only came on this trip because you were coming. I wanted to get to know you."

I searched Mac's eyes for malice, but only saw sincerity. I decided to let my guard down and be honest, too. "Looks like we have something in common then. I'm here because of you, too. You've been so sweet to me and I feel I can trust you."

Mac put his hand on mine. "Okay then, what do you say we forget about being married and focus on getting to know each other. We can just see what happens."

I was a little worried about the *see what happens* part because I didn't think I would be able to control myself with him if we were alone. His hand on mine made my insides squeamish and my heart rate increase. I nodded my agreement as Kate and Neil joined us at the table.

"Good morning," they both said in unison and then giggled. Being in love seriously agreed with Kate.

"Good morning," Mac and I each said separately.

"So did you guys end up having a good night when you left us?" Kate asked.

"Well, you know Natalie wasn't feeling well so I got her to her hotel room and she went to bed. Then I turned in, myself."

"Are you feeling better?" Neil asked.

"Yes, I'm good as new. Slept like a baby." *Was I overselling this?* I had no idea.

Neil poured coffee for Kate and himself. He was always so attentive to her. It occurred to me Mac was the same way with me. The way he held the chair out for me, and poured my coffee—it was just so instinctive to him. I could get used to having attention lavished upon me.

Charlie and Mitch showed up and we all made our way to the buffet. Everything looked so good but I didn't want to overdo it considering I felt like a train wreck. At least the coffee was helping my headache. When we sat down I observed that everyone's plate was loaded with food except for mine. I hoped no one noticed, but I began asking questions about the plan for the day, just in case.

"What time are we going for our massage?" I asked Kate.

"We're booked at noon. We should have just enough time after eating to get there on time."

The men began talking about golf and their anticipation about playing at the best course in Vegas. Kate continued to expound on the different massages the hotel had to offer. Both Kate and Charlie were excited to go shopping afterward and all I could think about was not revealing what happened between Mac and I.

I usually loved the idea of shopping, but I wanted to lounge at the pool and have Mac lube me up with suntan lotion instead. My cheeks flushed at my own thoughts. Where was this coming from? What had he unleashed in me last night? I hadn't felt like this since...Ty.

It was almost time for us to make our way to the spa and the men to depart for golf. Kate and Neil kissed goodbye as did Charlie and Mitch. Part of me felt a yearning to kiss Mac, but didn't act upon my impulse. Keeping things under wrap for a while might prove harder than I anticipated.

We made our way to the hotel spa and I attempted to keep the conversation light—about the pending nuptials, nothing about the prior night. Entering the spa, the scent of gardenia overtook me, soothing my frazzled nerves. I was looking forward to the massage—an hour of complete quiet, to be alone with my thoughts and have my troubles caressed away.

We walked up to the reception area to check in.

"Hi, I'm Kate Simmons. This is Charlie Andrews and Natalie Mason. We have massages scheduled at twelve."

The receptionist pulled up our appointments, then directed us to follow the woman standing next to her. The spa was a haven of tranquility and with every step I felt more at ease. We were directed to a seating area and told our masseurs would be with us momentarily. I had a feeling when we sat on the luxurious sofas the inquiry would begin.

"So, Nat. What happened when you and Mac left last night?" Charlie asked. Both Kate and Charlie stared at me intently.

"He brought me back to the hotel, made sure I got into my room, and I assume went to his room," I replied.

"That's it?" Kate questioned. "Nothing else happened? You two were making out pretty heavily at the bar."

"Yes. Mac was a perfect gentleman. He made sure I was safe and the next thing I knew I was seeing him for breakfast." I felt bad lying to my friends, but it had to be done. I didn't want to cast a shadow on their special weekend. The weekend was meant to be about them. I guess I also wasn't ready to divulge I had gotten married before each of them, to a man I'd known for a split second.

"Well, do you like him? Do you think you'll see him after this weekend?" Charlie asked.

A small smile crossed my face. "Yeah, I like him." Both Kate and Charlie squealed. Apparently if you are in love you want everyone else to be in love, too.

"This is so exciting," Kate said. "Mac is a great guy. I think you two would be really good together."

"Me too," Charlie chimed in.

Thankfully, the inquisition ended as we were each greeted by our masseurs. I had the next sixty minutes to attempt to silence my thoughts and just drift.

We each followed our perspective therapists to our own private rooms. Jackie, my therapist, instructed me to remove my clothes and lay face down on the table. As I laid face down on the table waiting for her to return to the room, it occurred to me this was the first day I hadn't cried over my little sister Jessica who had died so recently, in a senseless car crash. I dreaded the fact I was going to have to face the driver responsible for her death in court in a few weeks. The grief had washed over me every day, but today was different. The enormity of being with Mac had been an unexpected diversion from my overwhelming sadness. I knew life had to go on. It went on after each of my parents died, but I had Jessica to get me through it. Kate and Charlie assured me they were here for me, but with them both becoming wives, things were going to change. Then it dawned on me. Technically…I'm a wife. Surprisingly, I felt warmth overtake me as my mind grasped the concept of being Mac's wife. Mac reminded me of the kindest man I had ever known—a man I could trust and count on no matter what happened—my dad.

My massage therapist entered the room and began asking me questions about my preferences. I told her I liked deep tissue. She didn't talk during the massage except to check on the pressure. This was the first time since the accident I allowed my brain to surrender to nothingness, as she seemed to rub my troubles away. Between the calming sound of the ocean playing in the background and her expert hands, I was lulled into a tranquil state of mind.

CHAPTER 4: MAC

The distraction of golf was a huge relief after everything that happened this morning. I was, however, stoked Natalie admitted she came on this trip to get to know me. That was music to my ears.

Neil and Mitch did most of the talking on the way to the course. I gave the occasional acknowledgement token, but my mind was on Natalie. She had pierced my heart and I wanted to be with her, not here in the car with the guys. It was actually surprising that I felt this need to make everything right in her world. I felt driven to become her world. How had that happened so quickly? But I was stuck golfing instead. The irony wasn't lost on me—I loved the game, but I wanted Natalie more.

I was so preoccupied that I anticipated I would have a shitty round. That's the way it is with golf. If your head is somewhere else your game sucks.

Neil parked the car, we retrieved our golf clubs, and began walking to check in. Since there were three of us, we got two golf carts. I volunteered to drive alone, letting Neil and Mitch share. It was perfect. I didn't have to make small talk. My mind could have a chance to absorb everything I was feeling from the events of the last twenty four hours.

We got to the first tee box and when I hit the ball I hooked it to the left, into the trees. It was the lousiest shot I'd made in a long time.

"Mac, are you okay?" Neil asked. "I haven't seen you hit like that since we were in middle school."

"I guess I'm just tired from drinking last night," I said, hoping that would be the end of it. The good thing about golfing was we had to keep moving on and the lawyer in Neil couldn't question me for too long.

I tried to get out of my own head, but it was no use. Natalie was on my mind and there was nothing I could do about it. Flashes of the two of us in bed kept resurfacing, making it difficult to concentrate.

The round took just over four hours and we decided to stop at the clubhouse for a drink before heading back. This made me a little nervous because I had never been able to keep a secret from Neil. He was my best friend in the world—a brother. He had seen me through some of my darkest hours.

We sat at a table next to the window with an expansive view of the golf course. The waitress took our order and once she was gone, I knew I was in for it. I attempted to postpone the inevitable for as long as possible.

"So, how's Kate holding up with Roger still on the loose?"

"She's scared to death. He's got some pretty skilled stalker skills. But don't ask her about him. She doesn't want to talk about it," Neil replied.

"I can understand that. It's insane what a close call she had with him."

"Yeah, but that's not going to happen again. I'm going to make sure of it."

"She's lucky to have you man."

"Thanks," Neil said with a quizzical look. His brow creased and I knew the moment of truth was upon me.

"Mac, what's going on?" Neil asked. "You've been acting weird all day."

My first inclination was to lie and say I was fine. But I knew Neil. He was like a dog with a bone and he wasn't going to let go of this until I came clean. We'd known each other too long, and been through too much together, for me to pull one over on him.

"You can't tell anyone...including Kate and Charlie. Otherwise, I won't tell you."

Mitch put up his hands. "Bro, I won't breathe a word, I promise."

"Well, I think you know by now you can trust me," Neil said, a little exasperated.

I inhaled deeply, needing all the oxygen possible for what I was about to say. "Last night, after Natalie and I left the bar, we kind of got...married."

Neither of them said anything at first. The silence became deafening as they both sat there staring at me with their mouths hanging open slightly. The waitress returned with our drinks and I took a big swig. Natalie was going to kill me if she found out I said something.

Neil's brow furrowed more. "What the fuck are you talking about?" Now he was more than exasperated. He sounded pissed.

"We were drunk and somehow we ended up getting married. The worst part is, she was waiting until she was married to have sex and last night was her first time. She doesn't even remember it."

Mitch sat there shaking his head. "Shit, man. What are you going to do?"

"We decided this morning not to tell anyone because Natalie doesn't want to take the spotlight away from Kate and Charlie. I mentioned getting an annulment when we go back to San Diego. That's about all we discussed."

"I can handle the annulment if you want," Neil said.

"Well I'm not sure if I want an annulment. Nat and I had a few minutes at breakfast before you arrived, and it turns out we both came on this Vegas trip because of each other. I really like her and want to get to know her better."

"Natalie's in a vulnerable place right now and you've known her for what, five minutes?" Mitch snarled. "You hardly know anything about her."

"We can figure this out, Mitch," Neil said. "Everything is going to be okay."

"Natalie's been through more than most people and I don't want to see her get hurt, that's all," Mitch said, leaning back in his chair and crossing his arms.

"Well, I'd like to be there for her. I know she's lost her parents, her sister...she has to face the guy responsible in court. Maybe she could use my support and who knows, things could work out."

"There's more than that," Mitch said sighing. "She was in love with a guy who broke her heart pretty badly, and she hasn't dated since. He shredded her, man, and I don't want to see her get hurt again. So you better be damn sure if you are going to pursue her."

"Neil can vouch for me that I'm a stand-up guy and I'm not a player. The last relationship I had lasted two years." *Damn, who was this guy? Her attack dog?*

"Okay, fair enough. So what's your plan?" Mitch asked.

"I'm not sure. I really want to date her, but we're already married."

"Nothing's stopping you from dating her," Neil said. "Don't mention getting an annulment again and just see what happens. Pull out all the stops and sweep her off her feet."

I took in what Neil was saying. "I can always count on you to come up with a plan. Thanks, bro."

CHAPTER 5: NATALIE

The massage relaxed me and I was hoping I wouldn't have to answer too many questions about Mac. But, Kate and Charlie were so giddy about being brides it seemed they just couldn't help themselves. We had made our way to a fabulous shopping center and the questions began.

"So, is Mac a good kisser?" Kate wanted to know.

I smiled coyly. "Yes, he is." I didn't want to say too much on the subject, but feelings for Mac were beginning to well up inside of me.

"I could tell last night and this morning that he really likes you, Nat. Do you think you could see yourself with him?" Charlie asked, as we approached Victoria's Secret.

"Maybe…I don't know. It's been a long time since Ty, and I'm finally over him. I think I'm ready to move forward, and so far, Mac has been amazing." Staying vague might be the ticket here in this conversation. Plus, I wasn't sure if I was trying to convince them or myself I had moved on.

On one of the racks near the entrance, Kate found a beautiful white negligee and showed it to us. The entire bodice was lace with beads sewn onto it.

"That's gorgeous. You should try that on," I commented.

"I think you should try on some things too, Nat. I have a feeling you're going to need some lingerie in the near future," Kate said with a smile.

I looked bashfully at Kate and said, "I could use some new bras and panties." With that statement, my two dearest friends went into hyper-drive, selecting items for not only themselves but for me as well. A sales girl approached us, took our items, and started a fitting room for each of us.

After trying on what seemed like half the store, I had three bra and panty sets and two nighties. Kate and Charlie had an arm full of beautiful items. We made our purchases, and found a much-needed Starbuck's to refuel.

We ordered our drinks and each selected a sandwich. Once we sat down, my mind wandered to Jessica and the many times we went to Starbuck's. Charlie seemed to read my mind and asked, "How are you holding up, Nat?"

I knew what she was referring to, as with good friends, there was no need for elaboration. "Today is the first day I haven't cried," I said. "Being here with all of you, and getting to know Mac, has been a distraction I really needed."

Charlie reached over and grabbed my hand. "We're so glad you came on this trip with us. It wouldn't be the same without you."

"Me too," I admitted. "To be honest, as much as I want to support you both in your weddings, Mac was a motivating factor for coming this weekend. I wanted the opportunity to get to know him better." I just didn't have any idea how much better that was going to be.

Kate leaned back in her chair. "How are you feeling about going to court next month?"

"I'm not looking forward to it, but I want justice for my sister. If Justin hadn't been high, then maybe he wouldn't have lost control of the car. The District Attorney is going for manslaughter."

"I've decided to cut back my classes and be part-time next semester. I can go with you if you want me to," Kate offered. "When does the trial begin?"

"That would be so great, but it's scheduled to begin on January fourth. You'll be in Maui," I said, feeling the anxiety of this upcoming ordeal resting on my shoulders.

"Oh, Nat, I had no idea. Maybe the girls from work can take turns going with you on their days off," Kate said.

"I'll see what everyone has going on," I said. But the truth of the matter was I expected to go through the trial alone. Like usual.

We finished our sandwiches and decided to do more shopping. It was carefree and easy, and nothing had felt that way for weeks. Nothing, except being with Mac. Kate and Charlie each had an agenda of finding outfits to wear for wedding related occasions like bridal showers, rehearsal dinners, and honeymoons. It warmed my heart to see them so happy. When all was said and done we each had our arms filled with shopping bags. I found a few cute outfits which I hoped to wear on dates with Mac.

We returned to the hotel to relax before dinner. It was late afternoon and we knew the guys would be back soon. Walking into my room, I set the alarm, and immediately laid down. I was sleeping within minutes.

CHAPTER 6: MAC

The entire car ride back to the hotel all I could think about was Natalie. It was imperative I talk to her before we went out with our friends. Our conversation had been interrupted earlier, and I wanted to make certain she wasn't uncomfortable with our situation. I had dated enough women to know that sometimes they say one thing and really mean another, or they just changed their minds for reasons that were beyond my comprehension.

I knocked on Natalie's door uncertain of what I would find. After a moment, she answered wearing a robe. Her smile indicated she was happy to see me. I felt relief, as that was the response I was hoping for.

"Hey Nat. Did I catch you at a bad time?"

"I was just taking a nap. Come in," she said, opening the door wider.

I walked past her and made my way to the small living room area. I sat on the sofa next to her bed. She followed me and sat next to me which I took as a good sign. "I just wanted to finish our conversation from this morning. I want to make sure you're feeling okay. You know, about us, about everything."

"That's so sweet of you, Mac," she said, placing her hand on my arm.

The feel of her touch had more of an effect on me than I was expecting.

"I'll admit I was upset this morning, but our talk at breakfast put me at ease, especially since we both came to Vegas for the same reason." She looked so open and carefree all I wanted to do was scoop her into my arms and kiss her. "I'm going to lay my cards on the table, no pun intended. I like you. I have from the moment you walked into the Statton's kitchen. I'd like for us to get to know each other better and I want to start dating you when we return to San Diego. How do you feel about that?"

Natalie looked down at her hands for a moment. When she looked up at me she had a coy smile on her face. "I'd like that."

I was so happy I acted on impulse. I leaned in and kissed her, gently at first, but then I couldn't hold back and I invaded her mouth with my tongue, stroking hers in an erotic dance. My hands found her waist and I pulled her toward me, positioning her on top of me, her legs straddling my hips. She kissed me back with a passion I hadn't experienced before, like she had been dying to be kissed and I was the cure. I untied her robe and slid my hands around her ribs. She was wearing a tank top and boxers. I debated running my hands over her breasts, but in light of her inexperience, I didn't want to move too fast. So I just continued kissing her, pulling her body close to mine as she moaned in my mouth, causing my blood to overheat. I wanted her and I wanted her bad.

Natalie pulled away and said, "We should slow down. I'm not ready to go this fast." Her face was flushed, and her breathing, ragged.

I looked into her beautiful blue eyes and moved her hair off her face. "All I want to do is kiss you. Hold you. I don't want to do anything you're going to feel uncomfortable with. I'm not in any hurry."

Natalie put her forehead to mine. "Thank you. I know this isn't ideal for you, but I appreciate you being so considerate of my feelings."

"Well, my mom raised me to be a gentleman."

"I can tell. You've been amazing to me from the moment we met."

I nuzzled her delicate nose with my own for that compliment, and decided I better get out of her hotel room if I was going to have a shot at staying a gentleman.

"I better go since we have to meet for dinner in less than an hour."

"Okay," Natalie said, as she got off my lap and sat next to me.

I got up before I changed my mind, and made my way to the door. "I'll see you soon."

"See you soon," she echoed.

CHAPTER 7: NATALIE

The evening was going to be casual, so I put on my jeans and the off-the-shoulder black top I bought earlier while shopping. My black high heels finished the ensemble. Thinking about Mac kissing me left me breathless, and I knew I wanted more alone time with him. Being with him made me feel like life might hold a promise of light again. No games, no drama, only Mac and his sincere heart. He had a hold on me and it had nothing to do with our secret marriage. He was kind, considerate, generous, loving, and I was beginning to realize I wanted him. More than that, I needed him.

The agenda tonight was to have dinner and see The Blue Man Group. I took a moment to reflect and Jessica came to mind. A wave of grief crashed over me as I recalled the events of her death, and I couldn't stop the tears from falling. Dying in a car crash at the hands of her high boyfriend was so senseless. Her life was over and I was never going to see my baby sister again.

Mac understood my loss since his parents died when he was seventeen. He'd had Neil's family to look after him and Jessica and I'd had the Millers to look after us. They were our parents' best friends and had filled a void for us, had faithfully supported us through my mom's death, and then my dad's. They were a God-send in my life. Mac was, too. Strange how I had no idea how much I needed him until he came into my life. *I hope I don't lose him. It seems like everyone I love ends up leaving me.* I'm not sure if I could survive another loss, and already Mac seemed so important to me.

I made my way down to the lounge where we were meeting before going to Planet Hollywood for dinner. I was early, hoping to have a glass of wine and a few minutes to myself to calm my nerves. Sitting on a bar stool, I ordered a wine spritzer. Before I knew what had happened, a handsome gentleman, a few stools down from me, bought my drink. The bartender informed me my drink was paid for as I took out my wallet. I looked over and there he was, sitting right beside me, invading my space.

"Thank you for the drink," I said, taking a sip.

"No problem. My name's Cory," he said, extending his hand to take mine. I thought he was going to shake my hand, but he kissed it instead. "What's your name, gorgeous?"

"Her name is Mrs. Carter," Mac said, standing behind Cory. Cory turned and saw Mac there with a pissed off look on his face.

Cory put his hands up slightly. "Sorry man, didn't know she was married." He moved away quickly and that was the end of it, or so I thought.

"You let that man buy you a drink?" Mac asked, not knowing what had happened.

I shook my head. "He paid for it before I even realized. I took my wallet out to pay for it, but, he already had. I didn't know..." I couldn't seem to complete my sentence. It was as though I had cheated on him and felt guilty.

Mac sat down and took my hand. "I'm sorry. I saw that guy hitting on you and I wanted to beat the shit out of him. I didn't like that he was sitting next to you, talking to you, breathing the same air."

A small smile spread across my face. His jealously made me feel cherished...protected...in a caveman kind of way. I liked it and I wanted to have more of this feeling. "It's okay. I wasn't happy he was talking to me either, and I was just about to tell him I was waiting for my boyfriend. But, you saved the day and I didn't have to."

Mac's boyish grin melted me on the inside. Kissing him in my hotel room flashed through my mind and I blushed a little.

"So, you think of me as your boyfriend?" he asked, with a glint in his eye. He had interlocked his fingers with mine and placed our hands on his thigh.

"Honestly, I guess I do." The words came out, but I wanted to reel them back in. How was he going to react to my statement?

"Good, because I definitely want to be your boyfriend," he said, pulling my barstool closer to his. Our legs were touching and Mac planted a gentle kiss on my lips. His lips touching mine made me tingle all over and I suddenly wished we were alone. Our evening was already accounted for with our love-bird friends, however, who would probably be fashionably late.

Within seconds of each other, our cell phones rang. I answered mine, and it was Charlie calling to say she wasn't feeling well and they were going to stay in and order room service. When I hung up, Mac was just ending his call, too.

"That was Neil. Kate's not feeling well, so they are staying in and ordering room service."

I chuckled. "My call was from Charlie, saying she wasn't feeling well and they are staying in and ordering room service."

We both laughed at the transparency of our friends.

"Looks like we have some matchmaking going on. Neil made sure you and I were already together before he went into his explanation."

"So did Charlie," I said, with my eyes locked on Mac's. "What do you want to do now?" I asked, knowing that could be a loaded question.

Mac's devilish smile sent my mind in a thousand directions. I thought he might suggest we stay in and get room service too, but he didn't. "Let's go to dinner like we planned, but not Planet Hollywood. Maybe we can find a quiet Italian place," Mac suggested.

"I love that idea."

Mac called the bartender over. "Do you know of any out-of-the-way Italian places for a quiet dinner?" he asked.

The bartender told us about Mamma Mia's. He said it was old-fashioned home cooking with a romantic ambiance. Mac and I were off to get a cab within minutes. The evening was going better than I expected. We arrived at the quaint little restaurant that was off the beaten path. The serene atmosphere was calming and a woman's voice crooned *The Man I Love* in the background. I felt my shoulders relax as my surroundings washed over all of my senses. It had typical Italian flair, and we were seated in a circular booth toward the back. It was like being in my own private world with Mac. Having him all to myself was both scary and thrilling at the same time. We both scooted into the booth and Mac was so close to me, I could inhale his manly scent. It had intoxicated me earlier. I had no doubt my infatuation with all things Mac would continue throughout the night.

Mac ordered a bottle of wine for us and we perused the menus for a moment. I made up my mind quickly, so I could turn my attention to the delicious man sitting next to me. Mac closed his menu too, and took my hand in his. An electric current radiated through my body when he touched me. In that moment, I was glad we were married, so I could give myself over to him without breaking my promise to my mom. It was fascinating to feel relieved by that thought. Interesting turn of events from just a few hours before.

The waiter brought the wine and took our order. "Now that we've got that out of the way, I want to propose a toast," Mac said smiling. We each picked up our glasses and Mac began, "Here's to many quiet moments like this." We clinked glasses, each took a sip, put our glasses down, and Mac looked at me with blazing eyes. Before I could even breathe, he took my head in his hands and began kissing me. His tongue was sweet like wine as it stroked mine. His kiss was urgent and passionate, like he had been waiting a hundred years to press his lips to mine. My heart was beating so fast I thought it might pound right out of my chest. As the kiss slowed Mac put his nose to mine playfully nuzzling it. "I feel better now," he announced.

I laughed and said, "I didn't know you weren't feeling well."

"It's not that. I just needed to kiss you."

"I needed you to kiss me, too," I whispered shyly.

The waiter appeared with our bread and salads. The moment had been so powerful I was glad for the food to arrive. Kissing Mac was amazing, but I was torn between slowing down and tearing off his clothes. I was surprised at myself for having such extreme feelings. I was all over the place and I didn't know what to do about it.

"So, beautiful Natalie, could tell me more about yourself and your family? On our drive out here, it was fun talking about our childhoods and telling stories, but I want to know about the things that have made you who you are."

"I want to know more about you, too." I took a sip of wine knowing that sharing the tough times wasn't going to be easy.

"When I was nineteen, my mom was diagnosed with stage four ovarian cancer. It was a shock to all of us because we didn't have any family history and she was only in her forties. Usually women develop it later in life. At first, we were hopeful the doctors could help her. She had the best oncologist in San Diego caring for her. She was so sick when we took her into the hospital, the doctors decided to wait to do a hysterectomy until after several rounds of chemo. My dad was beside himself with worry, but he put on a brave front for all of us. He had always been my mom's rock."

Mac held my hand as I continued. "Chemo is a real bitch and my mom was sick as a dog. My dad used up so much of his vacation time from work staying at home, taking care of her. One day, when I got home from class, it occurred to me that I should take a sabbatical from college and take care of my mom. I informed my parents that evening that I was quitting school. They put up a fuss at first, but I told them there was nothing they could do to stop me."

"So you were in college at the time?" Mac asked.

"Yes, I was attending UCSD. Ironically, I was in the nursing program. Becoming a nurse had been a life-long dream until my mom became ill. Watching my mother dying right before my eyes changed me. It ripped my soul apart and I couldn't return to the program to become a nurse. The thought of watching people die was more than I could bear," I said, with tears welling up.

"Nat, if you're not ready to share this or it's too hard to talk about, I'll understand. We can talk about something else."

"No, it's okay." Mac kissed my cheek as the waiter brought out our food. For some reason that was beyond me, I wanted to curl up in his arms, tell him everything about myself, and just have him hold me forever. *What was it about him that caused me to feel so safe?*

"When the months of chemo were over, the doctors ran some tests before they could do the operation. The tests indicated the cancer had spread to my mom's lungs and lymphatic system. At that point, all they could do was prolong her life, not save her. I think if it had been just her, she might have opted out of chemo and just drifted away. But, she had my dad, sister, and me, who all wanted her to live as long as possible. We were selfish," I gasped out.

Mac put both his arms around me and held me as the tears fell from my eyes. He whispered in my ear, "Nat, I'm so sorry you had to go through all of that. If I could take it away, I would."

His arms and words were such a comfort. I knew in that moment, if he really wanted an annulment, it would rip my heart to shreds. Somewhere between morning and evening, I had fallen in love with Mac Carter. I knew I couldn't tell him, because it was way too soon to say such a thing, but my heart felt it. I recognized the feeling, because I had experienced it once before.

My tears stopped and I pulled back and looked into Mac's eyes, sincere concern visible in their depths. His hand caressed my face and words were rendered unnecessary.

"Natalie, have you ever shared this with anyone? Kate, Charlie?"

I shook my head. "They know my mom died of cancer, but I've never told them how painful it was to go through. It's hard for people to understand unless they have lost a loved one. I know Kate lost David so she would understand, but we didn't know each other when my mom died, so telling them all of this...it just hasn't come up."

"I know what you mean by people not understanding if they haven't been through it. Neil couldn't understand what I was going through when my parents died, but his mom could. She became my mom in so many ways, and she gave me so much strength. I have to admit I cried in her arms several times."

"How do you do that?" I asked.

"Do what?" Mac asked back.

"Share so openly and transparently. How do you make me so comfortable to tell you things I wouldn't tell anyone else?"

"Actually this is new for me, too. My last girlfriend was all about having a good time. But with you, I just feel...connected. Talking to you is easy, and listening to you, even easier."

Looking into his eyes, I was searching for anything indicating he wasn't telling the truth. But all I saw was a man with a genuine heart.

"So, how long after you mom passed away did your dad die?" Mac asked.

"It's such a tragedy," I said, shaking my head. "My dad was driving home from making some final arrangements for my mom's funeral, when he died in a car accident. It had been raining and he collided with an eighteen-wheeler. I think in his grief he wasn't paying attention to the road. They were both gone and it was just Jessica and me. Mac knowingly stroked my hand with his thumb. "She was four years younger than me, so I finished raising her. My parents had life insurance which helped with all of our expenses. After a couple of years, we decided to sell the house. It was big and there were memories around every corner that seemed to haunt both of us. With the money we made from the house, we were able to buy the condo outright. Not having a mortgage has been very helpful the last few years."

"Natalie, you've been through so much in such a short time," Mac said, shaking his head.

Being this close to him, and opening up as he listened so intently, made my heart flutter. My parents had been married after knowing each other only three weeks. Hearing the stories of their courtship when I was growing up, made me eager to be in love. Sitting here, next to Mac, I realized I had just embarked upon my own whirlwind romance.

"I feel like I have monopolized the conversation." As much as it was cathartic to share all this with Mac, I really wanted to know more about him.

"Why don't you tell me about your family?" I asked, desiring to shift the attention away from me.

Mac smiled. "I had the best parents in the world. Being their only child made me very close to them and we did everything together. The first trip my parents took without me was to Europe. I stayed with Neil's family while they were gone. It was a second honeymoon for them. On their way back, their plane went down over the Atlantic. Everyone perished. I'm just glad they had an amazing trip together before…"

Mac looked down for a moment. He took in a deep breath and then a sip of wine. We sat there holding hands, saying nothing else. Somehow, we didn't need the words to show that we knew each other in a way no one else did.

"We have the tickets for The Blue Man Group, if you still want to go," Mac finally said.

"Do you want to go?" I asked, hoping the answer was no.

"I'm up for it if you want to go. Otherwise, we could find a quiet piano bar and just talk some more."

"I vote for the piano bar. I'm sure The Blue Man Group are great, but I don't really care if I see them or not," I said.

***

The waiter from the restaurant suggested a place not very far away. Settling into the comfortable love seat, Mac put his arm around me and I rested my head on his shoulder. When the waitress came to take our drink order, Mac ordered a bottle of champagne.

"I think we should celebrate," he said, once the waitress returned with a bottle and two glasses. She opened and poured the champagne for us, then departed.

"What do you want to celebrate?" I asked, but somehow felt I already knew what he was going to say.

"Us," he simply said. "I want to celebrate what's happening between us."

"And what would you say is happening between us?" I asked demurely.

Mac looked at me with a fire in his eyes. A fire I had only seen in one other man.

"I'd say we are falling for each other, Natalie," he said, his eyes searing mine.

His words should have made we want to run for the hills, and if it had been any other man saying them to me, I would have. But I couldn't deny I was already there, falling, even though we hadn't known each other very long. I didn't say a word. I put my hands on his face and began kissing him. Telling him didn't seem like enough. I needed to demonstrate to this incredible man, that I was as into him as he was me. Mac's hands found my waist and moved toward my back. He pulled me close to him. There we were, in the little corner of the piano bar, making out like teenagers. There was nowhere else in the world I wanted to be, and no one else I wanted to be with.

***

Mac walked me to my hotel room door. My heart was beating rapidly, my breathing ragged, not knowing what would happen next.

"Would you like to come in?" I asked in a small voice, slightly uncertain if I was ready to venture in to this part of the relationship.

Mac looked at me intently, studying my face for a moment.

"I'd like nothing more than to come in and be with you, but I'm going to say goodnight right here instead."

The quizzical look on my face caused him to continue.

"I don't want you to feel rushed. I want you to be ready and I know that's going to take time," he said, as he wrapped his arms around me and whispered in my ear, "I am certain it will be worth the wait."

His words melted me and I didn't want him to leave, but he let go, kissed me on the cheek, and began walking toward the elevator. "I'll see you at breakfast, baby," he called back to me.

"See you then," was all I could muster.

Feeling like a cold shower was in order, I entered my hotel room alone, wishing Mac wasn't such a gentleman, but knowing I would be happy in the morning that he was.

CHAPTER 8: MAC

I entered my hotel room and went straight to the shower. I knew I had scored points for being a gentleman, but I wanted nothing more than to have Natalie's beautiful body stretched out before me, while I did all sorts of sensual things to her. Needing to alleviate the pressure that had been mounting, I turned on the cold water and stepped into the shower. My thoughts were racing about what it would be like when I finally did get to be with her, sober that was. I needed to think about something else before I exploded. But what? My mind was filled with images of licking Natalie's nipples while I slowly moved in and out of her. Her mouth devouring my hard cock. *Damn it.*

Jaws. Okay, the scene where the shark is attacking the boat and eats the captain. That ought to do it. Nothing sexy about that. I let that image resonate in my brain for a few minutes.

Heading to bed, I wondered if Natalie was thinking about me as much as I was thinking about her. I was already lost in the amazing woman, and I couldn't fathom how that had happened to me so quickly. I couldn't help but smile remembering we were already hitched.

All night I tossed and turned thinking about Natalie. Her heart had captured mine the day we met and I knew I was in deep. I had cared about women before, even thought I had been in love a time or two, but that paled in light of my feelings for her. Walking away from her had been so fucking difficult, but I had to put her first. I wasn't going to win her heart by being a selfish brute.

I also knew the word *annulment* wasn't going to depart from my mouth again. We'd only talk about it if she brought it up. I hoped to God she didn't and I had a chance to truly win her over. My thoughts puzzled me, since I wasn't ready to marry Cassie when she gave me an ultimatum. I easily cut her loose, but letting Natalie go was a different story. That was never going to happen.

I took out my phone and texted a catering service I had used in the past, asking for a romantic dinner to be prepared. I sent a list of what I wanted, knowing they would exceed my expectations. On the drive home, I would invite Natalie over for dinner. Following Neil's directive of pulling out all the stops, was my top priority, besides running my company.

I had plans in January to go to my London office and clean up some messes and finalize a merger. Sending my number two wasn't an option. I needed to be there and I knew I would be gone during some, if not all, of the trial. I could only hope Natalie would join me in London when the trial was over.

I decided to go to her hotel room so we could go down to breakfast together. Every moment I could spend with her meant she was closer to becoming mine. I had spent most of my time since my parents died pretending I didn't need someone to love, someone who would be willing to love me back. It had seemed safer than putting my heart out there, only to be hurt if they left me. Spending another minute pretending was out of the question with Natalie. Our marriage just made sense. She made sense. I couldn't imagine a life without her, now that I knew how well we fit.

Walking toward the door to leave my hotel room, I heard a knock. Opening the door, I saw my beautiful girl standing there, smiling at me.

"Good morning," Natalie said, her eyes beaming at mine.

"Good morning."

"I thought we could go down to breakfast together," she said, with a hopeful look on her face.

"Great minds think alike. I was just coming to get you."

We both laughed. "Why don't you come in? We have about fifteen minutes before we have to meet everyone."

She walked past me and I took in her intoxicating scent. My jaw tightened, knowing it was going to take a mountain of willpower to keep my hands to myself.

As I closed the door, Natalie asked, "Did you sleep well last night?"

I wanted to say that I would have slept much better with her in my arms, but I didn't. "I slept so-so. I always have a hard time staying at hotels."

"I know what you mean. I didn't sleep so well, either."

Was she giving me a hint or just making conversation? Being an optimist, I was going with hint.

We both sat on the sofa and a silence fell between us, but it wasn't awkward. I took her hand and kissed the back of it. She closed her eyes.

"I've had a...a good time this weekend, Mac. Thank you for spending so much time with me."

"All I want is to spend time with you," I said, realizing she was giving me green lights to proceed. "I hope you will join me for dinner tonight at my place. I've already made some arrangements."

"I would love to. Can I ask you a favor?"

"Of course, anything."

"In front of our friends, can we kind of lay low? I don't want to answer a bunch of questions from Kate and Charlie. I just want what is happening between us to be ours for now."

My mind flashed to my big mouth telling Neil and Mitch about our nuptials. I knew Neil would keep my confidence, but I didn't know Mitch well enough to be certain even though he gave his word.

I nodded. "We can tell them about us when you feel comfortable."

Relief flooded her face. "It's just...I feel like I have lost everyone in my life that I have been close to. I can't stand the thought of...of..."

"Losing me?" I said for her.

"Yes. I know it doesn't make any sense in light of how long we've known each other, how could I possibly lose you, I don't even have you."

"Oh, you have me Natalie," I said, moving closer to her. "I wanted you so badly, that I married you Friday night."

"We were drunk and didn't know what we were doing."

"No, don't do that."

"Don't do what?"

"Don't diminish what is happening between us. I meant what I said last night."

She searched my eyes with hers, her brow slightly furrowed. Then her face relaxed.

I lifted her hand and placed it on my chest so she could feel my racing heart.

"Your heart is beating so fast."

"Yes, you do that to me...among other things," I whispered. Then I couldn't take it any longer. My mouth found hers and I kissed her, thinking the whole time, I wanted to cherish the woman I had been lucky enough to meet. She welcomed my kiss and met my tongue with her own. I knew it would have to be brief, because I didn't have time for another cold shower. We were due downstairs any minute. Our kiss slowed and I put my forehead to hers. *What this woman does to me...*

"If we are going to keep things on the down low, then maybe we shouldn't show up to breakfast together. They might assume..."

"Oh, I didn't think of that. Why don't you go first and I'll come down after you?"

***

Approaching the table, our friends were talking amongst themselves.

"So, ladies, are you feeling better?" I asked, with one eye brow raised.

"Yes, we are," they both said in unison.

"Here, have a seat," Neil said, as he poured me a cup of coffee. "We were just waiting for you and Natalie before going to the buffet." The words no sooner rolled off Neil's tongue, when Nat showed up. I stood up and pulled out her chair.

"Good morning. It looks like you two are feeling better," she said, spying Kate and Charlie.

"Yes, we are," said Charlie. "It must have been a twenty-four-hour bug."

"Now that we're all here, let's hit the buffet," Kate said.

As everyone went toward the buffet, Mitch hung back with me. He had given me a look when I walked up to the table, so I thought it best I talk to him.

"Mitch, it's important to Natalie that no one knows about us."

"Don't worry. Bro code. I'm not telling."

"Good."

"But I will say this, if you fuck with her, you're fucking with me."

I put my hands up in surrender. "Understood," I said. Part of me was a little pissed he was giving me a veiled threat, but he was also looking out for Natalie's best interest, and I couldn't fault him for that. Maybe since Natalie had been without a boyfriend for so long, Mitch decided he was going to look after her.

Grateful Mitch was on board with keeping his mouth shut, I was able to enjoy my breakfast.

CHAPTER 9: NATALIE

Mac held my hand in the car as we drove away from the hotel. Looking down, and seeing our fingers intertwined, spread a tingling feeling throughout my body. I couldn't wait for dinner at his house later. Kissing him that morning had stirred me deep down, and I knew I wanted him.

"Do you think you could drop me off at home so I can freshen up before we have dinner tonight?" I asked.

"Sure. I think we'll be back in plenty of time for that."

"Great."

"You're kind of quiet. Is something on your mind?"

I debated for a moment if telling him about Ty was a good idea, but Mac had been nothing but wonderful to me since the moment I met him, so I decided I would tell him about the only other man I had ever been close to.

"Actually, yes. I was thinking about an old boyfriend. My only boyfriend with the exception of a few blind dates I have been set up on."

"Do you want to tell me about him?"

"Will it be weird if I do?"

"No. What's his name?"

"Ty."

"What happened?"

I contemplated the question for a moment. Somehow, part of what happened was still a mystery to me, too. "It's kind of a long story."

"We have hours to kill, Nat. It's okay to tell me. I want to know everything about you."

He had such a way of making me feel comfortable, so I began to tell him about the relationship that broke my heart. "I met Ty when I was a freshman and he was a senior in high school. I was friends with his sister Stephanie, and I spent a lot of time at her house, partly because I wanted to see Ty. At first, he didn't know I existed. I was his kid sister's friend. But the summer after my freshman year I blossomed, and he began to notice me. It was just flirting at first, but by July we were meeting secretly when I spent the night, and Stephanie was sleeping. We had a few stolen kisses, but nothing major happened between us. Ty was about to start college at UCSD and I had no idea if he would want a sophomore in high school as his girlfriend. His first semester, we didn't see each other much, but on Christmas vacation we got close again. Every moment we could find to be together, we did. I was head over heels for him," I said, remembering a simpler time in my life.

"We finally had an opportunity to go out on a date. My parents and sister had plans to see Phantom of the Opera in L.A. . I was supposed to go too, but feigned being sick. As soon as they left, Ty came over. We ordered pizza and watched a movie. We were finally alone and couldn't be caught by anyone."

"So, making out and heavy petting," Mac interjected with a grin.

"Yeah. He wanted to do more, but I wasn't ready to have sex. After that, it was another year before we were able to have another secret date."

"Why did you two have to keep it a secret?"

"We both agreed since he was so much older than me, my parents probably wouldn't approve. We wanted to wait until I was eighteen to go public with our relationship."

"Oh," Mac said, nodding.

"We were able to keep the secret until my senior year. Then Stephanie figured it out. She had been putting two and two together and she confronted Ty about our relationship one night. Once he explained to her that he loved me, she was excited for us and kept our secret. We told my parents the summer after I graduated high school."

"How did they take it?"

"We didn't fully disclose everything, but they took it well. We all started getting together for family gatherings at either Ty's house or mine. I was about to begin UCSD and Ty was about to start law school. He had applied to a ton of schools and had been accepted to several, but he wanted Harvard. His dad had a friend who made some calls and he was admitted last minute.

"Did the long distance thing break you two up?"

"Well, yes and no. I began applying to schools back east, hoping to transfer in my sophomore year. Ty was so busy with law school he didn't have time for a social life, anyway."

"So, what changed the plan?"

"My mom got sick and I couldn't leave her and my family. At first Ty understood and we decided after my mom was well I would go. But, she never got well and my dad died too, so I couldn't leave Jessica. Ty expected me to bring Jessica along, but I couldn't uproot her life with everything that happened. He was angry about it. Stephanie somehow got involved and we had a huge fight and haven't spoken since. Ty stopped all communication. When I finally got a hold of him, he said he was too busy for a girlfriend and it was over."

"Nat, that sucks."

"Both of my parents had died, my best friend hated me, and my boyfriend dumped me. It more than sucked. I was in pain for such a long time."

"That explains a lot. You've been through so much. I understand why it's hard for you to trust people."

Words got stuck in my throat when I heard Mac say I couldn't trust people. He was right, and I didn't know how to change that about myself, or if I could change it.

"Meeting Kate and Charlie made a difference. One night we were hanging out, Mitch was there too, and I told them the whole story. I think Mitch wanted to get on the next flight and go pummel Ty for hurting me so much. He's such a big brother," I said, smiling and shaking my head.

"Yeah, I've noticed that about him."

"Anyway, tonight at dinner, you'll have to tell me all about the women who have broken your heart," I said, giving his hand a squeeze.

"Well, I can tell you stories, but I am afraid I've probably broken more hearts than I have had mine broken. For a long time after my parents died, I didn't let anyone in. I dated, but didn't commit."

"So, what's changed?" I asked. Mac had been pretty open with me so far.

"It hit me that I'm almost thirty, and I want to have someone in my life I can share myself with, be myself around," he said, glancing over at me. "Honestly, I want what my parents had. They were an amazing couple who stuck it out no matter what happened."

Mac's declaration of wanting commitment sent tingles down my spine. I was feeling what Kate had described when she met Neil, and I craved to have someone love me like Neil loved Kate.

Mac dropped me off at my place so I could have some time to myself. He texted me his address, and we were set to have dinner in a couple of hours. While in the shower, I shaved my legs carefully, imagining his hands might roam my body that evening. The excitement of thinking of his touch made me yearn for him even more. It was going to be torture waiting for the time we agreed upon to have dinner. But would I be ready to make love to him again? I knew I was physically, but emotionally? Was I ready?

CHAPTER 10: MAC

I pulled into my garage, knowing the caterers would be showing up soon. When my parents died, I debated selling and moving into another place, but couldn't bring myself to do it. I needed to keep this part of them, and living in their house was the only way I knew how to do it. Deep in my heart, I believed my mom would love Natalie. That thought had never occurred to me when I was dating Cassie, nor anyone before her. It was good. Life was good. I just wanted to make sure I didn't blow it.

The caterers showed up with everything on my wish list and set the scene for a romantic evening. We were going to have dinner on the plush area rug in front of the fireplace. It just seemed like the perfect spot for us to relax and be together.

The time was drawing near and I expected Natalie at any moment. The doorbell rang, and as I eagerly approached the door, I was caught off guard finding Cassie on the other side of it. *What the hell was she doing here?*

"Cassie, I wasn't expecting you," I said in a slightly gruff tone.

"Well, life is full of unexpected surprises."

"What are you doing here?" I asked, hoping she would get to the point before Natalie showed up. I needed her gone before then.

"I thought we should talk. I hated how things ended between us. Can I come in?"

"Actually, I have plans for the evening, so we'll have to talk another time."

"I see. How about we meet for lunch sometime this week?"

"I'll have to check with my secretary. I don't know what I have available," I said, attempting to dismiss her.

"I already called Alice and she said you have Wednesday open. How about we meet at our place?" she asked with a coy demeanor.

"We don't have 'a place' anymore. We're broken up," I said, hoping she would take the hint and bow out gracefully.

She exhaled sharply. "We were together for two years and you can't give me a lunch date?"

As she asked her question, Natalie pulled up in her car. *Fuck. This can't be happening.*

"Of course. Let's meet at noon on Wednesday," I said, while Natalie got out of the car. "I'll see you, then," I said, motioning with my hand for her to leave. The last thing I wanted was for her and Natalie to cross paths, but it was about to be too late. Cassie turned, took one look at Natalie and then spun around toward me.

"Your plans, I take it?" she said, bitterness dripping from her lips.

Cassie had a sharp tongue and could unravel this night before it even started. Natalie approached and Cassie looked Nat up and down. "Are you next?" Cassie asked.

Natalie's brow furrowed, confusion spreading over her face. "Excuse me?" she responded.

"You know, the next woman Mac has set his sights on."

"Cassie, it's time for you to go," I said, intervening before this got out of hand.

Cassie began to walk away. "See you on Wednesday," she called out.

Natalie stood there staring at me, the hurt oozing from her eyes. Words escaped me and I didn't know how I was going to explain Cassie at my home or seeing her on Wednesday. Natalie just raised her eyebrows, waiting for an explanation.

"I...I don't know what to say. That was my ex-girlfriend, Cassie."

"She's just...lovely, isn't she?" Natalie said sarcastically. "It seems you have some unfinished business and I'm not good with complications," she said, as she began turning around to walk away from me. *What the hell was happening?*

This can't be ending, I thought, running after the woman who had already permeated my heart. "Natalie, wait," I called, but she kept walking. When we reached her car, I stopped her by putting a hand on either side of her, trapping her against the car. "Please, don't leave. Let me explain."

Natalie stared up at me with her gorgeous blue eyes. I could see the pain radiating from them. This precious woman had lost so much, but there was no way in hell she was going to lose me, or push me away. Words became useless and I pressed my lips to hers. It started off slowly, softly. But my desire for her took over, and my kiss turned urgent. I needed her like an addict needed his next drug fix. Natalie kissed me back and her hands glided up and down my back. Her caress stirred me and I wanted her hands to touch every inch of my body. My mind briefly scanned all of the women I'd dated in the past and there wasn't one I had ever wanted as much as I wanted the beautiful siren in my arms. Our kiss continued...lips, tongues, roaming hands. Her passion excited me, and I realized she was walking away because she was hurt, and she would only be hurt if she really cared about me. Making her mine forever, was all I could concentrate on.

Natalie's hand wrapped around my face. The kiss would be coming to an end and I hoped my demonstration proved my feelings for her.

She exhaled, slightly breathless, her chest rising and falling as she attempted to regain her composure.

"I'll give you one thing, Mac Carter, you sure do know how to kiss a girl." The smile spread across her face made my heart race even more.

"A woman like you should be kissed like that every day. I want to be the one...the one who kisses you and shuts out the entire world."

"I'm sorry I reacted to your ex-girlfriend. I have to admit, I am in unchartered waters here."

"You don't have anything to be sorry for. I'm sorry you had to meet her. She can be, well, unkind. I learned that first hand. One of the many reasons we're no longer together."

"So, what's happening on Wednesday?" Natalie asked.

"I'm meeting her for lunch."

"I see."

"I'm going to cancel. She caught me off guard coming over unannounced, and I just wanted her to leave, so I agreed to lunch."

"You know what? I don't want to give her another second of our evening. Besides, I'm starved and you promised me dinner," she said, looking up at me through her dark lashes.

I couldn't believe the incredible woman in front of me. How could she be so strong? How could I get so lucky?

"Yes, I did. Shall we?" I asked, as I released her and offered her my arm.

We walked back toward the house and I hoped the evening would go smoothly. This was our beginning.

CHAPTER 11: NATALIE

"Mac, your home is exquisite."

"Thank you. This is where I grew up. My mom went out of her way to make this a haven for us. This is my favorite place to be."

I looked around at the opulence that was Mac's home. It was clear no expense had been spared when his parents bought it. Surprisingly, it actually gave the Bellagio a run for its money. "It's clear your mom had a talent in decorating."

"Both of my parents grew up in working-class families. When my dad's business took off and began making a lot of money, my mom enjoyed the fruits of their labor. She worked alongside my dad, helping him make the business successful. Her hobby became decorating."

I was now standing in Mac's great room. The huge marble fireplace was surrounded by lit candles. Set up on the bear-skin rug, was a feast with a bottle of wine chilling in a bucket of ice. "I see you've been busy since you got home. This is amazing."

Mac smiled and my heart melted a little. He opened the wine and offered me a glass. All I could think about was how would I be able to resist him. I didn't want to hold back, but the truth was, I was scared out of my mind of being hurt—again. My poor heart couldn't take any more devastation.

Mac guided me toward the fireplace and we both laid on our sides, propping ourselves on our elbows, facing each other. He picked up a stuffed mushroom and fed it to me. Being with him was so effortless. Yet, this entire experience had me wondering how I let my guard down so quickly and allowed Mac to penetrate my heart with his charm.

"You seem a million miles away, Nat. What's going on in that beautiful head of yours?"

"I was just thinking...how easy it is to be with you. And how terrified I am something will go wrong and this won't work out."

Mac took my hand and kissed it. "What makes you think this won't work out?"

"I don't know, past experience," I said, attempting to keep my voice steady. I didn't want to break down in front of him, but being with him made me feel...safe. Safe enough to be real and not put up the brave front...the mask that kept me hidden. The mask the world expected me to wear. The mask I had worn for so long.

Mac moved the tray of food out of the way and laid closer to me. "It's okay to be scared." He picked up my hand and placed it on his chest. I could feel his heart pounding. "Come here," he said, as he began pulling my body close to his. He laid on his back and I placed my head on his chest. Having his arms around me again was just what I craved.

"Nat, we both know life doesn't come with any guarantees. I'm not perfect and chances are I could hurt your feelings at some point, but I'm crazy about you, and I want to be with you." Mac lifted my head so I was looking into his eyes. My emotions were running wild and I began blinking back the tears, but I couldn't stop them as they began rushing down my face.

"Nat, don't cry. I promise everything's going to be okay."

Before I could respond to his soothing words, Mac's lips found mine. His kiss sent shivers down my spine and my body was under his control again. He moved me to lay on my back and hovered over me, his chest pressing against mine. With each stroke of his tongue my panties became wetter. I wanted him more than anything in this world. Making love to him flashed through my mind as he expertly caressed me with his lips. With every passing second I became more enraptured with him. I wanted to do things with him that I never allowed myself to think about.

Mac positioned himself between my legs and feeling his erection against me caused me to moan in his mouth. The desire to have him inside of me continued to become more intense as his tongue swirled around mine. Was I ready, or would I possibly regret making love tomorrow? One thing I knew, I didn't want to do anything that would cause regrets. I already had too many from my past haunting me, like the last time I saw my sister.

I pulled away and Mac let me. He looked deep into my eyes, searching for anything that would reveal my thoughts. Then he smiled, kissed me on the cheek, and removed his body from covering mine.

"Natalie, I have no intentions of pushing you into anything. I want you to be completely sure when we do make love."

"Thank you," I said, feeling slightly ashamed. "It's just…I have so many regrets from my past, I don't want to do anything that will cause me to regret my actions with you."

He moved the hair off my shoulder so all of it was behind me. "What do you regret?" he asked tenderly, kindness flowing from his eyes.

As I thought about the best way to answer that question, we resumed eating and I decided to allow myself to open up to this captivating, caring man. "My sister and I had a huge fight when she stormed off to meet her boyfriend. I had met him and could tell he was high at the time. I was trying to talk some sense into her to stop seeing him, but she wouldn't listen. I'm the reason she's dead. If I had just kept my mouth shut she probably would have figured out on her own that he was a loser."

"Oh, Natalie, it's not your fault. You didn't put her in the car with him. Chances are, your sister had been using drugs as well, if she was dating a drug addict," Mac said, as he fed me another tasty treat. "Don't blame yourself."

"I can't help it. I was supposed to look after her, keep her protected…alive. I've failed my parents who were counting on me to take care of their youngest daughter."

"Your sister was going to make her own choices no matter what you said or did. You're not responsible for her dating, let alone, getting into a car with a high person. And I guarantee you; your parents know everything you did was with Jessica's best interest at heart."

I reached over and put my hand on his face. "How do you always know the right thing to say to me? Somehow, every time we're together, you make me feel better. Cared for."

"We've both had our fair share of heartbreak and the loss we've encountered has drawn us to each other. I feel closer to you than any other woman I've ever known. And yes, I care for you very much."

Mac pulled me into his arms and again I rested my head on his chest. He held me for a long time. Neither of us said anything as he stroked my arm with his hand. He had created the perfect evening and won more of my heart with each passing moment.

CHAPTER 12: MAC

It was getting late, so I kissed Natalie on the temple and said, "You better be getting home. It's past your bedtime." I flashed her a grin so she knew I was joking, but my resolve was weakening with each passing moment.

I wanted Natalie to stay the night with me so badly, but I knew waiting would ensure her that I was in this for a lasting relationship. That was at the top of my agenda—her falling in love with me, feeling loved by me. I had a ghost to live up to, in her perfect ex-boyfriend, who'd abandoned her. He had pushed too hard, been too selfish, stupidly lost her. I wasn't going to make his mistakes. If there is one thing my dad always told me, "A happy wife is a happy life."

I stood up, and held out my hand to her, helping her get up. I was secretly hoping she would protest, want to stay with me, but I wasn't surprised when she didn't. Just about every other woman I knew was more than content to go fast, but Natalie was unlike any other woman.

Her hand was intertwined with mine as we walked toward the front door and out to her car. When she looked up at me with her big blue eyes, I was a goner. Nothing was ever going to be the same again. I had given my heart to Natalie and the only way I was getting it back was if she broke it.

Kissing her goodnight was like savoring my favorite dessert. I wanted it to last forever, but I restrained myself before things became too heated, again. My hands, having a mind of their own, concerned me, so I gently ended our kiss.

"I'll call you tomorrow."

"I'd like that," she said, leaning her body into mine.

She had no idea what she was doing to me. Maybe she did. Who knows the mind of a woman?

"I had a wonderful time tonight. Thanks for inviting me over for dinner."

"It's the first of many dinners and evenings together, I hope."

Natalie looked down for a moment. When her eyes returned to mine, they were glistening with wetness.

"I hope so too, Mac."

Natalie opened the car door and climbed in. We shared one more glance and she drove away.

***

I woke up the next morning with thoughts of Natalie flooding me. Another cold shower was in order as parts of me were very aroused from the scenes my mind was creating. I knew a plan was in order. Everything was better if I had a plan. Winging it wouldn't sweep Natalie off her feet. Plus, I had really big shoes to fill with everything Neil had done to win Kate's heart. He had done countless things that were considered seriously romantic. And, I thought, Natalie loved romantic.

Doing all of the standard flowers and candy wasn't going to be enough, but that's where I would start, until I had time to get creative. The good news was we'd be seeing each other with Neil and Kate as well. The wedding and all of the festivities associated with it, were just around the corner. But, every great journey begins with the first step. I would send her flowers at work. It's a typical thing to do, but none the less, it would demonstrate that she was special to me. All I wanted to do was bring a smile to my girl's face.

I arrived at the office early, and as usual, my assistant was already there to greet me. Alice had been my father's assistant and I trusted her with my life. She had been there for me through thick and thin. I valued her opinion, which I asked for frequently. When I asked what she thought of Cassie and she was hesitant to say, I knew it was time to break things off. Cassie just made it easier with her ultimatum.

"Good morning, Alice."

"Good morning, Mr. Carter." She wouldn't call me Mac unless

we were speaking outside of work. Maintaining her professionalism was of the utmost importance to her.

"I trust you had a good weekend with your friends?" she asked.

"I had an amazing weekend," I said, barely able to contain the grin spreading across my face.

"So, where am I sending flowers to?" she inquired with a slight smile. She knew me too well.

"I need an incredible arrangement sent to Natalie Mason, at Nordstrom Fashion Valley, in the kids department."

"I will get that handled. Email me what you want the card to state."

"Will do," I said, as I continued my way to my office.

My schedule was packed, but all I wanted to do was think about Natalie. With Cassie on the warpath last night, I was certain Natalie would bolt. But, my kiss made her stay. How I loved kissing her soft lips.

I was proud of myself that I didn't let things go too far between us. I wanted her trust and I needed to know she was ready before anything actually happened.

"Mr. Carter, Harold Brody is here to see you," Alice said, via the intercom.

"Send him in," I responded. He did all of the legal work for Carter Industries.

He came in with sunken in shoulders and I could tell something was weighing heavily on him.

"What's going on, Harold?" I asked.

"I've done something I'm not proud of and it involves you."

I stared at him, waiting for him to go on. "What did you do?" I finally asked.

"Well, as you know, the entire trust to your parent's estate is to go to you on your thirtieth birthday."

"Yes, I am aware."

"What you don't know, is there's a stipulation in the trust that you are married by then. Your parents didn't want you to be alone if something happened to them."

"Why am I just hearing this now? How long do I have before I have to be married?" I asked, my heart pounding rapidly.

"You have to be married before you thirty first birthday."

"How is it you're just telling me about this now?" I asked with a gruff voice.

"This is the part I am ashamed of. Cassie found out about the marriage requirement in your trust. I don't know how, but she did. Then, she blackmailed me to not tell you until your birthday was approaching."

"How did she blackmail you?"

"Some creep took explicit photos of my daughter Rachel, and Cassie threatened to put them up on the internet if I didn't cooperate."

I rested my head in my hands. So that's why she wants to meet for lunch. She thinks I'm not going to have any other choice but to marry her.

"So, are you supposed to be telling me this now?" I asked.

"Not exactly. But, when I heard you broke things off with her, I knew she would pay me a visit."

"And?"

"She's doing whatever it takes for you to marry her. She threatened me not to tell you, but I couldn't keep this from you any longer. I feel just terrible about this whole damn thing."

I shook my head. "Harold, Cassie is a master manipulator. Don't feel bad. It took me two years to see the real her."

"I know I've let you down and it kills me that she's doing all of this."

No shit you let me down. You're my lawyer, for Pete's sake. That's what I was thinking, but instead, I said, "Don't worry, I'll handle Cassie. I'll also get back the pictures of your daughter."

"I'm getting too old for this. I think it's time to retire."

Harold filled me in on the rest of the particulars. When he departed, I immediately called Neil.

"I need to talk to you ASAP."

"What's going on?" Neil asked me.

"Do you have time for lunch? I need to strategize about some new information regarding my trust."

"I have a pretty full day, but if you want to bring sandwiches over, we can eat and talk in my office."

"Done. What time?"

"Noon."

"See ya, then."

"Alright, man."

As soon as I got off the phone with Neil, I realized I wouldn't be canceling the lunch appointment with Cassie. Getting Neil's take on it would help me be prepared. His mind was cunning and that's what I needed in dealing with her.

I was so pissed, I wanted to take out my aggression on the wall, but I had a feeling the wall would punch back as soon as my fist hit it. A broken hand wouldn't do me any good. All I could do was keep busy, until it was time to see Neil.

Time moved at a glacial pace. My biggest consideration was how this would affect my relationship with Natalie. I didn't want anything to get in our way. But, she may feel I tricked her into marriage because of the terms of my trust. Nothing could be further from the truth. I wanted her from the moment I held her on Thanksgiving. I was her moth and she was my flame.

I had Alice order up the sandwiches and picked them up on the way to Neil's office. His assistant Laura ushered me in.

"I see Laura still dresses provocatively for work," I said, as I motioned my hand toward her desk.

"Yeah, but I just try to ignore it."

Neil got up from his chair and we sat at the table in his office. I broke out the sandwiches, chips, sodas. It was just like being in college again.

"So, what's up?" Neil asked.

"You're not going to believe this, but I found out my parents trust had a stipulation I wasn't aware of."

"Lay it on me."

"I have to be married to keep control of the company. If I'm not married, the company will be divided amongst the shareholders."

Neil's brow creased as he processed the information. "Does that sound like your parents?" he asked.

"Not really, but who knows what was going through their minds at the time. Maybe they wanted to ensure I had a family life. They were so happy together."

"How is it that you didn't know?"

"Cassie found out, and blackmailed Harold by exploiting his daughter."

"Shit. She's crazy," Neil said.

"How would she even find this out? I mean, the trust was sealed. I have to be married within a year after turning thirty."

"Maybe she broke into Harold's office and found your file. Maybe there's more to the story than Harold is telling you. Hard to say."

"What should I do?"

"For starters, Harold is going to retire. He and his daughter are going on a long trip. I'll have Laura draw up the paperwork stating he is not to communicate anything about his retirement or whereabouts. You'll have it waiting on your personal fax, before you get back to the office. If he doesn't comply, then let Cassie do her worst to him."

"Good, but he will still have the problem of her having pictures of his daughter. What if he won't comply?"

"If he doesn't agree to retire, you won't give him severance, and you won't pay for the extended trip."

"He might go for it with that in mind."

"I'll get my tech guy to hack into her computer and find what she has on Harold's daughter. He can send a virus to destroy all of her files so it doesn't look like you did anything."

"Again. You're smarter than I give you credit for," I said, feeling a little more relaxed since Neil had a plan.

"I've had my share of dealing with dishonest people," Neil said.

"I also have to go to lunch with Cassie on Wednesday. She met Natalie last night when their paths crossed at my place."

"You are going to have to keep your cool with Cassie. She's unpredictable and you have no idea what she's capable of doing. Whatever happens during lunch on Wednesday, stay neutral."

"Easier said than done, bro," I chided. "I'm so pissed right now I could put my fist through the wall."

"You losing control gives her the power. Somehow, you're going to have to sit there and play nice. And under no circumstances, tell her that you're married to Natalie."

I nodded. Neil was right. He was always right. He had a clever mind for solving shit. "Okay, I'll keep calm. What do I do after she lowers the boom and tells me about the trust? I'm assuming that's why she wants to do lunch."

"I would say something like…I'll take that under advisement."

"Alright. Stay calm and say as little as possible. But how do I tell Natalie about this? She's going to think I tricked her in Vegas because I needed a wife. What if she doesn't believe me? Neil, I'm crazy about her."

"The last thing I would do is tell Natalie. That's why I didn't tell Kate about her and Elizabeth. I didn't think she would understand. But, I figured once she was in love with me she would forgive me."

"I hate keeping something like this from her, but you're right. Last night when she met Cassie, she bolted for her car after Cassie left. I stopped her and convinced her to stay."

"Natalie's in a vulnerable place. Any false moves and she'll be gone."

"Yeah, it almost all ended last night. All I could do was kiss her and hope she could feel how much she means to me. After we got past Cassie, it was a great night," I said, my mind wandering to the beautiful curves of her face and the feel of her body pressed against mine.

"Build on that, bro. I can tell she's totally into you," Neil said, nodding slightly.

"Alright. Then the next order of business is, will you take me on as a client? My company also needs to hire your firm."

"Consider it done. We're brothers, man. I've got your back."

***

I texted Natalie so she would have a message from me when she got off work. I wanted her to know I was thinking about her. Of course, the flowers would tell her that. Once we spoke on the phone, I'd invite her out to dinner if she was up for it. I wanted her just to come over and be with me, but I didn't want her to feel like I only had one thing in mind. The essence behind my dad's words, were to treat your woman well so she felt special…adored. That's what Natalie deserved. All I could do was pray all of Neil's advice would pan out the way he expected.

CHAPTER 13: NATALIE

My body was at work, but my mind was a million miles away. I volunteered to do some pricing in the stockroom so I could be in my own little world. Plus, my coworkers knew me so well, and keeping my true feelings hidden was practically useless.

Maria's voice startled me when she called out, "Nat, there's a huge display of flowers that were just delivered for you."

"Oh really?" I replied nonchalantly. I was hoping if I didn't make a big deal about it she wouldn't either.

"Sooo. What's going on?"

"I met Neil's best friend, Mac. He's really great and we're kind of seeing each other."

"What do you mean by *kind of*? Either you are, or you aren't."

"Well, it's all so new, I'm exactly not sure. We're taking things slow."

"I can tell you right now, the bouquet of flowers that just arrived for you, do not say *taking things slow*. I'm thinking they're communicating fast forward."

I couldn't help but laugh at Maria's enthusiasm. "Well, he's a very demonstrative man, like Neil," I replied, hoping to divert her interrogation.

"Neil pursued Kate pretty hard. They've only known each other since September and their already getting married. Now, don't get me wrong. I'm happy for her, but it did happen very quickly."

"It did. But if you saw them together you would see they're the perfect match," I responded, hoping the conversation would continue to be about Kate.

"When are you coming back to the sales floor? We're all dying to know what the card says."

"I'll be up in a few minutes," I said, wishing Maria's questioning would dissipate. Even though she was inquisitive, I couldn't help but feel loved by her. She and my other coworkers had always been so supportive and caring.

"Great. See you in a few."

I had never received flowers from anyone before. Mac's gesture made me feel warm, as if I were wrapped in cashmere, and sitting by a toasty fire. My whole body heated, and my thoughts wandered to the prior night, sitting in front of his fireplace. Well, not the sitting part. I closed my eyes and could almost feel his lips caress mine. His tongue dancing with mine. I wanted him and there was nothing stopping me from having him. I just wasn't sure exactly what he wanted from me. Waking up that morning, I considered that Mac and Cassie might have some unfinished business. Only time would tell.

I made my way back to the sales floor and was rendered speechless by the display sitting on the counter. It was extraordinary and must have cost a fortune. It was so big I didn't know how I was going to carry it and see where I was going at the same time. I opened the card and smiled as I read Mac's words.

Natalie,

Spending the last few days with you has meant everything to me. I'm looking forward to many more.

Mac

This card answered my question about what he was interested in. Maybe he really liked me and wanted to know me like he kept saying. *Why was I so distrustful?*

"Nat, you're killing us here. What does the card say?"

I handed the card to Maria and she read it out loud. Brenda and Lori had gathered around, and they were all a buzz about Mac.

"So, Neil's friend, huh? What's happened the last few days?" Lori inquired.

I couldn't hold back my emotions any longer. "I think we fell in love," I said, surprising myself that those words came out.

My dear coworkers, whom I had worked with for so many years, all smiled at me. "Oh, Natalie. This is wonderful," Brenda said. "We've all been waiting for this to happen to you. It sounds like Mac is a real catch."

"He is," I said, tearing up. I couldn't form any more words. Waves of emotion crashed over me like the turbulent sea in a storm.

Maria came and hugged me. "Nat, you deserve a wonderful man and a happy life. I have a good feeling about this."

"Thanks, Maria."

When my shift was over, I was glad to go. I loved my friends at work, but my emotions were all over the place and I hated crying in front of people. The brave front had been my mantra ever since I could remember. My need to please and make others feel comfortable, was deeply ingrained in me.

Maria and I went to punch out and get our handbags from security. She guided me so I knew where to go.

"Natalie, I know your instinct is to think something's going to go wrong."

I looked at her quizzically. "How do you know?"

"I've been watching you hide from life for a long time. You and Kate...two peas in a pod. Kate has found her happily ever after. Now, it's your turn. Open yourself up to this experience. Live Natalie. It's time."

Tears streamed down my face. I placed the enormous bouquet on the ground, and Maria pulled me close.

"Your parents would want you to go on and find happiness. Promise me you're going to give Mac a chance...a real chance."

"I promise," I choked out.

We let go of each other and Maria looked closely at me. "You deserve this, Nat."

I smiled and managed to say, "Thanks, Maria. I don't know what I would do without you and the rest of the girls. You're like my family."

"We are your family, sweetie. We all love you." She was right. I was truly thankful.

Maria guided me to my car and I buckled the flowers into the passenger seat. Then I took out my phone and saw Mac's text. He wanted to have dinner if I was up for it. I texted him back that I would love to, and to pick me up at seven.

"Keep being open. Things are going to work out," Maria assured me. In that moment, I felt so blessed for Kate, Charlie, the women I worked with, but most of all Mac.

"I'll see you tomorrow, Maria."

"I'll be waiting to hear how your date went," she said with a wink.

***

I got home with enough time to do all of the date preparations—I showered, redid my makeup, and scoured my closet for a great outfit. I put on my charcoal-gray pencil skirt with my pink off-the-shoulder top. It was fitted, and certain to get Mac's undivided attention. A few minutes later, there was a knock at my door.

Mac was wearing a navy blue suit that brought out his piercing blue eyes. "You look stunning," he said, picking up my hand to kiss it.

"You're looking pretty good, yourself," I responded back.

"I came here straight from work. Taking Friday off means putting in more hours this week."

"I'm sure as the boss, your responsibilities never end."

"It's intense to run an international company, but my staff is amazing."

Mac eyed the floral arrangement sitting on my dining table. I looked up at him and said, "Someone sent me an embarrassing display of flowers today."

"Looks like you have an admirer," he said, with a very serious look on his face. If his eyes could devour me I think they would have—his gaze pierced me.

"Perhaps I do," I said smiling. "You're very thoughtful and I love them. Thank you."

Mac lifted my hand again and kissed it. "They pale in comparison to you, Natalie."

A warm sensation flooded me. Still holding my hand, he pulled my body into his, wrapped his arms around me, and breathed me in. My body pressed against his, caused a tingling that gave me a jolt between my legs. I inhaled his essence and wanted him to do a whole lot more than hold me. I wanted his hands and mouth to cover every inch of my writhing body. The desire welling up inside me was scary, and normally I wouldn't take a risk, but Mac was worth the possibility of heartbreak, even though that seemed more and more unlikely.

Our embrace ended as I asked, "Would you like to come in for a glass of wine before we go?"

His eyes seemed to darken at my offer, as if he was struggling to stay committed to his original plans. I couldn't believe I had such an effect on him.

"Perhaps I will take you up on your offer after dinner. I made reservations at Pehoe's in Coronado."

"I've always wanted to go there, but never have," I said, beaming at the man standing before me, who had a way of anticipating what I would like. *How were we already kindred spirits?*

"Shall we, then?" he asked, extending his arm. I entwined my arm with his and we departed.

Pehoe's was an enchanting restaurant inspired by the Hawaiian Islands. The cuisine had a tropical flavor, with endless seafood to choose from. Coconut shrimp caught my eye and I felt goose bumps gazing at Mac while he perused the menu. My heart was pounding just thinking about the fact that he wasn't just my date...he was the man I married just a few days ago. Pondering that thought should have been overwhelming, but somehow it was comforting, like a favorite pair of jeans that have been washed a hundred times and are always just the right fit.

"Have you decided what you want?" he asked.

"I know exactly what I want," I replied, looking at his handsome face. But what I wanted wasn't on the menu. I had no idea how deprived I had been until I woke up Saturday morning in bed with this beautiful man. I didn't want to be too forward, but I also wanted him to know I was as interested in him as he was in me.

"Me too," Mac said, placing his hand on my thigh. His touch made me quiver on the inside and I only hoped he couldn't feel me shaking. My attraction had increased with such intensity; I wasn't quite sure what to do with it.

"So, now that we are back in reality and not in the fantasy world of Vegas, how are you feeling about everything that has happened between us over the last few days?"

The directness of his question took me aback a little. I picked up my glass of water and took a sip, to give myself a second to compose my thoughts. Mac had been pretty honest with me, so I decided to wear my heart on my sleeve and be honest as well.

I put my hand on top of his, smiled, and said, "I'm feeling good about us, Mac. I don't know exactly how everything's going to work out, but I want to explore the possibilities of our relationship."

"You know I want the same thing. What do you think are the possibilities?"

I took another long swig of water. It was getting hot in here and I was beginning to feel somewhat exposed. But Mac had told me in Vegas he was falling in love with me, and we had spent a wonderful evening together in his home. The romantic in me was imagining the fairy tale ending, but the practical side was scared out of my mind.

The waiter, thank God, interrupted us to take our order, so I didn't have to answer right away. We ordered our food and Mac's eyes again were piercing a hole right through me. He said nothing, waiting for my response to his question.

It was time to take a leap, and have faith a net would be provided to catch me. I swallowed hard and said, "I do want to stay married to you, as insane as that sounds to my own ears, and I want to create what we each experienced growing up." There. I said it. I said it, but part of me was committed and the other part was trembling on the inside as fear coursed through me. Death had taken so much from me. I was terrified of losing Mac. It was almost easier to not try at all than to have any more loss.

But, I was going to be quiet and see what he had to say. Mac didn't speak. Instead, he took my face in his hands and began kissing me slowly. His soft lips caressed mine, creating a surge of electricity between us. My mind was taking me to places I couldn't or shouldn't explore in public. His kiss told me everything I needed to know. Staying his wife was what he wanted...what we both wanted. Strange turn of events since waking up in his bed Saturday morning.

When our lips parted, he said, "I'm so glad you said you want to stay my wife. I know everything's happening quickly, but I know in my heart this is right. What we have is meant to be."

"I feel the same way, Mac."

He kissed me on the cheek and asked, "So do you still want to keep this from Kate and Charlie?"

"Actually, yes, I do. If that's okay? Kate is going through so much with Roger still being out there and the cops have no leads. I'm so worried he's going to find her. How did he go from being just a neighbor to a stalker obsessed with her? I'm so grateful Neil's protecting her."

"I know. Neil's going out of his mind. If anything happens to Kate, he won't survive it. I hope the cops get a lead."

"Me too. Then, on top of that, she's getting married so soon, I just don't want her to worry about me. Let's face it, our friends are going to think we are crazy."

"Well, I am crazy...crazy about you."

Mac's words made me gooey on the inside. I loved his honesty...it was such a good trait. My parents may have died when I was just a young woman, but their marriage taught me so much about relationships. Honesty was a key ingredient. If I could have a marriage like they had, I would be the most fortunate woman alive. Mac had an amazing example of marriage from his parents as well. The loss of our parents drew us together...like they had prearranged this whole thing somehow. It brought a smile to my face and warmed my heart. It also gave me hope; something that I could see had died in me with the death of my parents, and the loss of Ty.

"What are you smiling about, Mrs. Carter?" Mac asked.

My heart skipped a beat when I heard him call me Mrs. Carter, and I knew I would never grow tired of hearing it. "I was just thinking we are both blessed to have had parents who were happily married, that we could learn from them and have a shot of creating something similar."

Mac closed his eyes and let out a brief sigh. "Nothing in the world would make me happier than to have what my parents had. They loved each other so much."

"So did mine."

"I know it's been a short time, but this is what I know about you. You're a kind, loving woman who puts her friends before herself. You were strong for your sister during the worst time in your lives,

"I know it's been a short time, but this is what I know about you. You're a kind, loving woman who puts her friends before herself. You were strong for your sister during the worst time in your lives, giving up what you wanted to take care of her. You're willing to do whatever it takes to demonstrate your love for the people in your life. I admire those qualities and I want to know more about you...everything."

My eyes filled with tears and one escaped down my cheek. "Oh Mac..." but before I could say anything else, Mac wrapped his hands around my face and kissed me again. He was making me want him, need him, and it had been a long time since I had let my guard down. It was a relief to be this way with him.

After dessert and a decaf coffee, Mac drove me home. Holding my hand in his, I imagined what it would be like to be his full-fledged wife—with all it entailed. Waking up in his arms, making love to him, spending quiet evenings at home. I said a silent prayer for all of this to work out—knowing I may not be able to take it if it didn't.

Mac walked me to my door. "Would you like to come in?" I asked, longing to be alone with him.

"I do want to come in, but it's getting late and we both have work in the morning. I'd love to see you tomorrow night if you're not busy. We could just hang out, get a pizza, watch a movie?"

"I'd love that," I uttered, as his hands found my waist and he pulled me close. He kissed me goodnight and departed, leaving me wanting more.

***

I woke up the next morning eager for it to be evening again. I hoped work would fly by so I could be in Mac's arms—the only place I wanted to be.

I arrived at work about thirty minutes before the store opened and told Maria all about our wonderful dinner, leaving out the part about being married, of course. Maria would flip if she knew that. When the store opened, I had a surprise visitor...Cassie.

I was taken completely by surprise when she walked into the kid's department looking like she was on a mission. I didn't know what she wanted from me, but I did know she wanted Mac back.

"Natalie, so nice to see you," she said, with a sickeningly sweet voice. *How did Mac date her for so long?*

"Can I help you with something, Cassie?" I asked in a businesslike manner.

"I thought we could grab a cup of coffee since we have something in common."

I wasn't happy at the thought of having coffee with her, but I was intrigued to know what she wanted.

I looked at my watch. "I could take a fifteen minute break. Why don't we have coffee in the Café?"

"That sounds just charming, dear," she said in a condescending manner.

I glanced at Maria who had a scrunched up face. "Maria, I'm going to take a break," I said.

"Okay," Maria said. "Have a good time." Her voice went up at the end of her statement as if she was saying it as a question.

Cassie and I went to the Café, ordered our coffee, and sat down. I stared at her, waiting to hear the web she would spin.

"I just wanted to come give you a friendly warning. You seem like a nice girl, but Mac and I have been through break-ups before and we always get back together. I don't know what he has told you, but ultimately he can't stay away from me."

I wanted to wipe that smug look off her face, but I didn't want to give her the satisfaction of knowing she'd rattled me.

"Thanks for the heads up. But I'll wait to see what Mac decides."

"I just don't want you to get hurt, sweetie. Mac always goes through a couple of girls when we are apart and then he comes crawling back to me. So you should make it easier on yourself, and just walk away now."

I wanted to scream at her that we were already married, but I knew she needed to stay in the dark. Telling her wouldn't benefit me in the slightest. Even though, it would be great to see the look on her face and her jaw drop open. But, that just wasn't me, either.

"Don't worry about me," I retorted. "I can take care of myself."

"Oh, I'm sure you can. I'd just hate to see another girl get hurt by *my* Mac, that's all."

"Anything else?" I questioned before I stood up.

Cassie shook her head.

"I must be getting back to work. My break is over. Thanks for the coffee."

"You're welcome. Just keep in mind what we talked about."

I walked away with haste. How did Mac date her for two years? She was such a viper. I had a feeling this wouldn't be the last time we saw each other.

The rest of the day flew by. I answered all of Maria's questions about my unexpected visitor, but the person I really wanted to talk to about it was Mac. He would be at my place around seven for pizza and movies. I would get the 411 then.

I had picked up wine and beer on the way home, not knowing what Mac would prefer. My condo seemed so empty without Jessica and my thoughts turned toward our last conversation. I hoped the trial would provide some closure. I didn't know what I would be doing with myself right now if I didn't have Mac. I smiled inwardly, as I changed into my favorite jeans and soft grey knit shirt.

A knock on the door brought me out of my mental funk. When I opened it and saw Mac standing there, I couldn't help myself. I leapt into his arms, wrapping my body around his. He wound his muscular arms around me as my mouth met his. There we were in my doorway, passionately kissing. Perhaps Mac thought it would be better to be in private. He began walking us toward the couch. He must have memorized my apartment because he managed to not only find the couch, but he sat on it with me straddling him. Our tongues continued to swirl and every cell in my body had come to life. God, how I wanted him to make love to me. I had been thinking about it all afternoon.

"That's quite the welcome, beautiful girl. A guy could get used to this."

I smiled. "I'm happy to see you. I can tell you are happy to see me, too," I said suggestively.

Mac had a way of not only relaxing me, but also bringing out my sensual side. His hands moved from my waist to my hips. "So how was your day, baby?"

"It was interesting. I had an unexpected visitor."

Mac's brow creased. "Unexpected visitor?"

"Yes. Cassie, your ex."

"What?" Mac practically shouted. "She came to see you at work?"

"Yeah. I thought it was weird, but she's pulling out a last ditch effort to get you back."

"What did she say to you? Did she threaten you in any way? You didn't tell her we are married, did you?"

"No. What's going on? Why are you getting so upset?"

"I just don't want her to bother you. She's a little bit...crazy."

"I could tell. She told me that you two break up often and you come crawling back to her after you have had your fill of other women."

"Natalie, I can assure you, not only is that not true, but I don't want to have anything to do with her. She is my past and you are my future."

"I know. I kind of felt sorry for her today. She was grasping at straws to keep you in her life and the desperation just radiated off her body."

"You are being very generous right now. Did she say how she found you?"

What? "I assumed she knew from you. You didn't tell her I work at Nordstrom?"

"No."

"Then how did she know?"

"I have no idea. She's very resourceful and has a way of getting what she wants."

"Well, I have news for you...she's not getting you back. You're all mine, Mr. Carter."

Mac smiled. "Good to know, baby. Good to know."

Just then there was a knock on the door. "That must be the pizza."

"Let me get it," Mac said.

I moved off Mac's lap and watched him stride toward the door. Interesting that it wasn't exactly pizza I was hungry for at that moment. It was the pizza delivery guy, so I got up to get plates, drinks, and the salad I had made.

"I thought we could set everything up on the coffee table. I have several movie options."

"Great. What are the choices?" Mac asked, as he set the pizza down on the table.

I rattled off the choices and we decided on *The Princess Bride,* one of my all-time favorites. Mac put his arm around me and I snuggled into him. Being casual with him felt perfect. Natural. I watched the movie halfheartedly since my mind kept wandering to what might happen after the movie was over. Having Mac so close, touching him, breathing him in, was a deadly combination that heightened all of my senses.

When the movie ended, Mac looked at his watch. He seemed preoccupied. "Still thinking about Cassie?" I asked.

"Unfortunately, yes. I'll be seeing her tomorrow, and I will make sure she doesn't visit you again. It's getting late and I have an early morning meeting. I should get going," he said, kissing me on the top of my head.

"You really have to go?"

"Yeah. I've got some pressing matters to take care of at work. I hate to cut our date short, but it can't be helped."

"Okay. I'll walk you out."

I walked Mac to the door and before I opened it he took both my hands in his. "This might sound strange, but I don't know what your plans are for Christmas. We're going to spend it together, right?" he asked, eyebrows raised.

"I would love that," I said, hugging him. "What do you do for Christmas?"

"I spend it with the Statton's, at their home. Even before my parents died we always spent Christmas together."

"That sounds perfect. I just hope Mr. and Mrs. Statton don't think I'm an idiot for running out on Thanksgiving."

"I'm sure they don't. They're down to earth people and they've both lost people they loved."

"It's hard to believe it's almost Christmas. Everything's going by so fast."

"How about in the next couple of months we take a trip together and slow time down a little bit? We could sail to Hawaii on my yacht."

"You have a yacht?" I asked, surprise engulfing me. I knew Mac had money, but I no clue how much.

"Yeah, I love to be on the water. I haven't had the time lately to spend on it, but once I get the issues squared away in London, I'll be able to take a vacation."

I looked up into Mac's ruggedly handsome face. "A trip to Hawaii with you would be heaven." *How did I get so lucky?*

"Good," Mac said, kissing me again. "I'll talk to you tomorrow."

"Tomorrow," I said. Then he left.

CHAPTER 14: MAC

I called Neil first thing in the morning. "Neil, any word from the hacker?"

"Yes, he just called me a few minutes ago. He found the pictures on Cassie's computer, sent her a virus, and has destroyed every file. Cassie will have no clue how it happened. The only problem is if she saved it on a thumb drive or has hard copies."

"Yeah, that's a problem," I said, annoyed to have to deal with Cassie.

"I've got it handled. When you're at lunch, I'll have someone search her place."

"You're always thinking ahead, man. You're not going to believe what she did. She went to visit Natalie at work."

"That woman has some balls, man. She's not going to go easily," Neil said.

"I know. I'm furious and I hate that she's investigating Natalie. I have no idea how Cassie knew where Natalie works."

"They just met the one time, right?" Neil asked.

"Yes."

"Do you think Cassie wrote down Natalie's license plate number when they were both at your house?"

"That could explain it." It didn't sound like the Cassie I dated, but the woman pursuing me so urgently, was vastly different from the girl I went out with.

"Don't freak, but maybe she's had Natalie followed. The info from the license plate would only give her Natalie's name and

"Don't freak, but maybe she's had Natalie followed. The info from the license plate would only give her Natalie's name and address, not where she works," Neil said.

"Yeah, it crossed my mind. I'm going to hire security to watch over Natalie. I'm just not telling her."

"Good plan. I'd say hire Paul's firm, but Natalie has probably met most of the guys when she's been with Kate. It can't be anyone she would recognize."

"I'm already on it. I have a meeting with Silverstone Securities this morning."

"When are you taking care of Harold?"

"I'm seeing him first thing when I get to the office, so I better go."

"Alright, later, bro."

"Later."

When I arrived at the office, Harold was already waiting for me in reception. He sat across from Alice because I had instructed her not to let him into my office alone. His story didn't resonate with me as being completely truthful, and I wasn't certain of what he was capable of doing.

We exchanged the common pleasantries and he followed me in, taking a seat in the first chair.

"Harold, you dropped a bomb on me yesterday. I've thought a lot about how to handle this. It's going to go like this. You're going to retire with a severance package. You and your daughter are going on a long trip wherever you want, but there will be no contact with anyone. Under no circumstances is anyone to know where you are going. Time to disappear for a while."

"I see," said Harold. "I know I have completely failed you and if you want me to leave, it's the least I can do."

"I know you're worried about your daughter and I can assure you I'm doing everything in my power to locate the pictures and have them destroyed."

"I appreciate that very much."

I pulled out a folder with paperwork Neil had drafted. I slid the folder across the desk. "I need you to sign these. I don't want any problems."

"Of course. I'll just read through them and get them back to you as soon as possible."

"I want this wrapped up today. Your resignation, and the paperwork signed."

Harold nodded. "It will be done." He stood and walked out.

I was glad to see him go. His betrayal was like a noose around my neck, suffocating me. I was so disappointed, but I could understand him wanting to protect his daughter. I understood more, now that I had someone to protect, too.

Alice buzzed me. "Mr. Silverstone has arrived," she said.

"Please send him in, Alice."

"Mr. Silverstone, thanks for meeting me on such short notice," I said, extending my hand to shake his.

"Please call me Gavin. My firm is at your service."

"Yeah, call me Mac. Let's get down to business. The young woman you will be protecting, Natalie Mason, is very important to me and I don't want her to know you are following her. I need invisibility."

"We are more than capable of blending in. She'll never know we're there."

"Good. Also, here's a picture of the possible threat," I said, handing him a picture of Cassie. "She has been blackmailing my lawyer and she paid a visit to Natalie yesterday at work."

"Okay. Do you want me to have someone tail her as well?"

I thought for a moment. "Yes, I do. I have a feeling Cassie could become dangerous and I have no idea what she is capable of doing."

I gave Gavin all of Natalie's info along with Cassie's, and he was on his way.

I had a mountain of work to do, so I sent Nat a text letting her know I wanted to take her to dinner tomorrow night—anywhere she wanted to go. I knew I'd be at the office late to finalize everything with Harold, and the deal I had been working on in Europe. Excitement and frustration both, poured over me knowing I'd be going to London in a few weeks. The trial prevented me from taking Natalie along. I'd have to plan a wonderful honeymoon for us in the very near future. She was all I could think about. Not just how much I wanted to make love to her again. She was just so much more to me. She was mine and I would do anything to protect her.

CHAPTER 15: NATALIE

Work had been hectic with all of the Christmas shoppers. My feet were killing me, and I was looking forward to a night to myself to regroup a little after a whirlwind weekend with Mac. Mac and I had been together several nights in a row and as much as I loved his company, I had grown accustomed to being alone. Not that I preferred to be alone, it had just become my norm.

My phone began ringing and I saw it was Kate.

"Hey Kate."

"Hi Nat. How's it going?"

"Good, just tired from work. We were so busy today. I only took fifteen minutes for lunch."

"I know. I miss being with all of you at Nordie's. In so many ways it was fun."

"Oh, sweetie. We'd love to have you back. Any word from the police about Roger? Have they found him yet?"

"No, he's still out there somewhere. I'm constantly looking over my shoulder. I just want him to be caught," Kate said with a sigh. "I'm also terrified he's going to do something to Neil. Roger is seriously deranged."

"I can't even imagine what you are going through. You both still have security, right?"

"Yes, as we know, security isn't a hundred percent guarantee of safety. Roger is on a mission and he's so much more cunning than I ever imagined."

"Have you been able to sleep at night?"

"Not without having nightmares that Roger has taken me. I'm going to see my doctor today to get something for my anxiety."

"I had to take anxiety meds when my parents died. They help take the edge off. I'm glad you're getting some."

"Me too. I really need to relax. I feel so jumpy all of the time. God, when I think about moving in next door to him, he seemed so normal. Never in a million years would I have thought he was a mad man and would become obsessed with me. I shudder to think about what could have happened if I hadn't gotten away from him."

"I know. I'm so grateful you have Neil to keep you safe."

"Yeah, Neil has been amazing. I don't know what I'd do without him. I'm so lucky Nat. If wasn't for Neil, I don't know what would have happened," Kate said, with a hitch in her voice.

"Oh, Kate. He'll be caught soon. It's going to be okay." I was hoping to console my dearest friend, but I knew she was crying on the other end. How could she not be? The stress of having a stalker who the police thought had killed people was enough to put anyone on the edge.

"I'm sure you're right Nat. Anyway, I don't want to give Roger any more time. Let's talk about something else. I had a great time last weekend with you, Charlie, and the guys. Have you heard from Mac?"

How was I going to get out of this question without lying? "We've been in touch."

"That's good. I think you two would be great together."

"Well, we'll see what happens." Hopefully being vague would get me off the hook for answering any more questions. I didn't want to burden Kate with my worries. She had enough on her plate.

"I wanted to ask you, and of course you can say no if you'd prefer not to, but would you like to spend Christmas with us at the Statton's?"

That was perfect. Now I didn't have to explain that Mac had invited me. Plus, it made me feel so good that Kate was inviting me again after I abruptly left on Thanksgiving. She was always there for me. "I'd love to."

"How are you holding up with everything? I know you were a trooper over the weekend."

"I'm doing okay. I just want to get the trial over with so I can begin to move on. It's hard to grieve when I still have to face court."

"I wish I could be there with you. I hate that you're facing this alone. Have you had a chance to talk to the girls at work? I'm sure whoever is off will go with you."

"It's been so busy, I haven't had a chance. But something will work out."

"It will. It'll be hard, but at least you'll have some closure."

"Thanks, Kate. I'm so glad I have you and Charlie."

"Nat, you and Charlie are my best friends. I just want to get through this and I want you to be happy."

"I know, Kate. I have a feeling I'll find my happiness soon."

"I think so too, Nat."

We talked about wedding details and the rehearsal dinner. I was so happy for Kate and I was surprisingly happy for myself for a change. After our call, I got into bed with my Kindle, and fell asleep reading *Eyes Wide Open*. If Brynne could find her happily ever after, then so could I.

When I woke up in the morning, I thought of two things. One, I was going to see Mac, look into his beautiful eyes, kiss him senseless, and feel his arms around me. Two, he was having lunch with his ex-girlfriend, a very beautiful woman, who wanted him back. That thought was very unpleasant, especially since she'd paid me a visit spewing her web of lies. I had downplayed my feelings about her visiting me at work so Mac wouldn't think I was jealous or insecure, but the reality was, I felt ill knowing he would be spending time with her. It was going to be a long day.

CHAPTER 16: MAC

I woke up dreading lunch with Cassie. How was I going to sit there and not tell her off for being so despicable? I kept telling myself it was the only way I would get the upper hand. If she thought this craziness was going to work, she was sadly mistaken.

My morning was busy and lunch seemed to arrive instantaneously. As I drove to the restaurant, I kept replaying Neil's words. Stay calm and don't tell her a thing. Seeing Cassie was the last thing I wanted to do.

Walking into the restaurant, I spotted Cassie sitting at a table she and I had shared many times. She had ordered a bottle of wine, and was already drinking it when I walked up.

"Mac, so lovely to see you," she said in a sugary sweet voice. I never noticed that about her. *Was she like this before?*

"You indicated when you came over to my home, that we needed to talk. So, here I am."

"There's no rush. I took the liberty of ordering our favorite appetizer and wine," she said, pouring me a glass. She lifted her glass to make a toast. "Here's to us finding our way back to each other."

I shook my head slightly. "I'm sorry, but that's not going to happen."

"Mac, I forgive you for impetuously breaking up with me. I shouldn't have pressured you into marrying me. Why don't we just pick up where we left off and put this whole stupid break up behind us?"

"Cassie, I appreciate your candor, but I don't want to get back together."

"It's that other woman, Natalie, isn't it?"

My blood began to boil even more when I heard Cassie say Natalie's name. "Let's leave Natalie out of this. She's a friend of Neil's and you don't need to be concerned with her."

"I see. So you're not romantically involved with her? She's an awfully pretty friend," Cassie said, making air quotes when she said friend.

The waiter brought the appetizer and asked for our order. I was seething, but I kept hearing Neil in my head, so I stayed composed and ordered a sandwich. I popped a stuffed mushroom in my mouth so I didn't have to respond right away.

"Mac, I don't want to argue about an inconsequential girl. I want to discuss us getting back together. I have something to tell you that might come as a shock."

I sat there, staring at her, knowing she was about to tell me her dirty little secret—at least part of it.

"I found out some very important information about your trust. Your parents put in a clause stating you have to be married when you are thirty to keep your company. That's why I suggested we get married. I was looking out for your best interest."

"My best interest?" I said, raising my eyebrows.

"Well, of course. You know how much I love you and want what's best for you."

"I see," was all I could muster.

"So, when do you want to get married?"

"Like I said earlier, I'm not getting back together with you. Your disclosure changes nothing. I'm not the one for you," I said, beginning to rise. "You deserve someone better than me and I hope you find him soon."

"Mac, you're the one I want. No one is better for me than you. Besides, this is a win-win. You get to keep what is yours and I get to be your wife."

"I'll take what you've said under advisement. Right now, I need to get back to work."

"But you haven't eaten anything or…"

"I'll take it to go," I said, flagging down the waiter. I asked him to wrap up my food and then I paid the bill. "Take care of yourself, Cassie." I then turned and walked toward the entrance of the restaurant. The waiter brought me a bag and I was out the door. I knew if I hadn't left when I did, I would have lost it.

I got back to the office and immediately called Neil to fill him in. I honestly didn't know what to make of Cassie. She was more unstable than I realized.

"She sounds so fucked up. Did the security start today?"

"Yes. I have two men covering Natalie at all times."

"Good."

"I need to convince Natalie to go public with the fact we're married and move in with me."

"Yeah, but somehow I don't think that will detour Cassie. She's been blackmailing your lawyer, after all."

"This is worse than I anticipated." Then it hit me. Neil had his own mental person to be concerned with—Roger. "Neil, I'm so lame. You don't need to solve my problem with Cassie. You've got your own irrational lunatic to deal with."

"Don't sweat it, bro."

"But what you're dealing with is so much worse."

Alice buzzed me that some board members were here to see me.

"I've gotta go. I need to talk to some of the board members."

"Alright, later."

Alice ushered the board members into my office. Mrs. Langstrom was the first to speak. "We've been informed of the clause in your parents' trust. When are you planning on getting married?"

Damn, Cassie worked fast. She had a master plan and I was beginning to understand I needed to start playing offense instead of defense. "Soon, Mrs. Langstrom."

"Well, we haven't seen any announcements in the paper. So what does soon, mean?" Mr. Billings questioned.

"I'll let you all know when I am ready. Is there anything else?" They all just stood there staring at me. "Okay then, I have work to do. If you will excuse me," I said, motioning toward the door.

The day couldn't end soon enough. I had texted Natalie about dinner at seven. She replied that she'd be ready. Putting the day behind me was easy, knowing I would be spending the evening with her, and I had planned, what I hoped, would be a memorable one.

CHAPTER 17: NATALIE

When I opened the door, Mac's face lit up. I was wearing my black dress with a low V-neck, showing off a little bit of cleavage. Hearing a slight groan escape from him, I knew my outfit was just right.

"Hi, baby," Mac said. "You are looking very beautiful this evening." Seeing him react like that to me, and call me baby, almost had me swooning. *Mac was good for my heart. I hoped.*

"Thank you," I said, blushing. "Where are we going?"

"It's a surprise, but you're going to need your coat."

After I grabbed my leather coat, Mac extended his arm to me. On the drive over, we briefly talked about his lunch with Cassie. Without saying too much, he explained Cassie had become accustomed to a certain lifestyle...a lifestyle he could provide. It seemed she wasn't willing to give up without a fight. He had made it clear to her at lunch they weren't getting back together.

"How did she take it?" I asked.

"I'm not sure. Somehow I have the feeling it's not the end of things. But maybe once we go public with being married, she'll give up."

Mac pulled up to the harbor and said, "We're here."

I looked around a little unsure of where here was. "Okay," I said.

Mac got out and went around opening my door. "What are we doing here?" I asked.

"We're having dinner on my yacht."

"You're full of surprises, Mr. Carter," I said.

"You have no idea, baby. I plan on keeping you guessing for the rest of your life."

Looking up into his big blue eyes, I could see love resonating from them. I knew Mac had completely given his heart to me and I had given mine to him. As we walked along the dock hand in hand I didn't feel my feet touch the planks. I was walking on air.

Seeing his yacht, I remarked, "Mac, it's so beautiful."

"Thanks. My parents bought it a couple of years before they died and we had some amazing times on it. My favorite was cruising to Hawaii."

"I'm looking forward to our trip to Hawaii," I said, as Mac helped me onto his yacht.

"Me too, Nat."

"Wow, this is huge."

"It sleeps eight people, so it's a fun party boat. We'll have to have our friends out in the near future."

I heard what he said, but that meant our friends knowing we were married. I thought I would feel adverse to the idea, but I was beginning to really like it. Mrs. Mac Carter had a lovely ring to it.

"Do you go out often?" I asked, as we approached a romantic table set for two, champagne chilling beside it.

Mac pulled my chair out for me. "I don't take her out as much as I would like."

A server came up from below and greeted us. "Good evening sir, miss. May I pour some champagne for you?"

"Yes, Miles. Thank you."

"Do you have a full-time staff as well?"

"Miles is here full-time. The rest of the staff joins for excursions when needed."

Mac lifted his champagne glass. "To a beautiful night with an even more beautiful woman." We clinked our glasses and each took a sip. The bubbles tickled my nose. My heart began racing, especially after reading about the erotic images when the heroine had been seduced, when reading the night before. I wondered if Mac and I would be engaging in some shipboard romance of our own. I flushed at my thoughts.

I set my glass down as did Mac. Music began playing in the background, with the smooth voice of Harry Connick Jr. singing *It Had to Be You.* "We'll be having dinner in about fifteen minutes. Would you like to dance in the meantime?"

"I'd love to."

Mac stood and extended his hand to me. I took it eagerly. I wanted so much to be in his arms, feeling his heart beat against mine. His boyish good looks were so sexy to me.

Mac pulled me close and nuzzled his nose in my hair. "Natalie, you smell so delicious, I just want to eat you up."

That was my undoing. I wanted to kiss him so badly. Who was I kidding? I wanted to do way more than kiss him. I looked up at him, and watched his mouth plunging toward mine, enrapturing me, controlling me, devouring me. His tongue tangled with mine as our bodies swayed to the music. Every part of me was alight, and all I wanted was to find a cabin down below and be with him. My body was pressed hard against his as our kiss continued. I was beginning to feel faint, the passion between us overwhelming me. Our kiss continued until Miles brought up our salads, interrupting our moment. Part of me was relieved, because I didn't know how long I could continue without more happening. I wondered if Mac would make love to me, again.

"Shall we?" he asked, motioning toward the table. I was still breathless from our kiss, so it took me a moment to even consider food. Mac, ever the gentleman, pulled out my chair for me. I looked down at the decadent food, then back up at the man before me. He took my breath away. It was almost as if he was holding back on my behalf. *I hoped that's what it was.* We began eating our salads.

"This is so delicious. I love the mix of pears with gorgonzola cheese and walnuts."

"Me, too," Mac said. "But I love kissing you more, though. You taste way better than this salad." His piercing blue eyes seared me. I imagined leaping over the table and into his arms. I needed to get a hold of myself. All I could do was look back at him with the same intensity.

To break the spell he had on me, I began questioning him again, although it was hard to find my voice. "So, when was the last time you took your boat out?"

Mac thought for a moment. "It's been about three months."

"Did you take Cassie out? On the boat, I mean?" *Why was I asking him this? So stupid.*

"Oh, yes. We dated for almost two years."

"What broke you up, if you don't mind me asking?"

"My assistant, Alice."

"Seriously? How did that go down?"

"One evening when Cassie was leaving my office, I overhead Alice say goodnight to her and wish her a pleasant evening. Cassie didn't even acknowledge Alice. I was standing at the door, but Cassie didn't know it. So, once she was completely gone, I called Alice into my office. She sat across from me and I asked her point blank what she thought of Cassie."

"Wow, what did she say?"

"Alice attempted to be diplomatic. She didn't want to say anything negative about Cassie. She probably assumed I would be asking Cassie to marry me."

"How did you get the truth out of her?"

"By telling her the truth. That I needed her opinion on whether or not Cassie was the one for me. I told her I trusted her implicitly and wanted her thoughts about Cassie. Alice has known me for a long time. She's like family to me."

"What did she say?"

"Alice is a very wise woman. She told me I would never be happy with a woman who treated other people so poorly. Cassie had no consideration for anyone but herself and I would eventually be miserable if I married her."

"That took a lot of courage on Alice's part."

"It did. But Alice has never steered me wrong. I trust her with my life and being married to someone is a big part of life. Plus, I already felt Cassie and I wouldn't have a relationship like my parents. She was spoiled and selfish. It just took a while to see it."

I sighed. "Well, when you have feelings for someone it's sometimes difficult to see the real them, if they are hiding things they don't want you to know."

"That's a very good point."

Our server brought out the lobster tail with melted butter, halting our conversation momentarily. I pulled off a piece of lobster with my fork, dipped it in butter and fed it to Mac. As the fork entered his mouth, he closed his eyes and moaned slightly.

"Delicious, baby," he said, as his eyes opened and he gave me a mouthwatering look, his eyes blazing, locked on mine. He was so sexy and I was so attracted to him. But not just his looks, I was attracted to his personality, honesty, generosity, sense of humor. Did I just make a list for myself? Yes. He was all of those things and so much more. I smiled slightly when the thought came to me, that he was all mine.

"I have to admit, it doesn't hurt my feelings any, that things didn't work out with you and Cassie," I said, looking at him coquettishly. "Her loss is my gain."

Mac didn't say a word. He stood up and held his hand out to me. As I took his hand, he kissed it sending shivers through my body. He pulled me close and whispered in my ear, "Baby, I've gained everything by having you in my life. You are more important to me than you can imagine. I'm so glad I get to prove to you what you mean to me."

"Oh, Mac," I breathed. His words had caused more stirring inside me. I felt both hot and chilled simultaneously.

"Let's get you inside baby. You're shaking."

I wasn't sure if I was just cold or if his words had caused me to quiver. We went down below to the living room. Mac asked for Miles to bring our food to us. While we waited, he sweetly kissed me on the sofa. I kept wondering if he was going to make a move, but he stayed a gentleman. I wasn't normally such an indecisive person. However, being with Mac both confused and delighted me. I was cautious by nature, so waiting still felt right. But, with a sexy man like Mac kissing me, my resolve was weakening. Choosing to let nature take its course, I firmly believed we would both know when it was right. Then, it would be perfect timing, and I would have no doubts whatsoever. Our meal was brought to us and we continued eating. It was so hard to keep from launching myself at him, so I did what I did best. Hid. Hid behind the mask of social decorum.

"So, it sounds like you've had this boat for a long time," I said.

"Yes, my parents bought it when I was ten. We mostly did day or weekend excursions except for a vacation to Hawaii. I didn't take it out on a long journey until the summer after I turned eighteen. After my parents died, I stayed with Neil's family and finished high school. A few days after graduating, I took her out with a crew on board. Neil came with me and we cruised down to Cabo. We had a blast for the month we were gone."

"Oh, that sounds so exciting. I haven't had much experience traveling so far, but I'd love to see the world."

"You will, Nat. I'll gladly be your tour guide. We can go anywhere you want."

"I leaned into to him and put my head on his shoulder. "How did all of this happen?"

"What do you mean?"

"I mean, on Friday we were just two people driving to Vegas together. Well, obviously more than that, but not much. How did we get from there to here, in each other's arms?"

Mac pulled my chin up to look into my eyes. "I'm just one lucky man. You're truly an amazing gift I wasn't expecting."

Again I found myself searching his eyes for any malice, but I only saw sincerity, and love. We kissed for a while on the sofa...sweet, soft, beautiful kisses. I was glad Mac wasn't in any rush. Feeling cherished by him only heightened my desire.

"Nat, it's getting late and I know you have to work in the morning. I'm sure you're going to have another slammed day."

"Yes, it's going to be insanely busy until Christmas Eve at six o'clock when the store closes. But, in the six weeks before Christmas, I make about thirty percent of my income, so it's all good."

Mac had a frown on his chiseled face.

"What's wrong?" I asked, thinking I had said something that offended him.

"Nothing. It's just...you know you don't have to work anymore. I mean, look around, I obviously have enough money. I'd like to look after you, Nat."

He had just thrown me for a loop. "I know you have money, but it doesn't mean it belongs to me or I can quit my job." I could tell by the look on his face and his jaw slightly dropping that he knew he

"Actually, yes it does. We aren't staying a secret forever, right? You've told me that you want to stay married."

"Mac, everything is happening so fast. I just need a little time. I'm not ready to discuss quitting my job or what the future might bring. I just want to enjoy getting to know you."

Mac looked down toward the floor. He had been so open toward me and expressed how much he wanted me in his life, and I had just shot him down. *What was wrong with me?*

"Mac…"

"You know what, Nat? I'm going to have Miles drive you home. I feel like staying here tonight," he said, as he released me and began walking toward a door I presumed led to the kitchen.

I ran after him and grabbed his hand. "Mac, please. Please stop. I didn't mean to push you away. I'm so attracted to you that it scares me to death. I…I just…I can't take getting hurt. I hope you can understand." My eyes were filled with tears from the possibility he could give up on me.

Caressing my face, Mac paused, as if considering what to say. "I'm a patient man, but I have to admit, waiting to go public about our marriage is difficult. I just needed you to throw me a bone. So, you're so attracted to me, huh?" A grin spread across his handsome face, and I found myself pushing him in the shoulder feigning annoyance at his arrogance.

"Come. Let me take you home."

We walked hand in hand back the way we came. Our drive to my house was quiet, but Mac held my hand the entire way. Him walking away from me proved something to both of us.

"Before we say goodnight, I wanted to invite you to the ball the Statton's are throwing on Saturday night. They are doing a fundraiser for the San Diego Children's Foundation. I would love for you to go with me."

"That sounds amazing. Is it black tie?"

"Yes."

"Well, I'm sure I could find something to wear from work."

"I have an idea. How about I take you shopping tomorrow night? We'll find the perfect gown."

A man after my own shopping heart. "I love that idea."

"Me, too. You can be my own personal Barbie doll," he said, with a salacious grin.

I shook my head with a smile on my face. "I get off work at six."

"I'll pick you up at work, then. Do you want to shop at Nordstrom or somewhere else?"

"I'll peruse the store and see if there's anything I want to try on. We can take it from there."

Mac kissed me lightly on my lips. "I'll see you tomorrow."

"See you then."

CHAPTER 18: MAC

I wasn't sure what to expect from Cassie. She wasn't just going to ride into the sunset quietly. My phone lit up and it was Neil.

"Hey bro, any word from the guy searching Cassie's place?"

"He texted me that he'd hit the jackpot. Cassie had a secret compartment in her bedroom wall. He took the pictures and some other things. He's bringing them to me this morning."

"Great," I said, relieved.

"Come on by whenever you get a chance."

"I'll bring lunch later if you're available."

"Yes, I'm here all day."

The morning was busy and lunch arrived before I knew it. Alice ordered take out and I picked up on the way. I couldn't wait to see the look on Cassie's face when she realized her leverage was gone.

Neil's assistant was away from her desk, so I peered into his office. "Hey, ready for a break?"

"Yes," Neil said, wearily. I have been busy today. Lawsuits."

"I know what you mean. I'm frantically working on the merger with Merrick Electronics. Now that Harold's retired, I'm going to need your help."

"Have your assistant send over the files so I can become familiar with everything. You do have a lawyer in London who's helping to broker the deal, right?"

"Yes. He's really sharp. I just want to be prepared and know everything that's being stipulated in the contract."

Neil moved to the table in his office as I placed the food on it. We began eating and he opened the box of items from Cassie's apartment.

"No wonder Harold did what Cassie said. These pictures are so graphic," I said, getting an eye full of his daughter.

"I thought it was strange only her face can be identified, not the man. Whoever she was with, didn't want any pub if they did go public. Now the question is, do you think Cassie would have another set of pictures?"

"Hard to say. She had them on her computer and hard copy. I would imagine she would have been satisfied with that. What else did he find?" I asked.

"Falsified identification."

"What?"

"She has a birth certificate, passport, and a drivers' license under the name Kimberly Montrose. Have you heard that name before?"

I searched the crevices of my mind. "No, not that I can think of. God, I wonder why she would have that?"

"It's hard to say. It could be someone she was planning on becoming or who she actually is, or maybe, neither."

"This is so fucked up," I said, staring at the passport.

"I'm doing a background check on Cassie and her alias, to see if anything comes up. Hopefully it will give us some clues."

I slumped in the chair. "I'll let the security team know the threat to Natalie is more serious than I thought. I don't think she's crazy. It seems more like she's had a plan the whole time."

"That's what I was thinking, too. I want you to start writing down what was happening in your life and in your business when you met Cassie. Maybe you'll be able to pinpoint something to help unravel all of this," Neil suggested.

"Okay. But it was two years ago. It's easier said than done."

"How did you meet her again?"

"Oddly, we met at the grocery store. She asked me a question about something and we struck up a conversation. Afterwards, we went for a drink."

"A random encounter that could have been designed by her," Neil said. "We'll get to the bottom of this. On a happier note, how are things with Natalie?"

"We had dinner on my yacht last night."

"Just dinner?" Neil asked, raising his eyebrows.

"Yes, just dinner. I'm not a hundred percent convinced she's ready to be my wife, so I'm trying to go slow, but it's definitely a challenge. I want her so damn bad."

Neil nodded. "I know the feeling. Kate had me from our first phone call."

"I just have to be patient until Natalie's ready to go public. I did, however, invite her to your parents' ball on Saturday."

"Good. Maybe with Kate and Charlie seeing her as your date, she might break down and tell them. I'm not loving keeping this secret. Kate is eager to see what will happen between you two."

"As long as Cassie doesn't screw it up, I think Natalie and I will stay married."

We talked about the highlights from ESPN and finished eating. Neil had a client coming in and I needed to get back to the office.

***

I couldn't get the smile off my face as I drove toward Nordstrom to pick up Natalie. She was waiting for me at the employee entrance. When I pulled up, she gave me her dazzling smile. Damn, I was a goner. She had such a sweet innocence about her, but at the same time, was alluring as hell. *Shit. Waiting is hard.*

"How was your day?" I asked her as she got into my car.

"It was long. We had some difficult customers today. One actually threw a gift box at me that was on display. We were so busy; we couldn't give very good service. I'm pretty sure she went to personnel to complain about me."

"Oh, Nat. That sucks. Are you going to be in trouble?"

"I'll be talked to, but that should be it. One customer complaint isn't going to get me fired."

"Well, you can resign anytime, baby."

"You're a typical man, Mac Carter. Always angling to get your way."

"True. I have to warn you, I'm an only child and used to getting what I want."

"Well, we'll just see about that," she said with a giggle. I could listen to her laugh all night. I could think of a few other things I could do with her all night, too.

"So, did you find anything you wanted to try on here at Nordies?"

"No. I did look during lunch and tried on a few things, but nothing was quite right."

"I'm assuming you have an idea of other stores for us to try."

"Yes, there's a shop here in the mall that has only evening attire. But it's on the other side, so let's drive so we can park close. My feet are killing me."

"Your wish is my command, Mrs. Carter," I said smiling. I couldn't wait to see her in an evening gown.

We parked the car and I came around to open her door. She took my hand getting out, and then I was able to envelop her into my arms. Feeling her pressed against me caused an ache only she could fulfill. I inhaled deeply, smelling the gardenia-scented shampoo she must use. The best part about all of it was her hugging me back.

"So, where's this store of yours?" I asked, nuzzling her nose.

"This way," she said, taking my hand.

Natalie was right about the store. It was wall to wall dresses and I was content to see her try on every single one of them. The store owner was very smart and had provided a sofa for the men while waiting for their women. Natalie began selecting dresses, and within a few moments, her arms were full. The sales lady put her in a fitting room and I eagerly waited.

While she was in trying on dresses, one in particular caught my eye. It was a white halter-neck dress that looked like it would hug every curve on Natalie's gorgeous body. I hoped one day to see her in something sexy like that. I more than hoped...I was counting on it.

Modeling dress after dress, Natalie's face was lit up like a Christmas tree with twinkling lights. She looked incredible in every one of them, but the one that made my heart skip a beat, was the purple backless dress. It caressed her body, but still had an elegant tone. For me, that was the one.

"I love this one and the black one. What do you think?"

"I think they're both great, but the one you are wearing now is sensational. Purple is quickly becoming my new favorite color."

"Good to know," she said, as she turned toward the fitting rooms. Watching her walk away, I wanted to follow her into the dressing room and have my way with her. A few moments later, she returned with the purple dress draped over her arm.

"I see you've made a decision."

"Yes, I have."

Somehow, it felt as though her response seemed to be more than just about the dress, but I wasn't sure.

"Let's buy it and go eat dinner."

She begrudgingly let me pay for the gown and we began walking toward the car.

"Can we just pick something up and go to my place?" Natalie asked.

"Sure. What would you like?"

"Chinese sounds good. There's a Hot Wok near my house. I usually go there for take out."

We took the food back to Natalie's. I dished it up while she changed out of her work clothes. I so wanted to assist her in disrobing, but I already had my plan in place for sweeping her off her feet, so I wasn't going to make any moves. Returning in a clingy, long-sleeved knit top and yoga pants, I almost changed my mind about the plan. *Fuck.* She looked so damn hot, even in her comfy clothes.

"I have *The Big Bang Theory* recorded if you want to watch it while we eat."

"I love that show."

"Me, too. I just need to wind down. I'm so tired."

We sat, ate, and watched the show. Natalie kept yawning and I knew that was my cue to leave after the show was over.

We both laughed out loud at the witty banter between the characters. "I love Sheldon. He's my favorite," Natalie said.

"Me too," I replied, picking up her soft hand and kissing the back of it. We held hands throughout the show and when it ended I stood to take my leave.

"Leaving so soon?" she asked.

"Yes, baby. You need to get to bed and get some rest. I know you have more long days ahead of you until Christmas."

She nodded. "I just need a hot shower. But going to bed does sound like a good idea."

I desperately wanted to be in the shower with her, rubbing my hands all over her soapy body. I nearly moaned out loud thinking about her wet soapy body, and tried to banish the thought before she could pick up on it. She looked up at me with her beautifully expressive eyes, and I almost crumbled. Time to go. Swiftly, I walked toward the door. Natalie followed after me. I needed to tell her what I was feeling. I didn't want her to think I didn't want to stay. She had looked disappointed when I announced I was leaving.

"Thank you so much for the beautiful dress and dinner. I had fun tonight."

"Me too, baby," I said, as she leaned into my body. "You know I don't want to leave you, don't you? I don't want you to feel pressure, gorgeous girl, but I do want you. So much. But, I'm keeping my promise. I just needed you to know that, okay?"

My comment seemed to appease her somewhat, and she sighed quietly when I hugged her, and kissed her on the forehead. As I turned the doorknob, I said, "What time shall I pick you up on Saturday? The party starts at eight."

"How about seven?"

"Perfect."

We said our good nights and I fled. I was beyond tempted, but knew sticking to my plan would be a romantic overture she would never forget. It might give me the worst case of blue balls, but, for Natalie, it was worth it. I needed her to know I would be there for the long haul.

CHAPTER 19: NATALIE

I could hardly wait to see Mac and spend the evening with him. We had texted back and forth on Friday, but I didn't see him, which felt strange. I wanted to be with him and texting didn't cut it at all. His comment about wanting me, and respecting my wishes, only heightened my longing to make love to him. *Damn, the sexy man.*

I got off work at six, raced home, and began getting ready for my Cinderella evening. It had been a long time since I'd had an occasion to dress up. I put on the purple gown and gazed at myself in the mirror. I checked myself from different angles to make sure everything was right. Walking out of my bedroom, I heard a knock at the door.

Opening the door, I heard Mac inhale. "Damn baby, you look so beautiful. I'm going to have to watch you like a hawk tonight. Every man there is going to have his sights on you."

"Oh Mac. You're so sweet, but I highly doubt that."

"No. You're exquisite and I'm very proud to be your escort this evening."

I blushed, but my heart filled with love for this man. I was eager to see what the night, and the following weeks would bring. *Bring on the romance.*

"Shall we go?" Mac asked, extending his arm.

I had butterflies in my stomach fluttering their wings the entire way there. I wasn't nervous about being with Mac, I was nervous about Kate's questions. This would be harder to wave off than us spending time together in Vegas.

We arrived at the party with a few minutes to spare. Mac picked up my hand and kissed the back of it. "You are dazzling tonight. I'm going to be the most envied man at the ball. So glad I found you, baby."

"Oh, Mac. I feel so fortunate to have found you as well. Thank you for being so loving and caring toward me. And patient."

"Baby, you're easy to love. Patience…not so easy." Mac smiled as he said the last part, but he sweetly kissed me on the cheek, and proceeded to get out of the car.

We walked up the long driveway, tastefully flanked with Italian Cypress trees. They had been decorated with white lights and red ornaments. I expected the entire Statton home was decorated to perfection.

Mac held my hand as we walked up the steps to the house. The party itself was going to be under a tent in their expansive backyard. Mac didn't knock, he just went on in. At first it seemed strange, but then it occurred to me that he was family.

"May I take your coat?" he asked.

"Yes," I said, turning my back to him so he could slip it off my shoulders. Once he had it off, he trailed kisses from my shoulder to my neck. His lips on my skin made me tingle all over.

The entire house was decorated with lights, ornaments, and even mistletoe. We were standing right underneath it. "Look Nat, we're under the mistletoe," Mac said with a wicked grin. Before I could respond, he scooped me up in his arms and kissed me. My body was pressed up against his and I could feel my muscles clench deep below. Mac Carter sure did have an effect on me that caused my panties to sizzle.

He put me down and I steadied myself against his chest. As I was regaining my composure, Kate and Neil were headed straight for us.

"Nat, I'm so glad you're here," Kate said, as she hugged me tight.

"Me too, Kate," I said, holding my dear friend. She was glowing with happiness, something I was just beginning to really understand.

Mac and Neil were shaking hands as Kate released me. Neil hugged me as well.

"How about a drink?" Neil asked.

"Lead the way," Mac responded.

We all began walking toward the kitchen, but Kate grabbed my arm and brought me into the parlor. "Natalie, what's going on with you two? Is it getting serious?" she asked, giddy with excitement. It almost felt cruel hiding this from her.

"Mac invited me to the gala and I accepted. We're just getting to know each other."

"Come on. There's got to be more to it. I see how you two look at each other."

"Oh, Kate. You're about to marry the man of your dreams so it's only natural you want everyone else to be in love, too. Mac and I are just hanging out."

Kate didn't seem satisfied with my answer. "I don't know Nat…I think we're going to be planning your wedding very soon."

Thinking about how apropos her statement was, I laughed.

"Don't laugh, Nat. You know I'm right."

Neil and Mac returned with a glass of wine in each hand. I was so grateful when Mac handed one to me. I was going to need large quantities of alcohol to survive Kate's questioning. Neil had rubbed off on her a little and she was more relentless than she'd been in the past.

More guests arrived, but they were ushered to the white tent by the service staff. Neil extended his arm to Kate, "Shall we, baby?" They began walking out toward the party and Mac and I followed in toe.

The tent was its own outdoor room, set up with round tables seating eight, a dance floor, and a stage where the band was ready to play. Poinsettias were everywhere and the table centerpieces were huge clear bowls with an array of decorations in them. Each ornament had a child's name attached and I couldn't wait to choose one for myself. It would be good to do something for someone else. We followed Neil to our assigned table. The only problem was, there was someone already sitting in my seat.

"Cassie," Mac said, louder than he probably expected to. The frown on Neil and Kate's faces, said they had been unaware of her presence.

"Hi Mac," Cassie said, in a voice that almost seemed unnatural. I'm not a violent person, but I felt the urge to punch her.

"Cassie, why are you here?"

"You invited me, silly."

"Cassie, I invited you when we were a couple. Us breaking up should have clued you in on the fact you were no longer invited. And that was months ago."

Cassie looked up at Neil. "I'm not allowed to donate to the children's fund?"

Kate stood there, her hands balled up and her brow furrowed.

Neil tilted his head and said, "Of course we would love your donation to the fund and so would the children. But we don't need a scene, Cassie. This is a charity event."

"I'm not going to make a scene, Neil. I'm going to enjoy the party, dance with my Mac, help some children, and go home."

At that moment, I started to lunge at Cassie, but Mac pulled me closer to his body, restraining me. My breathing was rapid. I was especially infuriated by the words "my Mac" reverberating in my mind. *What is wrong with the woman?* She was in for a rude awakening, and I couldn't wait to see the look on her face when we revealed the truth.

Neil leaned over and said something to Kate. Kate nodded and made her way to my side. "Let's go powder our noses," she said, stretching her hand toward mine.

I took her hand and we walked away from the whole scene. Part of me wanted to stay, to hear what she could possible say to justify herself, but the other part of me was grateful Kate had whisked me away. We found the downstairs bathroom which easily could have fit ten people in it.

Once the door was locked behind us, I breathed a sigh of relief.

"Nat, are you okay?"

"That woman is crazy. First she visits me at work and now she's here? She's a stalker." As soon as the words came out of my mouth I thought about Roger stalking Kate and all she had been going through. "Oh Kate, please tell me the police have found Roger?"

"No, but let's not talk about him. I'm concerned about you. You said Cassie came to see you at work?"

"Yes, she paid me a visit a few days ago saying she and Mac break up all the time, he fools around with someone else, and then they get back together."

"I can't believe that. He's not a player. But I can ask Neil if that sounds like him."

"No, I don't want you to ask Neil. I believe Mac. I just don't want to be caught up in all this drama with Cassie. It's just too much with everything else."

Kate shook her head. "Don't give up on Mac." She put her hands on my shoulders and looked into my eyes. "Nat, you deserve to be happy and I believe in my heart Mac can make you happy. He's not going to run out on you and he's not going to hurt you."

My eyes filled with tears. I knew she was right. He had already made me happy. I wanted to tell her right then he was my husband, that I was falling in love with him, but I held back. Why couldn't I share that? Kate hugged me.

"Your family would want you to have the best life possible, sweetie. Try to trust that everything is going to be okay. Look at how I have been blessed with Neil."

"You're right. I'm not going to let Cassie ruin things for me." I checked my makeup, making certain my tears hadn't streaked my face. When Kate opened the bathroom door, Mac was standing outside waiting for me.

"Kate, may I talk to Natalie?"

Kate looked back at me, giving me a smile of reassurance. Then she turned and walked away.

Mac stepped forward, effectively causing me to step back into the bathroom. He locked the door just like Kate had done, but it felt different being in here with him. Like a wool coat, warmth surrounded me. I felt safe, somehow.

"Cassie is refusing to leave, so I was thinking we should go. We can go to dinner downtown at the Hyatt and have drinks up at the top. We'll have a view of the bay and the city," he said, putting his hand on my face. "I just want you to feel comfortable. That doesn't seem likely with Cassie here."

"I don't want to spoil the night you had planned," I said, placing my hands on his chest. Mac's hands found their way to my waist.

"Baby, my only plan is to be with you. I'll just give a check to Neil's mom, and she can take care of the rest. We can also pull some names off the trees at the mall, and do some shopping together, or drop off toy for tots, whatever you want.

Jessica came to mind. She and I always loved to choose some children to give presents to. It was something we did together every year...until this year. Thinking of her just made me want to curl up in a ball and cry until there were no more tears left in my body.

Mac's hand found its way up my arm to my face. He gently cradled my face in his hand. "I know you miss her terribly, and if you don't want to socialize I will completely understand. I can take you home, or the yacht, or my house, or out. Anything," he said.

"I'm not sure what I exactly want to do, but I don't want to be here with Cassie."

"What time do you have to work tomorrow?"

"I'm off tomorrow," I sighed.

"That's great. How about we get what you need from your place, go to my yacht, and we can go to Catalina? Miles will captain the boat while we're sleeping and we can spend the day shopping, hanging out, hiking, whatever."

I smiled up at the beautiful man doing everything in his power to make me happy. "I love that idea."

"Great, baby. Let's go."

Mac opened the bathroom door and we walked out straight to the car. Once we were driving away, I texted Kate that we had decided to leave. She understood. It would have been a fun night since Charlie and Mitch were due to arrive any moment, but Mac's idea of going to Catalina was beyond perfect for us. I wanted to be curled up with him, forgetting everything else in the world existed.

After packing what I needed for our voyage, we made it to the yacht. Since Mac had called ahead, Miles was ready and he had a couple of crew members with him for the journey. I looked at Mac quizzically, and reading my mind he said, "They will be helping Miles with everything we will need for our trip."

I nodded, too mentally exhausted to say very much. My legs felt heavy, as if I were wearing concrete boots, as I walked into the cabin of his yacht. One of the crew members, Trina, offered me a glass of champagne. I almost took it but decided on water instead. The other crew member, Alan, brought in my bag.

"Mac, don't you need to pack for our trip?"

"I keep everything I need in my cabin, so I never have to pack."

"Where would you like me to stow Miss Mason's belongings, Mr. Carter?" Alan asked.

"I'll take them from here, thanks."

I followed Mac down the hallway. I didn't know what he had in mind, but I was so tired it didn't matter. I was having trouble keeping my eyes open. He brought my things into what appeared to be the master suite.

"I thought we could keep your things in here, if that's okay?"

"Of course," I said. My feelings were lighting up around my body like a ball racing through a pinball machine. I wanted him to make love to me, but I also wanted things to go slow. I couldn't have things both ways and I was frustrated with myself for being so indecisive.

Mac placed my case on the bed. "Let's get you unpacked and comfortable. Miles has prepared dinner for us."

"Good. I think that's why I'm so tired, from not eating."

Within minutes, my things were stowed away and we headed to the main cabin for dinner. Everything was set up with silver covers keeping the food hot.

After eating salmon, wild rice, and broccoli, I began to feel human again, but my exhaustion hadn't dissipated. The stress of everything was just too much. Mac seemed to understand I just needed some quiet, and he sat next to me while eating, instead of across from me, placing his hand on my leg when he wasn't using it to eat. A couple of times he leaned over and kissed me on my cheek.

Trina took our plates away and left a large piece of chocolate cake on the table. Mac picked up my hand and kissed each of my knuckles. His touch sent sparks through my body.

"Baby, you look so tired. I know things have been very stressful. Let's get you to bed."

I nodded, but nothing more. We walked into his cabin, where I took out my pajamas and headed into the bathroom to get ready for bed. I felt so nervous being alone in such an intimate setting with Mac. He had brought the cake with him, so I figured we were going to have some of it before…

Mac knocked on the door. "Are you okay, Nat?"

"Yes." I managed to get out.

"I'm not convinced."

I opened the door to see him standing there in nothing but pajama bottoms. My eyes scanned his chiseled chest and I wanted to run my fingers down his abs. His physique was…perfect. Perfect to me.

"Looks like you've been keeping up with your workouts, Mr. Carter," I said, looking up at him through my eyelashes.

Mac smiled and slightly shook his head. "I work out with my trainer four days a week. He's a drill sergeant."

"I can attest all of your hard work is paying off."

"Well, you're looking pretty fit yourself, Mrs. Carter."

Hearing the words Mrs. Carter, made me mushy on the inside. I looked at Mac's mouth and all I could think about was how much I wanted it on every inch of me. Mac put his hands on my face and said, "You are so beautiful, Natalie. I'm such a fortunate man." Then his mouth descended upon mine and he began kissing me, his mouth claiming mine for his own. I was putty in his masterful hands as my body began to fall toward his. He scooped me up and placed me on his bed. He lay to the side of me and continued kissing me, igniting the passion I had buried so long ago. I wanted him, and in that moment, nothing else in the world existed.

After a few delicious moments, Mac released me from his kisses. "Natalie, I want to make love to you, but I want it to happen when you can tell me, without reservation, that you love me. I want this to be real and not just a technicality. I'm not completely certain you and I are in the same place, yet."

"What are you saying?"

"What I'm saying, is I need to know I'm the only one for you. The only man you want…the only man you love…the only man you need. When I know that to be true, then I will make love to you."

"How do you know it's not true, already?"

"I can sense you are holding back. You're not completely ready and I'm not going to push you. You. Are. Worth. The. Wait," he said slowly, looking deep into my eyes.

I placed my hands on his face and said, "How do you always know what to do and say to make me feel treasured?"

"It must be one of my many gifts," he said, and we both laughed. "Now I want you to get some sleep and when we wake up, we'll be docked in Catalina. It will be a beautiful day."

"I can't wait. Thank you for treating me like I'm something precious."

"You are, Natalie. You're my wife. That makes you incredibly precious. To me."

CHAPTER 20: MAC

Natalie drifted to sleep almost immediately, surrendering to her exhaustion. I watched my beautiful girl for a long time, inhaling her essence, aching for her to love me. I never knew I could feel this much intensity and love for someone. I just wanted her to be happy, feel safe, and know beyond all measure, that I am the man for her. If she had been any of the other women I had dated, I wouldn't have hesitated to take her to bed. But my mom's words echoed in my head about treating the right woman like a precious jewel. Natalie was my dazzling jewel.

The next month was going to be brutal, with getting through the first Christmas without her sister, and the trial of the man who took her sister away. It made sense she was so worn out. And on top of it all, she had her job keeping her on her feet and customers to please.

I got under the covers with my darling bride and snuggled up close to her. I wanted her to awaken in the morning wrapped in my arms. There was no place else I'd rather be, and I was going to do everything in my power to make her feel the same way.

The sun peeked through the folds in the curtain that didn't quite restrain its brightness. Natalie began to stir, but she was still cradled in my arms. I knew she could feel how much I desired her as I was pressed up against her backside. Nothing in my world would have been better than making love to her.

"Good morning," I said, as she began to stir.

"Good morning," she murmured back.

Neither of us moved and she let me hold her for a while. "Did you sleep well, Mrs. Carter?"

"How could I not, being nestled in your arms?"

"How about you, Mr. Carter?"

"Never better. I could sleep like this every night and wake up this way every morning." Nothing was better than this. Well, maybe one other thing would be, and God knew I was ready. My hard cock was pressed against her perfect backside. I better get up or things were going to happen.

"Coffee is waiting for us and Trina will make anything we want for breakfast."

"Great, but I need a shower first to wake up," she said, her eyes still half shut.

"Okay. I'll have Trina whip up some omelets for us if you like."

"Mm. That sounds good." She had better not groan like that again, or I may not be able to resist her.

Natalie went to shower, and after getting dressed, I went to place our order with Trina. When breakfast was ready and Natalie had still not come up, I decided to check on her. As I approached the bathroom, I heard sobs coming from within.

"Baby, are you okay?"

She just cried more.

"Can I come in?"

"Okay," her trembling voice answered.

I could see her gorgeous body shaking through the clear shower door. I grabbed the towel off the rack, opened the door, and took her by the hand. Stepping out of the shower, I wrapped both the towel and my arms around her. Continuing to cry, she choked out, "I'm sorry."

"Shh. There's nothing to be sorry about. It's only natural for you to be sad."

"I just miss her, Mac. So much."

"I know, baby, I know."

"After our parents died, Jessica and I made our own tradition. We spent Christmas Eve with our parents' friends, the Millers, but on Christmas day we would go downtown and help at the homeless shelter. Knowing there would be children there, we always brought a trunk full of gifts. It always worked out that we had just the right number of gifts for the homeless boys and girls. It was all Jessica's idea. In many ways, she was so selfless and so loving. I hate how our relationship ended. Angry…hurtful. Each of us saying things we can't take back now."

We stood there in the bathroom, my arms encircling her petite frame, her head resting on my chest. There was nothing I could say to take her pain away, so I didn't say anything.

"How did you get through your first Christmas after your parents died?"

"Neil's mom got me through it. I just wanted to stay home, but she wouldn't let me be alone. She convinced me her family was my family, and they were there for me no matter what. They got me through everything." Her grip on me tightened. "I'm here for you and I'm never letting you go."

After a few moments, Natalie looked up at me with her sad, but beautiful blue eyes. "I'm sorry I can't give you what you want just yet. I'm just overwhelmed and can't seem to make decisions…" she said, her words drifting off.

"Baby, I'm not some dumb young guy who just wants one thing. I want the real thing…a marriage, a family, a life-long commitment."

Natalie smiled, making my heart melt. She didn't respond to my words, but she stood up on her toes and kissed me. Her kiss said everything I needed to know.

"I'm okay, now," she said, hugging me again. "Is breakfast almost ready?"

"Yes. I'll let you get dressed."

A few minutes later, Natalie met me out on the deck for breakfast. We soaked up the sun and devoured our omelets. "I thought we could go zip-lining this afternoon if you'd like. I checked and they can take us at four. Is that something you would be interested in doing?"

Natalie's eyes lit up. She squealed with delight. "I've always wanted to do that."

"Awesome, me too. So, you want to explore until we have to meet for the tour or would you prefer to just lounge on the boat?"

"I'd love to check out the shops."

"Let's go, then."

We strolled hand in hand down the main street toward the shops. I was interested to see what Natalie liked, so I'd have an idea what to get her for Christmas.

After a few hours, we meandered toward the beach. It was the perfect set up with cabana's available so we could relax. A waitress from the adjacent restaurant took our order of appetizers and drinks. We both sat back, gazing out at the ocean.

"There's something so calming about the ocean. It's just my favorite place to be. I love everything about it. The sound of the waves crashing against the rocks, the salty scent wafting through the cool breeze, sand between my toes."

I watched Natalie talk, but kept thinking about how much I wanted her and how this morning had been a herculean task not picking her up and taking her to bed.

"Mac, what are you thinking about?" she asked me with a coy grin.

My heart was beating rapidly and I almost couldn't contain myself. "This morning... holding you...feeling your body against mine."

Natalie's lips parted and she let out a soft moan. An urgent look crossed her beautiful face. Reaching for my hand she said, "I enjoyed being in your arms, too."

Our waitress arrived as I was kissing the back of Natalie's hand. We ate our food and drank our margaritas without speaking. It was strange, but we didn't need words to be comfortable with each other. We just needed to be together.

CHAPTER 21: NATALIE

Mac had penetrated the hardened exterior that protected my heart for longer than I could remember. He was so open and I found that to be very sexy. I was beginning to believe I could have what Charlie and Mitch and Kate and Neil had—true bliss.

We made our way to the tour company for an adventure of a lifetime. At least, it was for me. There were six other people in our group and the guides gave us the 411 as they drove us up the mountain. After driving as far as we could, we hiked up another mile or so. The view was beyond astounding and I felt like I could see right into Heaven.

Ryan, our first guide, demonstrated what to do as he glided across the first line. He made it look simple enough, but I wasn't feeling so brave. I kept letting the other guests go before us and pretty soon it was just Mac, Steve, the second tour guide, and me, left on the platform.

"Okay, you're next," Steve said to Mac. He set Mac up in the harness, attached him to the line, and Mac jumped off, floating effortlessly to the other side.

Then it was my turn. Why did I wait to go last? My nerves were getting the better of me. Steve secured me to the line and I stood at the edge. Fear had taken over.

"Steve, you're going to have to push me. I can't jump off."

Steve smiled. "You're going to love it. Just relax," he said, and then pushed me without warning. Looking out at the panoramic view of the ocean and shoreline beyond rendered me speechless. Within seconds, I arrived on the other side of the line and Ryan caught me just like he had everyone else. The rush was intoxicating and the fear had vanished. My only regret was there were only four more lines left and we'd be done. Mac took my hand as we climbed down the stairs to make our way to the next launching area.

"I was getting worried you wouldn't do it," he said.

"Me too. I had to ask Steve to push me. I couldn't jump."

"Now how do you feel?"

"Like I'm on top of the world," I said, looking up at Mac's ruggedly handsome face.

"Good. This is amazing, isn't it?"

"Yeah. It's more than my brain could fathom when you suggested it."

We crossed a few more lines with everything going exactly like it should. I could do it all day if they let me.

I was the last person to cross the last line. As I came in for the landing, Steve caught me, but then let go and I drifted back toward the middle of the line. Ryan yelled from the other side, "Don't move. Just stay where you are."

I yelled back, "Thanks for the tip," rolling my eyes.

I heard Steve say to Mac, "Sorry, man. You're not going to like what I have to do to bring her back in."

Mac crossed his arms over his chest and said something to Steve I couldn't hear. Then Steve attached himself to the line and began moving toward me. When he got to me, he had to wrap his legs around my body and pull me to the platform using his hands. So there we were, our bodies entwined with each other and the expression on Mac's face was not one of amusement. Quite frankly, he looked pissed off. Once I was safe on the landing, he pretty much took me out of Steve's hands. The ride back was a quiet one, with Mac saying very little.

When we returned to the yacht I finally couldn't take it anymore.

I knew he was mad, but I couldn't understand why.

"Mac, he had to come out to get me. How else was he going to do it?" I asked slightly annoyed.

Mac sighed. "This is going to sound irrational, but I couldn't stand him touching you. I don't want any other man to touch you again," he said, pulling me into his body as we stood on the deck.

The jealously that exuded from him was unfounded, but also endearing in a caveman sort of way. I put my hands on his face. "Mac, you have nothing to be jealous about. I don't want to be with Steve. I want to be with you. I'm here with you."

Visibly relaxing, Mac said, "I needed to hear you say it, Natalie. I haven't been sure about what you are thinking or feeling today."

"I know. Everything is happening so fast and I haven't caught my breath yet."

Mac furrowed his brow. "We have all the time in the world, but I can't help how I feel. I want to be with you."

I wanted to return the feelings, tell him exactly what he wanted to hear, but I couldn't just then. Nothing made sense to me. One moment, I wanted to tear his clothes off, the next, I wanted to take things slow. I hoped Mac would understand. I rested my head against his chest and he held me for a long moment. Miles interrupted us with word that we were departing in fifteen minutes. "Trina has prepared everything if you are ready to dine, Sir."

"Thanks, Miles."

Down below in the dining compartment, Trina had set a romantic scene for us. The table had pink rose petals strewn around it, fine china and crystal, wine in an adjacent ice bucket, and two plates enclosed with silver covers. The candles were the final touch that drew me in.

"I see Trina's been busy," I said. "Looks like she's prepared everything you asked for and then some."

Mac grinned. He looked so young and handsome. "She aims to please. Shall we?" he asked, motioning toward the table. The patience and care of Mac amazed me.

Mac pulled out my chair for me. We ate and reminisced about our adventure zip-lining in Catalina. It had been a perfect day and I wanted to savor every moment of it. Despite it all feeling a little surreal, and the confusion I was experiencing, I was glad for the taste of wonderful.

CHAPTER 22: MAC

Seeing Natalie's beautiful face by candlelight mesmerized me. How could a woman look so sweet and innocent, but be sultry and alluring at the same time? I watched her animated expression as she expounded upon conquering her fear of zip-lining. I could watch her forever.

"I've been monopolizing the conversation. Tell me something about you," she said, sipping more wine. "I know, who was your first girlfriend in high school?"

"That would be Heather. We were the typical high school couple. She was a cheerleader and I was a football player. We naturally gravitated toward each other in our junior year, but before that it had been flirting and hanging out with our group of friends."

"So, how long did you two date?"

"We were together for two years."

"What broke you up?"

"Heather was accepted to Oxford, so she moved the summer after graduation. She wanted to study art history and restore paintings."

"Aw. Did she break your heart?" Natalie asked with a sympathetic look.

"At the time I thought she did, but now I know there is only one woman capable of doing that." Natalie's eyes grew wide and her lips parted. "You have that kind of power over me, Natalie. Your heart has captured mine and I never want to be released."

Natalie inhaled deeply. Her eyes said it all. She was touched by my openness. Hopefully by New Year's she would be able to tell me she loves me. I wanted to hear those words from her desperately.

"Oh, Mac. You're penetrating my heart, too," she said, taking my hand. I caressed the back of her hand with my thumb.

I got up, keeping her hand in mine and walked her over to the sectional. I just wanted us to feel comfortable together like a favorite pair of shoes. Putting my arm around her, Natalie put her head on my chest. I stroked her arm. "Natalie, what do you hope for…for your future?"

"I don't know if I can answer that question. I haven't thought about my hopes for a long time. My life became about Jessica and what she needed. I had to be strong for her, so I didn't allow myself the luxury of hopes or dreams. I guess, in a way, if I didn't hope then I wouldn't be disappointed."

It saddened me to hear her say this. I wasn't sure how to respond, so I kept silent.

"How about you, Mac?"

"I've wanted a family for a long time and I have been longing to find the right woman to share everything with. I guess you could say I'm a hopeless romantic."

I heard Natalie exhale and knew there was a smile on her face. "I can agree with that. I didn't think any man could be as romantic as Neil has been to Kate, but I must say you are giving him a run for his money."

"Glad to hear it, Mrs. Carter. I aim to please."

Natalie sat up and looked into my eyes. "Everything you have done since we met has been beyond…beyond what anyone else would do or has ever done." Her eyes stayed locked with mine. "I am so grateful that all of this has happened between us. I have to admit, being with you makes me want things."

"Like what?" I asked, hoping she would open up more.

"Things I haven't dared wish for…for a very long time. Someone to spend my life with, a family. The usual things people want in life."

"So, you could see yourself having those things now?"

"Yes, I could."

I couldn't contain my smile. I moved the wave of hair that gently cascaded over her face. I pulled her close and just held her. "Baby, you already have those things now."

"I'm beginning to believe that," she whispered.

Unbeknownst to us, we were already docked and back in San Diego. Our time together had been so intimate that I was completely distracted. Miles carefully wandered in to inform me.

When he left I decided it might be better to take Natalie home rather than spend another night torturing myself in bed with her. "How about I take you home?" I suggested.

"That might be good. I have some things I need to do before tomorrow. Mundane stuff like laundry."

"Yeah, I have a few things I want to do as well."

I drove my beautiful siren home. Since she had been with me, I had security watching her condo. They blended in pretty well and I might not have noticed them myself if I hadn't been paying attention looking for them. I kissed my girl goodnight and departed.

I can't believe Natalie has come into my life and reshaped my world. My focus. My heart. She is my forever. I had no doubts whatsoever.

CHAPTER 23: NATALIE

Waking up Monday morning, I took a moment to let it sink in that I was going to have a man in my life for Christmas. Then it really hit me. I could have Mac forever if I wanted to. The thought heated me like a cup of my favorite tea on a chilly day. He kept telling me that he wanted me, but somehow it hadn't seemed real until this morning. He was everything I could ever wish for in a man and more. I just needed...I needed to trust again...completely. Mac deserved that, and I was going to take the plunge. Closing my eyes, I imagined moving in with Mac and beginning the New Year with a new husband and a new life. After Kate's wedding, we could share our news with our friends.

It was so nice to have two days off in a row, but I knew the days leading up to Christmas were going to be very busy. So, I had to make the day count. Getting up, I got dressed, made coffee, and ate breakfast. I wondered what I should get Mac for Christmas. After being on his yacht, I realized he probably had everything. What would I buy a man who owns a yacht? I thought about something personal...something from the heart. Maybe I was just corny, but I decided to make Mac a Christmas stocking and fill it with small gifts. Michael's had all the items I needed and I spent the afternoon with glitter and my glue gun. I cut out a felt Christmas tree and glued on tiny decorations. Cutting Styrofoam into small squares, I wrapped them with wrapping paper and glued them under the tree. A star on the top completed the front of the stocking. On the back I had already written with a gold pen, "All My Love, Natalie."

Feeling satisfied as I admired my work, it dawned on me the hard part was going to be filling it with items. That was going to take more consideration. Perhaps a visit to Best Buy for the latest gizmo on the market would work as the main gift, and I could add in some funny things like cute socks. Then cuff links came to mind, and I knew I could find those at work tomorrow.

Mac and I had been texting back and forth all day, and even though I wanted to see him, I decided having some plans of my own would be good.

So, I called the Millers. They had been best friends with my parents since before I was born. Basically, they had become Jessica's and my surrogate parents after... . They were on a cruise when Jessica died, but made it back for the memorial. Their love and support had been a constant in my life that I was so grateful for. Without them, Jessica and I surely would have fallen apart.

"Hey Beverly," I said. "What are you and Daniel up to tonight?"

"We just bought a tree and were planning on having dinner and decorating it. Why don't you come over? We'd love to see you. Plus, Daniel seems to have issues with putting the ornaments in the right places so we could use your help."

I could hear Daniel in the background protesting, but Beverly just laughed. "So any news? Did you have fun in Vegas with your friends?"

"It was a great getaway. I have so much to tell you guys."

"Well, good. I want to hear all about it."

"I'll be there in about thirty minutes. I can't wait to see you both."

We said our goodbyes and I made my way to the Miller's home.

When I pulled into their driveway, so many wonderful memories flooded my mind. Every significant event in my life had been shared with them. Beverly and my mom had been friends since grade school. Their friendship had carried them through the rough times, being each other's strong tower in times of trouble and the ray of sunshine when all was well. Beverly had been there with me when my mom died. She had held one hand, and I, the other. We never talked about that day, but we shared a bond that was unbreakable.

As I walked up the pathway to their cape-cod style home, Daniel opened the door before I reached it, gave me a hug and ushered me inside. The scent of cinnamon wafted through the air and I knew we would be enjoying apple pie after dinner. Beverly was a great cook and apple pie was her specialty. She didn't make it that often, since their sons had moved to the East Coast a few years back.

Entering the Miller home, I went to the spot I always went, the kitchen. Beverly was stirring the pots, but gave me a big hug and told me how much she missed me. I decided to ask them about their trip since I hadn't even mentioned it when they returned. I had been dealing with too many other things.

Daniel poured me a glass of iced tea and Beverly told me all about their cruise around Italy. In ten days, they went to eight ports. It sounded amazing and I found myself imagining taking a trip like that with Mac.

Sitting down for dinner, Beverly eyed me. She knew me so well.

"So sweetheart, what's going on?"

I looked at her and then at Daniel. "I do have some pretty big news." Informing them of my recent nuptials and the romantic, sweep-me-off-my-feet dates, left them both staring at me, speechless. I kept looking back and forth between them to see who was going to speak first.

Daniel rubbed his chin slightly, "Wow, you've been busy."

"It sounds way more than busy," Beverly expounded. "You're married."

"I know. It's been overwhelming and my emotions are all over the place."

"Question. Do you like him?" Daniel asked.

I smiled and nodded. "He's a wonderful man and I'm beginning to more than like him."

"Tell us about him, hon. What makes him wonderful?" Beverly inquired with a loving look on her face.

"The best thing I can tell you is that he reminds me of my dad. Mac is kind, loving, and generous. He's also very expressive with his feelings and has made it clear to me that he wants to stay married." I thought for another moment. "It's weird, but he's very in tune with my needs…he has a way of reading me."

"Those are good qualities, but you haven't known him for very long. How do you feel about staying married?" Beverly continued.

"At first, I wasn't sure. I mean, waking up married was quite a shock and I figured we would get an annulment when we returned home. But spending time together has been so comfortable. Exhilarating. I can be myself around him."

Daniel nodded like he knew what I meant. "When do we get to meet him?"

"Why don't you two come over on Christmas Eve? We can have dinner together and get to know him a little?" Beverly suggested.

"Okay. I'll ask him. We are already spending Christmas Day together. I'll let you know what he says."

Telling Beverly and Daniel about the escapades that had been happening in my life felt like a weight had been lifted off my shoulders. I hadn't realized how I had been carrying the burdens alone, until I shared them with the loving couple. I was glad I had them to confide in, but even more, I wanted their opinion on Mac. If they liked him I would take it as a good sign.

After dinner, Daniel put on some Christmas music and we decorated the tree, this simple task gave me a sense of coming home. Being with them filled my heart with hope that I could have my own tree to decorate in the near future. It wasn't about the tree, it was about the feeling of belonging. I belonged to them because of their connection to my family. In that moment, I thought about how I belonged to Mac as well, and my mind drifted to decorating the tree with him next year, and all the other things we would do together as our relationship grew.

I looked at my watch thinking it was much earlier than it was. The day had flown by and I had to be at work by seven a.m. . The store was opening early this week to accommodate shoppers before their time to buy gifts was up.

"I need to get home," I said, sighing. "I have an early day tomorrow."

Beverly put her arm around me. "Okay. We'll walk you out."

Approaching my car I called out, "I'll be in touch about Christmas Eve."

CHAPTER 24: MAC

Cassie hadn't contacted me since our lunch and security hadn't noticed anything unusual while surveying Natalie. Relief washed over me, but I knew deep down in the pit of my stomach Cassie wasn't quite done. I was just waiting for her to emerge after regrouping.

Taking the afternoon off work, I headed to the mall to do my Christmas shopping. I would have loved to ask Kate what to buy, but that would have made her question what was going on between Natalie and me. So, I did what any man in my position would do, I went to the best jewelry store I knew. I needed more than one item for the plan I had in mind. I couldn't wait to surprise my girl. Thoughts rambled through my mind: seeing her adorned in diamonds and nothing else. I wanted her in the worst way. *Shit.*

It occurred to me how in some ways Natalie was as strong as steel, but in other ways, as fragile as a flower in the hot scorching sun. I found her to be so intriguing, and she captivated all my thoughts. The sales girl at Tiffany's showed me several exquisite items and I found just what I had wanted. Then she wrapped them up and I was on my way.

As I was exiting the store I ran right into Cassie. There were no mathematical odds to explain that, the only explanation being she had followed me.

"Mac," she cried, hugging me. I didn't hug her back. Her hands on me felt revolting.

"Cassie," I said through clinched teeth.

"Doing your Christmas shopping?" she inquired.

"Yes."

"Wow. The little blue bag from Tiffany's. Natalie is one lucky girl. I don't recall getting any blue bags from you."

If I could have breathed fire on her I would have, I was so angry when I heard her say Natalie's name. I didn't respond because I had nothing to say.

"Are things getting serious between you two?"

"Cassie, what do you want?"

"I told you at lunch what I want…us back together. Of course there's also your trust to keep in mind."

"Cassie, I already told you that I'm not interested in getting back together. I'm not going to change my mind."

"Oh Mac, always so determined. I admire that quality in you."

"Gotta go. Have a nice day," I said, as I turned and walked away. If she had been a man, I would have beaten the shit out of her. Walking to my car I wondered if she had followed me or if she had someone tailing me.

When I got home I decided to call Natalie to give her the heads up about Cassie.

"Hey, baby. How was your day?"

"I'd say it was productive. I got a lot accomplished. How about yours?"

"Good. Mine was productive, too. Listen, do you think I could swing by? I have something important to talk to you about." Telling her about Cassie over the phone just didn't seem right.

"Sure. I'm just getting ready for bed."

"I'll see you soon."

Driving toward Natalie's house, I tried to figure out what I was going to say. Nothing sounded good. It all sounded like she was being stalked by a crazy woman. That was the last thing she needed to hear, especially with all she had to deal with.

I took a deep breath before knocking on her door. I knocked and she answered it almost at the same time.

"Hi," she said, her blue eyes lighting up. Even with no makeup on, and in her pajamas, she was hot.

"Hi, baby," I said, moving toward her, holding her in my arms. She hugged me back, hard. I didn't want that moment to end.

She escorted me into her living room and we sat on the sofa.

"Would you like something to drink?" she asked.

"No, I'm good. I don't want to stay too long since you are getting ready for bed."

"The next few days are going to be insane. I have to be at work at seven. If it's busy, I'll end up staying late."

I took my beautiful girl's hand and kissed it. "I went shopping today, myself."

"Did you find anything good?" she asked, beaming.

"I did, but I also found Cassie. She was waiting for me when I walked out of the store."

"Well, I know it's a small world, but it's not that small. Do you think she followed you?"

"I'm assuming she did, but I can't be certain," I said, rubbing my jaw.

Natalie stared at me with a questioning look on her face.

"I'm just going to come out with it. After she went to see you at work, I hired security…to watch over you."

"What?"

"I know I should have said something, but I didn't want to scare you. I asked them to stay invisible so your life wouldn't be interrupted."

"Do you think that's necessary? That Cassie is going to hurt me?"

"I have no idea what she's capable of doing. I just know that she's crafty and determined."

Natalie rubbed her temples. "So you've had security following me for days? I seriously had no clue. Why didn't you tell me? I think I have the right to know if I might be in danger."

"I didn't tell you because I thought I might be overreacting. But now, I know I made the right decision."

"This is wild. I wasn't expecting you to say anything like this."

"I know, and I'm hoping it's just for a short time until I figure out how to make her understand that she and I are not getting back together."

Natalie shook her head. "There seems to be a fine line between love and obsession. I'm glad you told me, because I would have freaked out if I realized someone was following me."

I put my arm around her and pulled her close. "I was concerned you might be upset with me."

"I probably would be if Kate hadn't just been through so much with that certifiable crazy man, Roger. I would have told you security was overkill. But in light of how deranged he has turned out to be, I think anyone is capable of just about...anything. So, thank you for protecting me."

I kissed her on the head. "I'll always protect you." I pulled her chin up and pressed my lips to hers. She moaned softly and I knew that was my cue to leave before I acted on my impulse. Until we had a real marriage I wanted her to stay true to her promise she had made to her mother.

"I should be going. It's getting late and I want you to get your rest." I got up and Natalie walked me to the door. I put my hand on her face and she leaned into it.

"Text me when you get off work tomorrow. If you're not too tired I'd love to see you."

"I will," she said.

I kissed her goodnight and left. The next thing on my agenda was beefing up the security protecting her.

CHAPTER 25: NATALIE

Work had been slammed and I ended up working twelve-hour days, so Mac and I communicated by phone over the next few days. Understanding that things were out of my control, he called me every night before I went to bed. I had invited him to the Miller's for Christmas Eve and of course we had Christmas day at the Statton's.

I didn't let Mac know it, but the whole Cassie thing kind of freaked me out. It seemed like I saw her around every corner or expected her to jump out of the bushes and do…I don't know what. She knew where I worked and most likely where I lived. But, she hadn't come around or made any threats, so all I could do was be on guard. I had always wanted to learn a martial art, so I would be signing up for classes after the trial.

I was scheduled to work from seven to four on Christmas Eve and I hoped to be out of work on time. Mac was going to pick me up around five so we could go to Christmas Eve services at my church before having dinner with the Millers. I had been looking forward to it all week. Since Daniel and Beverly knew we were married, I didn't have to be careful around them like I would be with Neil's family.

When I arrived home, I found a box on my welcome mat. A rush of heat coursed through my body just thinking about how romantic Mac had been the whole time. I brought it in, placed the box on the table, and opened the card. It simply said, *Nothing lasts forever.*

I opened the box to find black roses. These weren't from Mac...they were from her. Bile rose up in my throat...the threat of Cassie was now very real in my mind. Mac had warned me about Cassie's instability. Before this, I probably wouldn't have been so sure of his assessment. What kind of woman does this? Why? Is there more to this than Mac is telling me? I am not made for this.

I called Mac. He said security would be on my doorstep and he was on his way. Within a moment, Streeter was at my door, introducing himself.

"I'm Natalie. I guess you've been looking after me," I said, extending my hand.

"My pleasure Miss Mason. May I see the card?"

I handed the card to him and he read it, slightly nodding.

"What do you think?" I asked.

"I don't want to alarm you, but we definitely have a problem."

I didn't answer him or ask any more questions. My problem had just delivered herself to my front door and was making it clear that she wanted to scare me off to get Mac back.

I walked into my kitchen and took out a bottle of wine. I offered some to Streeter, knowing he wouldn't take it, but he did accept a glass of water.

I sat on my sofa and waited for Mac. Before I knew it, my glass was empty, and Mac was knocking on my door. Streeter let him in and he came directly to me and covered my body with his as he sat next to me. He practically crushed me. But I didn't care. I needed him to feel safe. Being in his arms meant everything to me at that moment.

The stress of the situation overtook me and I ran to the bathroom. I began heaving and finally threw up. Mac was at the door to see if I was okay. I knew he could hear me which made it all the worse. I didn't want him to see me like that. I swished my mouth with mouthwash to remove the horrible taste and wiped away the mascara that had smeared from my eyes watering. When I came out he asked me if I had ginger ale or 7 Up on hand.

"7 Up," I said.

"Go lay down. I'll bring you some."

I peeled my clothes off, tossing everything onto the chair in my bedroom. Climbing into bed, my bones felt heavy; keeping my eyes open was a struggle. I was so tired from the last few days and the episode with the roses had undoubtedly pushed me over the edge.

Mac came in and put the glass of 7 Up on my nightstand. Then he went to the bathroom, returning with a wet washcloth, placing it on my forehead.

"Baby, you look exhausted. Do you want me to call the Millers and cancel?"

Looking at my alarm clock I thought if I could just sleep for a little while I would feel as good as new. "My phone's in the living room. Maybe we could just postpone dinner and go over later, after I take a nap."

"Okay. I'll grab it."

Mac retrieved my phone and I called Beverly. She completely understood and said to just call if we were going to come over. Hearing the love in her voice made me feel better. Ending the call, I placed my phone on the night stand, and picked up my drink. I took several sips while Mac stood there hovering over me. A beautiful man stood before me and I could barely focus my eyes on him.

"Scoot over," he said. He lay on the covers and spooned me from behind, warming my body with his. I began drifting…

Kisses started at my shoulders and trailed up toward my neck. Mac whispered, "Baby, I love you so much. You're my world and I can't imagine my life without you. I don't want to date you any longer, I want you to move in with me and be my wife. Let me love you."

I turned toward him and whispered, "Yes." I looked into the eyes of the man who loved me as he descended toward my mouth. He tugged on my lower lip with his teeth and began sweet, slow kisses that caused a jolt between my legs. Flashing back to the morning I woke up in his bed, my body heated, I felt myself begin to pulse slightly. My heart was pounding in anticipation of what would happen next. Mac's hand found its way to my bare breast and he began swirling his fingers over one of them. As my nipple responded, he tugged on it, causing it to become hard and making me gush between my thighs. His kisses were sweet perfection and my body started to tremble, my desire for him coursing through my veins. My hand slid up his arm, found its way to his neck, finally running through his sandy brown hair.

Mac moved on top of me, kissing me all the way down my neck, to my breast that he had been teasing and tantalizing with his hand. The closer his mouth came to my breast the more ragged my breathing became. I thought I was going to scream out when his tongue began swirling around my nipple, the sensation was so powerful. He used his knee to get between my legs and I could feel his erection against my thigh. Mac moved to my other breast, making sure not to neglect it, as his hand slid down my body, over my stomach, into my panties. I moaned again when his fingers glided between my tender folds of flesh, becoming sticky from my arousal. He lightly scraped and licked my nipples while his finger made a circular motion over my clit. My muscles clutched deep below as his fingers mastered my body.

"Oh…oh, Mac," I uttered.

Mac's eyes met mine. He exhaled sharply. "Natalie, you're so beautiful. I want to make you feel things you have never felt before." He slid a finger into me and I thought I was going to convulse, it was so intense. He licked and kissed his way down toward the apex of my thighs and before I knew it he was removing my panties. He maneuvered between my legs, spread me apart and gazed at me. He made a primal sound as his tongue made its first lick of my clit. Moaning, my fingers gently grabbed his hair as he began the onslaught of swirling round and round. He slowly slid a finger in and out of me as he kept licking. In and out…in and out.

"Mac," I cried out. Sitting up in bed, I realized I had been dreaming. My bedroom door was shut and I was completely alone. The one thing that wasn't a dream, were my drenched panties and I flushed at the thought of what my mind had been doing in my sleep. I turned on my lamp and looked over at my clock. It was nearly seven, so I must have been sleeping for a couple of hours. I could hear soft voices coming from the other room and I assumed Mac and Streeter were talking.

Getting up, I went to my dresser to don fresh panties and a bra. I put on one of the sets I got in Vegas with Kate and Charlie. I got dressed and went into my bathroom to make myself look presentable by touching up my makeup and styling my hair a little.

Coming out of my bedroom, I found Mac watching the news. He

looked over at me and asked, "Are you feeling better?"

"Yes, I feel back to normal. I haven't thrown up in years, but with everything that's been happening, I'm not surprised."

Mac reached his hand out, "Come here, baby."

I took his hand and sat beside him. My sex dream had unearthed many emotions and I simultaneously wanted to rip his clothes off and run away from him. I was still all over the place and didn't quite understand my range of feelings.

"Do you still feel up to going to the Miller's house?" he asked.

I nodded. "I do. I'll call them right now."

As we made our way to Beverly and Daniel's home, it occurred to me that I forgot to ask about Streeter.

"Mac, where's Streeter?"

"I told him he could take the rest of the evening off. Westin will be guarding you during the night."

Parking in front of the Miller's home, Mac turned toward me. "It means so much to me to spend Christmas with you. I know the way things started between us made you a little scared... but there's nowhere else I'd rather be or anyone else I'd rather be with. You have my heart, Natalie Carter."

My eyes teared a little. He was so transparent and I had been wary of returning his sentiment. He seemed to strip me of my defenses every time we were together. I was choked up by his words and stupidly didn't say anything back.

"Natalie, I need you to say something. Am I making a fool out of myself here? Do you feel anything close to how I feel?" he asked with a slight crease between his brow.

I swallowed hard. "I do have feelings for you, Mac. I do want to be with you and I'm sorry I haven't been as expressive as you about how I feel."

Mac grinned. "It's okay. I just needed some confirmation."

He got out of the car and came around, opening my door. I took his hand as I got out and Mac embraced me, pressing his muscular body against mine. I could feel his love for me radiating in his touch. I hoped the gift I made for him for Christmas would demonstrate my feelings, since I was having trouble saying them.

We knocked on the Miller's front door. Daniel answered with a big smile on his face. He was such a kind man and I loved him like he was my own dad. I couldn't remember a time that he had ever been cross with me, and he always made time for me.

I hugged Daniel and he welcomed us in.

"Daniel, I'd like you to meet Mac Carter...my husband," I said, astonished that I had just used the word husband.

Daniel extended his hand. "Glad to meet you."

"It's a pleasure to meet you as well," Mac replied.

We walked in toward the great room. Beverly was just finishing setting the table.

"Mac, it's wonderful to meet you," she said, giving him a hug. Then she hugged me and whispered in my ear, "He's hunky."

I giggled and Mac raised his eyebrows at me.

"Everything looks amazing. Have you been cooking all day?" I asked.

"Not all day, but you know how I love to cook. Daniel, would you open the champagne?"

Daniel proceeded to get the champagne while Beverly had us sit at the table. She went into the kitchen and grabbed two glasses and Daniel brought in the other two.

"I'd like to make a toast," Beverly said, raising her glass. "May you both have all the happiness and love you each deserve." We all clinked our glasses and took a sip.

"Thank you, Beverly," Mac said. "I'm going to do everything in my power to make Natalie happy. She's a very special woman."

Beverly reached out and took my hand. "Yes she is," she said, squeezing it.

We passed around the roast, potatoes, green beans, and rolls. Once everyone had their food, Daniel said grace.

We ate dinner and talked. Daniel told us about the time he and Beverly were in London and they saw Ringo Star from the Beatles walk right past them. My parents had loved the Beatles, so I knew most of their songs. Mac shared one of his childhood Christmas memories about finding his wrapped Christmas presents in the closet one year.

"Neil and I found my Christmas presents when I was eleven. My mom had gone shopping and we had the house to ourselves for about an hour. We carefully unwrapped all of the presents to see what was inside. Then we carefully put the wrapping back on. Of course, when

Christmas morning came and I opened my presents, my parents were expecting me to be surprised and excited. But I had already seen everything," Mac said, shaking his head.

"Did your parents figure it out?" I asked.

"Not at first. But my dad kept watching me, knowing I should have been bouncing off the walls. Finally, when my mom was in the kitchen, he pulled me aside and asked me what was going on. I tried to lie my way out of it, but he knew me too well. He didn't want to disappoint my mom, so he secretly grounded me. My mom never found out."

After dinner, I helped Beverly clean the kitchen while Daniel and Mac talked in the living room. I figured Daniel would be pulling the dad card and grilling Mac a little. Strangely, knowing that was possibly happening made me feel special. I was so blessed to have these two wonderful people in my life who looked out for me.

Beverly pulled me out of my reverie. "I think you've found a good one, Natalie."

I smiled. "He is a good man."

"Are you still planning on staying married to him?"

I looked into Beverly's loving eyes. "It's all happened incredibly fast, but I'm about ninety percent sure I am staying Mrs. Mac Carter. As you know, my parents were married quickly."

"I know. I was there. Every relationship develops in its own time. Daniel and I dated for a year before he proposed. Your parents dated for like a minute."

"They loved each other so much, didn't they?"

"They sure did, honey. I do see some of your dad in Mac. He has a certain warmth about him. I can tell he's completely in love with you. It shows on his face when he looks at you."

"You really see that?" I asked. "You can see he loves me?"

"Yes, honey. He can't keep his eyes off you. But, it's more than that. He just seems tuned in to you and your every need."

I nodded, taking in what Beverly was saying. I felt I needed her motherly insight. We joined Mac and Daniel in the living room for an after dinner drink. The Miller's had always been my family, but having Mac here sitting next to me made everything different, brighter somehow.

We said our goodbyes and the next thing I knew, we were in front of my place and Mac was waking me.

"Baby, you fell asleep," he said, gently rubbing my arm.

I halfway opened my eyes. "I don't know why I'm so tired."

"Nat, you've had so much stress between work, your sister, us...it's not surprising that you're completely exhausted." I sighed, knowing it was true, but also amazed at how the man cared for me so attentively.

CHAPTER 26: MAC

Westin was waiting for us when I brought Natalie home. My poor girl was so exhausted from everything and I knew she needed to sleep. I'd see her in the morning when we had breakfast together and I could give her the little blue box from Tiffany's. I couldn't wait to see the look on her face when she opened it.

I drove home knowing Natalie was safe, but not happy about Cassie and her antics. I wasn't sure if Cassie was being dramatic or seriously disturbed. Considering I had no proof Cassie was the culprit, going to the police would be a colossal waste of time.

Waking up early, I reached over in bed groggily, thinking I would feel Natalie's body next to mine. All I wanted for Christmas was her to come home with me and be my wife, but until Neil and Kate got married, she was going to use them as an excuse to hide from her feelings. The fire in her kiss told me she wanted me. If I didn't have an idea of what she was going through in losing her sister, I might have considered giving up.

Arriving at Natalie's door, I expected to see Westin standing outside. When I didn't, my heart began racing and panic set in. I knocked briskly on the door and just as I was about to take out my cell to call 911, Westin opened it. I know I hired the guy and I wanted him to protect my girl, but son of a bitch…I didn't want him spending the night inside her apartment with her.

"Good morning, Mr. Carter," Westin said.

"Good morning," I managed.

Natalie was in the kitchen and the aroma of coffee brewing invited me in. When Westin closed the door behind me, I decided he and Streeter could have the day off. As long as I was with Natalie, I could protect her.

Natalie came toward me with a sweet sexy smile on her face. *How did she always look so gorgeous?* Seeing her sent all of my senses into overdrive.

"Good morning, Mac," she said, kissing me on the cheek.

"Good morning," I replied, grabbing her at the waist, pulling her close to my body. "Did you sleep well?" I asked.

"I did. I feel better."

I glanced over at Westin who was looking in another direction, clearly uncomfortable with the situation. Maybe he could sense that I was feeling territorial, who knows. "I can take it from here, Westin. You and Streeter can have the day off. I'll call you when we need one of you to come back."

"Okay," he said. He began to leave.

"Merry Christmas," Natalie called out after him.

"Merry Christmas, Miss Mason, Mr. Carter."

I watched him leave without uttering a word. My annoyance must have come through because as soon as he shut the door, Natalie looked at me with raised eyebrows.

"Is something wrong?"

I exhaled sharply. "I wasn't expecting him to be inside with you, drinking coffee, hanging out."

"Where were you expecting him to be?"

"Standing outside your front door, not in here ogling you."

"What? He was hardly ogling me," she said, rolling her eyes.

My jaw tightened and she was pulling away from me, but I wasn't letting her go. "Natalie, I've never been the jealous type before…I want you all to myself."

"Mac, don't you think you're overreacting a little? You hired him to protect me from your deranged ex-girlfriend."

"Natalie, I know I hired him. I just don't want him getting cozy with you."

Natalie's face relaxed. "Mac, I wasn't with Westin. I just gave him some coffee. Nothing else."

I put my forehead to hers, knowing I was acting like a teenager.

"I'm sorry. I'm just used to things being different."

"What do you mean by different?"

"Most women make it clear when they are interested in me. I'm not used to the guessing, like I have been with you."

Natalie looked down for a moment. Then she looked back up at me with tears in her eyes. "Maybe this will show you how I feel," she said, going toward the wrapped present on her coffee table. I followed her into the living room. She handed the gift to me. "Open it."

We both sat on the sofa as I unwrapped my gift. Seeing the stocking she obviously had made for me, touched me in a way no other gift ever had. I knew I was hard to buy for, since I am a man of means. Natalie put a lot of thought and effort into my gift.

"Baby, I love it. No one has ever made anything for me before."

"Look at the back," she said sweetly.

On the back she had written "*All My Love, Natalie.*"

"I'm sorry I'm not ready to shout from the rooftops how I feel about you, but I hope this helps you to know I want you in my life and I do have feelings for you."

I smiled at my girl. "Yes, Nat, it does."

"It's one week until Kate and Neil's wedding. Can you give me a week?"

I took that question as a good sign. I knew then. I knew she loved me. So that's what I would give her, a week. I nodded and kissed her on the lips.

"I want you to have your present now, too." I pulled the Tiffany's box out of my coat pocket and handed it to Natalie.

"I've never gone into Tiffany's before," she said, staring at the blue box. Natalie lifted the lid of the box, revealing the earrings I had selected for her.

"Oh my God, Mac, these are beautiful," she said, gazing at the tanzanite and diamond earrings. "But, they must have cost a fortune. You shouldn't have bought me something so…"

"Stop. Nothing is too expensive for you. I want to give you everything, and when I saw these, I thought of your beautiful blue eyes," I said. Natalie began putting the earrings on.

"How do they look?" she asked.

"Gorgeous, just like the woman wearing them."

"I'm gonna go look in the mirror."

Natalie returned a minute later. "I love them, Mac. Thank you," she said, melding into my arms, her head on my chest. Holding her for a while, I imagined how things would go when I gave her the other blue box I had from Tiffany's.

We made our way to the Statton home after enjoying our breakfast and just hanging out. Later that night, we had plans of watching *It's a Wonderful Life.*

I held Natalie's hand walking up the driveway, but then realized she'd probably prefer I not be affectionate at that point. Approaching the door, I let go of her hand to open it.

The sound of laughter, and the aroma of bread baking, made us both smile at each other. I felt pretty lucky to have Natalie. Something had been missing last year, celebrating Christmas with Cassie. The whole experience, looking back, seemed contrived, fake, artificial. With Nat, the day seemed rich and alive. Worth celebrating again. I love my girl.

Entering the kitchen, we were greeted by the whole Statton clan. It dawned on me as Neil's sister Jessica was hugging me, that Natalie's sister had been named Jessica, too. Oh, shit. I hoped my girl was going to be okay. Thanksgiving had been a disaster.

"You're here," Kate said, hugging Natalie. "Did you show up at the same time or come together?" she asked, raising one eyebrow.

"I offered to bring Natalie today when I heard you had invited her."

Natalie cleverly created a diversion. "How are things coming along for the wedding? I'm sorry I haven't been that involved."

"Oh, Sadie has it all under control and I know you have been swamped at Nordies, so don't give it a second thought."

"Well, I wish you were there with us. We all miss you so much. I'm assuming there isn't any news on Roger."

"No," Kate said, shaking her head. "He's still at large. I would have called you if they had him in custody."

"They're going to find him. It's just a matter of time," Neil said, pulling Kate close to his side and kissing her on the cheek.

Neil's parents, Sophia and Magnus, hugged each of us. "Would you each like a glass of wine?" she offered.

"That sounds great, but I'll get it. You have your hands full with the meal. Sophia put her hand on my shoulder and gave me her motherly smile. She walked with me over to the refrigerator and took out an unopened bottle of white chardonnay. She looked at me expectantly, like she knew something I hadn't told her.

"You love her, don't you?" she asked in a hushed voice.

"Yes," I said.

She hugged me. "I'm so thrilled both my boys are happy. I look forward to your wedding."

Hearing her say that made me realize Natalie hadn't gotten the wedding she had been dreaming about since she was a little girl. Time to do some investigative work and find out what her dream wedding might be.

I poured the wine and Sophia got back to the oven to check on the Cornish hens that were baking.

I took the wine over to Natalie and began questioning Kate about the wedding.

"So, who did you say was your wedding planner?"

"Sadie Phelps. She's the best in San Diego and my handsome fiancé was smart enough to hire her to coordinate everything," Kate said, glancing at Neil with a gleam in her eye.

"Well, Neil is a smart man. So, I take it you're not having a big shindig?" I continued.

"I've been to both large and small weddings and I preferred the smaller ones. They're just more intimate."

Out of the corner of my eye, I saw Natalie nod her head. Then, I knew two things. Natalie would be okay with a small wedding and I needed to hire Sadie Phelps.

"So, what are the popular colors for weddings these days?"

Kate laughed. "Mac, you're so sweet to ask. But, I have no idea what is popular. I mainly did neutrals, but with red roses."

"Oh," I said, looking over at Natalie. I guess I was going to have to look at her closet to see what colors she liked. I was pleased with myself for at least finding out a little bit of info on the down low. Making the fairy tale wedding, that my beautiful girl had always wanted, will have to be my focus, despite how busy I am at work. My girl deserves a special day.

"Why don't you fellas come outside with me? I want to show you where I'm going to put the new putting green," Magnus suggested.

We followed him out and left the ladies inside. After Magus described all the intricacies of the newest addition to the Statton estate, Neil and I hung back a little to talk.

"How's it going?" Neil inquired.

"Man, I'm crazy about her, but she still doesn't want to go public until after you and Kate are hitched."

"That's only a week from today. It'll go by fast."

I went on to inform Neil about everything that had been going on with Cassie, how I had to tell Natalie about security, and my plans for New Year's Eve. He listened intently like always, and then we were called into the house for dinner. Confiding in him made me relax a little. I wanted to find out what was happening with Roger, but it would have to wait until we were alone again. I didn't want to bring it up during dinner.

The dinner conversation was lively, with Neil's parents telling stories of Christmas's when Neil and Jessica were small children. Kate was having a ball listening to the antics Neil pulled when he was a boy. Not much had changed since then. He was still tenacious as evidenced by the beautiful woman sitting by his side. He knew what he wanted and he always went after it.

Natalie didn't say much, but I didn't expect her to. Since we were seated next to each other, I was able to check in with her by touching her leg periodically. Each time, she put her hand in mine and squeezed it, signaling she was okay.

After about four hours at the Statton home, I could tell Natalie was growing tired. I just wanted my girl to quit her job so she could relax, get through her losses, and begin a life with me.

"Do you want to get going soon?" I asked her quietly.

"That would be good. I'm feeling a little drained."

We said our goodbyes to the Statton family. On the way home, Natalie told me how much she'd enjoyed herself and how Sophia had gone out of her way to make her feel at home. We arrived back at her place and cuddled on the couch to watch It's a Wonderful Life. Glancing over at my girl intently watching the movie unfold, I wanted so much to tell her I loved her, and ask her to come home with me, but I had promised to give her one more week.

CHAPTER 27: NATALIE

Between the bridal shower, engagement party, rehearsal dinner, and Neil's sister having her baby, the week between Christmas and New Year's flew by. The merger Mac was working on kept him busy as well, so we had very little time alone together. The security guards kept shadowing me and I hadn't received any other unexpected surprises from Cassie. I was hoping she had given up, but having seen the resolve in her eyes when she had come to Nordstrom, I knew that was too much to ask for.

Fortunately, Mac was my date for the wedding and I was looking forward to some time alone with him. Standing up in the wedding party, I imagined us before a minister saying our I do's, slipping rings onto each other's fingers, and kissing when we were pronounced man and wife. Kate and Neil's was probably the closest I was going to get to a wedding, but I didn't mind, because I knew the important thing was the marriage, not the party before it. A few times I caught Mac eyeing me during the ceremony, causing my cheeks to burn. He looked so handsome in his tux and I just wanted to be in his arms.

Once the ceremony was over we proceeded to the reception. After Neil and Kate's first dance, I knew I'd have my wish of being in Mac's arms dancing with him. At least I could borrow some things from the special night and make them my own.

Finally, the right song came on and Mac asked me to dance. He held my hand as he guided me out to the dance floor. Once I was secure in his arms, he told me in my ear how beautiful I looked.

Then our eyes met.

"So, you still haven't told them anything?" he asked me. "I can't believe you've made it this long without telling them."

I shook my head. "No, I'm really good at keeping secrets."

"You don't think Kate and Charlie suspect anything?"

"They've been so distracted with wedding planning that they haven't asked much about you until today, after you removed that horrible woman from Kate's suite. I'm so glad you made her leave."

"I've had experience with obsessed women. I hope she resigns, or Neil is going to have to fire her. She's too unstable to keep around."

"No kidding. So, you've had a stalker other than Cassie?"

"Yes, one old girlfriend tried to sabotage the relationship I had after she and I ended."

"Wow, you really attract the crazy ones, huh?" I said laughing. "Good thing she didn't take a page out of Roger's book."

Mac chuckled at my joke. "I can't believe Kate is going through all of that. You never know who's unstable. Did you ever meet Roger?"

"Yes. Once, when Kate, Charlie, and I had gone to lunch. Kate and Charlie had already moved and we just happened to cross paths. He seemed normal at first, but I could tell he was way too into Kate. Charlie kept intervening to answer his questions. We ended up taking our lunch to go to get away from him. Fortunately, he was with his son, so he couldn't follow us. Kate was a wreck."

"Poor Kate. She's had a really tough time."

"Yes, she has." I tilted my head to one side, but my eyes were downcast.

Mac lifted my chin. "Tell me," he said.

"I do have something to tell you, but I want to wait until we are alone."

"Is everything okay?" he asked with a concerned look.

"I'm not sure."

"Nat, you're scaring me."

"Just hold me, Mac."

Mac pulled me close and I rested my head on his shoulder. The music changed to a fast song and he promptly escorted me off the dance floor and out of the ballroom.

"Where are we going?" I asked.

"Up to your hotel room to grab your things, and then to my suite."

I didn't speak. I was feeling breathless with what it would mean to be in his suite with him for the night. Especially with what I needed to tell him. Mac led me by the hand to my room. I fished out the key from the small bag I was carrying. Mac opened the door and we collected my things quickly, the tension between us rising with each passing moment.

When we arrived at the door to Mac's suite, he looked down at me and said, "Mrs. Carter, I want you to be with me every day and every night from now on. I don't want to spend another minute without you."

I searched his eyes like I always did. I didn't know why, he hadn't lied to me so far, but everything seemed too good to be true and I was anticipating something going wrong. I knew he was waiting for me to respond to his declaration. "I want to be with you too, Mac," I said, my voice slightly shaking. I didn't know how he was going to react once I told him my news.

Mac opened the door, scooped me up in his arms, and carried me over the threshold. I felt... like a bride. He had a way of making me feel special, adored, and protected, all at once. I loved him for that. My own thoughts made my blood pressure spike as I was finally admitting to myself that I loved Mac Carter.

Mac placed me on the bed and then went back into the hall to grab my suitcase. When he returned, his face looked worried and his demeanor was serious.

"Okay, what's going on?" he asked, as he sat on the bed next to me.

I exhaled and gathered my thoughts. How was I going to tell him? What if it changed things?

"Natalie, please tell me what's going on."

"I'm not sure how to start."

"Start from the beginning."

"I'm just...just worried about what you are going to think," I said, swallowing hard.

Mac took my hand. "Baby, there's nothing you can tell me that will take me away from you. Is that what you are worried about?"

I nodded.

"Well, you're not going to tell me something like you're actually a man, are you?" he asked with a grin.

"No, I'm not a man," I said, not being able to contain my laugh.

"Then anything else we'll face together."

"I'm late." There, I said it.

"Late for what?" Mac questioned.

"Late," I said, giving him a hard look.

"You mean…we might be…pregnant?" he asked, his eyes alight with what I desired to be hope.

"I haven't taken a pregnancy test, but I bought one. I just didn't want to be alone when I found out."

"Where's the test? Let's do it now."

"It's in my makeup bag in my suitcase."

Mac brought my suitcase over to the bed. He placed it on the bed and opened it for me. I found my bag and took out the test.

"You know, before I do this, I probably need to get out of this gown," I said, moving toward the edge of the bed to stand. I found my silky robe in my luggage and turned my back to Mac, indicating he could unzip my dress. Under my dress, I was wearing a bustier and a thong. As the dress slid down my body, I heard Mac's breathing accelerate. He was seeing me without clothing for the first time—at least, the first time he would remember.

Turning to face him, I saw the fire in his eyes. Desire was coursing through my body and I wanted to make love to him so desperately, but I slipped on my robe and proceeded to the bathroom to take the test. I followed the instructions and carried the test out with me when I was finished.

"How long will it take?" he asked.

"A couple of minutes."

Mac had put on some music while I was in the bathroom. Michael Buble crooned in the background as we stood there staring at each other. I put the test on the nightstand and Mac pulled me into his arms saying, "No matter what the test indicates, I love you and want to spend the rest of my life showing you how much."

"Oh Mac, I love you, and I want the same thing. I was so worried that you…"

"Baby, no more worrying. I've got you and I'm never letting you go. Hang on, did you just tell me that you love me?"

The love pouring through my husband's eyes and his words drove away my fears.

I sighed, "Yes, Mac, I did. You've made me so happy and I can't believe I get to have you in my life."

"Believe it, because I'm all yours. Always. And you're all mine. Always."

I smiled at my adoring husband. "Always."

Mac grinned, "Dance with me, Mrs. Carter."

I wrapped my hands around his neck and began slow dancing with my husband who continually reassured me that he loved me. His words might have said it, but his actions had screamed it loud and clear.

Mac whispered in my ear, "I hope we have a daughter just like you."

If I wasn't already desperate for him before, his words caused me to crave him in a way I had never experienced before. I had fallen hopelessly in love with this gorgeous man and I was going to completely let my guard down and show him.

The song ended and so did the few minutes we needed for the test to give an accurate response.

"Are you ready to see the results?" he asked me.

"Yes," I answered, courage welling up inside. "I'm so happy you're okay with this, that you're not freaking out right now."

Mac put his hands on my face. "Natalie, I want you, I need you, and most importantly, I love you. Never doubt that. Nothing can change how I feel about you."

Mac picked up the test and held it between us so we could both see it at the same time. "It's positive," I said, looking up at him. He was beaming as he looked down at me.

"Let's celebrate, baby," he said, sweeping me off my feet.

"What did you have in mind?" I asked coyly.

"You'll see," he said, placing me on the bed again.

Mac got down on his knees and pulled another blue box from his coat just like on Christmas. Taking my hand, he said, "I've been planning this and it's been so hard to wait, like a kid waiting for Santa to bring him a puppy."

"Mac," I began.

"No don't say anything yet," he said, putting his fingers lightly on my lips. "Natalie, I love the way you laugh…the way you always surprise me… . I love how you think of others before yourself. I love the way your mind works. You're secretive sexy side; how you love your friends fiercely. I see my life with you, a family, Christmases with our children. You are the only one for me. Do you know why I'm so certain?" he asked.

I shook my head, too choked up to speak as I looked into his adoring face.

"I know, because I can't see my life without you."

Tears escaped my eyes as I looked into the handsome face of the man who was proposing to me, professing his love—the man I wanted to spend the rest of my life with—the man who had become my everything.

Mac took an exquisite emerald cut diamond ring out of the box and said, "My beautiful Natalie, will you spend the rest of your life with me…be my wife?"

"Yes, Mac. I want nothing more," I responded. Mac slid the ring onto my finger and then moved up toward the bed to sit beside me.

"I promise I will always love you, be strong for you, take care of you, and make you feel cherished. I love you so much, Natalie Carter."

"I love you too, Mac Carter," I choked out. Mac's mouth plunged toward mine. His kiss knocked me off my axis and I felt light-headed—drifting on a sea of ecstasy—his mouth overtaking mine. He kissed me for several minutes before pulling away. Standing up he began taking off his tux, and before I knew it, he was standing there only wearing his boxers. Mac's body was lean and muscular. I gazed at his abs and wanted to run my fingers over them. Seeing him and knowing what we were about to do excited me, the intensity causing a throbbing deep down.

He climbed into bed with me. "I've wanted to make love to you since we woke up in bed together, but I didn't want to push you. I wanted you to feel ready. Are you okay with us being together? Now?" he asked in his boyish Mac way.

"Yes," I said. "I want you so much." I untied my robe and Mac slid it off my shoulders. Feeling his hands on my body sent shivers down my spine. I could feel the heat between my legs and my heart rate quickened. I had been dreaming about this moment and finally had arrived.

"Mac," I said, hoping to God that I didn't sound scared.

"Don't worry, baby. I'm going to go very slow."

How did he do that? He always seemed to know what I was thinking. He could read me so well.

Before I could say anything else, Mac swallowed my words with his mouth ravaging mine. I surrendered to him completely, having a desperate need to be with him...to be his wife in every way.

Mac's hands glided over the bustier I was still wearing. As his hand made its way toward my breast, I felt a jolt of pleasure surge throughout my body. He pulled me forward, wrapped his hands around my body, going to work on the hooks at the back of my garment. My heart pounded more at the thought of Mac seeing my breasts for the first time and what he was going to do to them. Within seconds, they were freed as Mac pulled the bustier away from my body.

"God, you are so beautiful, Natalie," he said, looking with undisguised desire at my exposed body. All I had on was my thong underwear. I could feel Mac's ridge pressing more firmly into my thigh. He was still in his boxers, and I so wanted him to remove them.

Mac made his way to my neck and began sliding his tongue along the side. He found a spot that made me moan and the sound I made caused him to linger there, increasing the intensity of the feeling. His hands glided from my hips up my waist, finding their way to my breasts. Mac barely touched my nipples yet they responded to him. Eagerly. His kisses continued down my neck to my shoulders until his hot mouth found its way to my right nipple. He gave my breasts attention like a man eating a fine delicacy at a banquet. His tongue. His teeth. His hands. They were all becoming too much and the throbbing sensation at the apex of my thighs was sending me to the edge. I let out another low moan. Mac's eyes met mine as he began moving his body to cover mine. His mouth departed from my breast and made it's decent down to my stomach. I knew where he was headed and excitement sparked in me like fireworks on the Fourth of July. He was almost there and I didn't know what to expect, but I trusted him implicitly.

Mac spread me apart and made a deep, low groan. "Baby, I've been waiting to taste you...all of you." With that, his mouth descended upon me and I surprised myself by moaning loudly. Cries of pleasure left my throat as Mac's tongue swirled around and around. He slid one finger inside me slowly, giving me a glimpse of things to come. His finger began slipping in and out of me while his tongue licked my tender folds, creating more desire than I could have imagined. I could barely catch my breath, as deep within me, a gentle pulsing began between my legs. Mac's other hand slid up to my breast to lightly pinch my nipple. The onslaught of his mouth and hands sent me over the edge, I began feeling the intense vibration, squeezing his finger, as I yelled out in pure gratification. Mac made a few more licks as I began coming down from what he had just done to me. Everything had fallen away and all that remained was my quivering body, eager for more of him.

Mac's nose nuzzled my belly button while he moved up my body. He began sliding his boxers down his hips and I decided to help him by hooking my toes between the waist band, pushing them down more. Suddenly, it all became very real to me that Mac and I were about to become one. His body would be inside my body. I hoped I would make him feel as good as he had made me feel.

"Are you okay?" he asked with glistening lips.

I touched his face and stared into his eyes. "I'm not okay...I'm amazing. You made me feel... so... there are no words."

Mac's face softened. "Trust me, baby. This is just the start; we're just beginning our lives together. There's going to be a whole lot more of what you just experienced."

Mac's mouth invaded mine again and he began rubbing his iron hard rod against the slippery flesh between my thighs. He slipped inside of me just a little and then pulled out, rubbing his head against me entirely. Each time he did it, I felt more and more tightening deep down. I ached for him to be all the way inside of me...to feel him...to make love to him.

I began lifting my hips to meet him when he entered me, but he kept taunting me with his short insertion and a rubbing of my clit. Finally, I couldn't take it anymore, and I placed my hands on his firm ass, pulling him inside of me, not letting him depart. "Make love to me, Mac," I said. "I need to feel you. Now."

Mac slowly moved in and out of my drenched core, filling me each time. Between his intent movements and his tongue finding its way to my left breast, I exploded again, making sounds that echoed the ones from moments earlier.

"God, Natalie, I love hearing the sounds you make when you come," he said, his breathing ragged. "You. Feel. So. Damn. Good."

His pace quickened and within seconds Mac was moaning in my ear, finding his release.

He stayed on top of me for a few minutes and I relished the feeling of our bodies joined together. I never wanted the incredible feeling to end.

I was so glad I had waited until I was sure. I knew I loved Mac, and I was now certain of his love for me. Making love with him was so worth the wait. I couldn't believe the bundle of tingling mess I had become. Coming apart twice like that. Was I okay in bed for him? He has had many lovers before me, so I just hoped I hadn't let him down.

CHAPTER 28: MAC

Our evening together had been incredible. I had been captured by her dazzling beauty, the feeling of her body connected to mine, the tasting of her sweetness, but mostly, knowing she wanted me and loved what I was doing to her. She communicated that loud and clear with each erotic sound escaping her juicy lips. I was completely intoxicated by my beautiful girl in every way…until Natalie laid her head on my shoulder and began to cry. She tried to cover it up at first, but her body began trembling and a small whimper left her voice. Then I felt a tear drop onto my chest.

"Baby, what's wrong?" I asked, as I began sitting up so I could look into her eyes. *Damn it. She wasn't ready for this. How could I have been so stupid?*

A long pause descended between us as I waited for Natalie to speak. After several deep breaths, she regained her composure.

I traced the curve of her face with my index finger and rested my hand on her shoulder. "You don't regret that we made love, do you?" I asked, hoping the answer was no. Please let the answer be no. Making love to her had been life changing for me. I needed her more than anything.

Natalie shook her head. "It's not that. Being with you tonight was incredible. You are an amazing man, Mac."

I looked down toward the sheets, anxiety rising up inside me at what she was going to say next.

"Are you not sure about us, Natalie?" I somberly asked.

Natalie pulled my chin toward her so I was looking her in the eyes. "It's not you, it's me."

"I don't understand."

She exhaled loudly. I was beginning to brace myself for the worst.

"I'm scared," she said in a quiet voice.

"Baby, I'm here. There's nothing to be scared of."

"I'm afraid at some point you won't be here. That something will happen or you will leave me. Everyone I've ever loved I've lost. I couldn't take losing you."

I put my hands around Natalie's head and pulled her to me for a kiss. "You're not going to lose me," I said reassuringly. "I'm in love with you and I want to be married to you the rest of my life." I pulled her body closer to mine and held her for a long time. Her fear was understandable since she had lost so much in her life. Then it dawned on me. "Is this why you wanted to keep our marriage a secret from Kate and Charlie?"

The forlorn look on Natalie's face said it all. "For so long, I have shielded myself from having a relationship. I didn't want to tell Kate and Charlie because I knew they would be excited and they would do things to push us together. I love them for being such great friends, but in all honesty, being in self-protective mode, I haven't let them be close to me either…at least, not the real me. But then you came along, Mac Carter, and broke through all the walls I have built around my heart."

I had to admit hearing her words made me relax a little. I didn't know why it worked out the way it had, but from the moment I held her on Thanksgiving, I had a need for her…a desire I couldn't quite understand. Perhaps it was love at first sight…a concept I always thought was a little hokey, but now it had happened to me.

"You broke through my walls too, Natalie. When we met on Thanksgiving I was instantly drawn to you, but not just because you are so incredibly beautiful. There was something radiating from the inside you that I wanted to know…needed to know. Then when you excused yourself to the ladies room and Kate informed me about your sister and your parents, I felt connected to you. I knew the pain you were experiencing from all you've lost," I said, wiping her tears away.

"When I found you alone on the terrace and you let me hold you and comfort you, I felt like the luckiest man in the world. You were letting me in and that so rarely happens nowadays."

Natalie looked at me with her big blue eyes. "I don't know why, but when I met you that day I knew I could trust you. I have no reason for it and I still don't know how or why all of this has happened between us. I'm beginning to understand why they say God works in mysterious ways."

"Yes, He does," I said, placing my hand on her waist as I leaned in to kiss her. Wanting so much to relieve her of her worries, I said, "Everything is going to be okay. You'll see. You've had more bad things happen to you at such a young age, more than most people experience in a lifetime, so it's completely understandable that you are worried. But I believe all of this is happening for a reason." I picked up her hand and placed it on my chest so she could feel my heart beating. "I know in my heart we're going to have a long and happy life together. Plus," I said, putting my hand on her stomach, "we have this little nugget we've created and having a baby with you is going to be the greatest thing I ever do."

"Oh, Mac," she said, her eyes filling with more tears. "How did you get so deep into my heart?"

"It's probably my good looks and boyish charm that did it for you," I said, waggling my eyebrows. Natalie laughed as I grinned at her. Hearing her laughter lightened the mood. I wanted my girl to be carefree and happy. She had been bogged down by life's most tragic circumstances for far too long. She's been alone for just as long. Not any longer. The girl was mine. She won't know another moment of loneliness.

"I definitely think it must be your modesty, too, that attracted me," she said, looking at me through her long lashes.

I chuckled. "Yeah, there's that, too," I said, as my breathing became heavier. We had been laying there in bed together, totally naked and the sheets had pooled around her waist, revealing the breasts I wanted to do all sorts of things to. I just wanted to get my hands and mouth on her luscious body again. "Come here, baby," I said, pulling her close.

Natalie's body became draped over mine, her breast pressed against my chest and her thigh wrapping over me. Having her body so close gave me an array of ideas of what we could do right now.

"Baby?" I whispered.

"Yes," she whispered back.

I ran my hand up the back of her thigh, over her perfectly heart-shaped ass, and said, "Do you want to make love again?"

Natalie shifted her body on top of mine, straddling my hips. Her hands were on the bed on either side of my chest, effectively pushing her breast together. This was a sight I could behold forever.

"Yes, baby. I want you over and over again," she said, as her mouth descended to mine.

CHAPTER 29: NATALIE

Dreams of Mac, carried me through the night, and I awoke thinking about all of the delectable things he had done to me. A few weeks ago, I couldn't have imagined I would be waking up in bed with my gorgeous, sexy husband, pregnant with his child. Surreal was a gross understatement in the scenario that was playing out before my eyes, and I felt like I was a bystander watching my new life take shape. I wanted to just believe Mac that everything was going to be okay, but my experience was life kept throwing curve balls, some of which I had no way of swinging against. During the next few days, there would be another ball when the trial started for the death of my sister.

I rolled over and looked at Mac, much like I did in Vegas. Except this time, I felt blissful, not confused. It was time to let our friends in on our secret. We were having an early brunch together, so that would be the time to tell them. Knowing Kate and Charlie, they would be ecstatic for me. I could always count on them to be supportive.

I snuggled up to Mac and drifted for a few more minutes in the arms of the man I loved. I wondered if my feet would touch the ground when I got up. I was so happy in that perfect moment.

Half an hour later, Mac was beginning to stir. His hands glided up my thigh to my hip and he pulled me back toward him. Pushing his erection against me, his hand found its way to cup my breast. Kissing my neck and shoulder, he said, "Good morning, Mrs. Carter."

"I think it's about to be a really good morning," I responded. Mac's hand slid down my abdomen to the apex of my thighs. His hand meandered its way to my hot core and he inserted two fingers inside me.

"Baby, you are so hot and wet for me," he said, spreading my slippery juice up the tender folds of flesh he had acquainted himself with the night before.

Needless to say, we weren't in any hurry to leave the bed. Not for a good hour. Not until both of us were almost asleep from being sated so deliciously.

***

Our friends were already sitting in the dining room when we arrived for brunch. I wasn't sure who was glowing more, Kate or I. Kate and Charlie had huge grins on their faces as they watched Mac and me walking hand in hand. It was time to let the cat out of the bag.

Mac pulled my chair out and we both sat at the round table with our best friends in the world. I had kept my hands hidden under the table.

Kate looked at me, she looked at Mac, and then back at me. "Natalie, so help me if you don't start talking…"

I blurted out. "We got married in Vegas." I never saw such shocked expressions in all my life.

"What the hell are you talking about?" Charlie asked. "You went back to Vegas and got married…without telling us?" she shrieked.

"Not exactly," Mac said, stepping in. "The first night there, when I took Natalie back to her room because she was drunk and I was tipsy, we stopped by a chapel and got married. Natalie didn't want to take the limelight away from you Kate, so she kept it a secret."

Kate's eyes filled with tears. "Nat, you put me before your own happiness? You have to stop doing that. What you want, matters. What you need, matters." Kate and Charlie got up, came around the table and hugged me. It was the first time since I could remember I truly let them in. I was going to work at not being shut off, but I knew it would be a process. At least, this was my first step in being transparent—something I had learned from Mac. His transparency was so evident in the way he loved me so unconditionally, so patiently, so passionately.

Neil and Mitch shook Mac's hand, but they didn't seem to be as shocked.

"This is so incredible," Kate said. "So, what's going to happen now?"

"I'm not a hundred percent sure. We haven't gotten that far," I said, glancing at Mac. "Last night, we decided to stay married and let you all in on it this morning. Mac even officially proposed," I said, lifting up my left hand so they could see the ring. A flash of the first ring he had given me made me smile. I would always have that ring. It signified the beginning of our whole romantic love affair and would be precious to me forever.

"Wow, it's gorgeous," Charlie said, taking my hand in hers. She gave my hand to Kate who just stood there shaking her head. "It's just stunning." They both sat back down.

"I was thinking," Mac interjected, "That we could have a dinner party on my yacht tonight to celebrate. Can you come around four? We'll have cocktails, dinner, and watch the sunset."

"Bro, we'd love to," Neil quickly replied.

"Yeah, we're in, too," Mitch chimed in.

Kate and Charlie sat there nodding and smiling.

"Excellent."

The waiter took our order and I went into detailed explanation about what had been going on over the last few weeks. Kate and Charlie beamed at me from across the table, absorbing every word I said. I had finally joined them in the "being in love" status.

I was taken aback by their pure happiness and love for me. It had been there the entire time of our relationship, but I hadn't truly felt accepted. But it was my own fault for letting fear of rejection and loss run my life. Sharing so openly, I felt relieved, but also accepted in a way I had only received from my parents…and from my Mac too, of course.

After breakfast, we all went our separate ways. Mac and I went back to his suite to pack up so we could check out of the hotel.

Mac took me in his arms. "Mrs. Carter, it's time to go back to your place and pack up some of your things. I want you to move in with me today."

"Mm," I purred. "That sounds perfect."

When we got to my condo, I saw a familiar face guarding my door.

"Streeter, any activity?" Mac asked.

"No sir," Streeter replied.

I breathed a sigh of relief as we walked through the door. It had been a week since the black flowers were delivered. I was hoping Cassie had given up and moved on, but I knew I was only fooling myself. She wasn't the type to go peacefully into the night. I just wish I could understand why she had been so insistent.

"Baby, why don't you take what you need for the next few days and I'll have someone come, get the rest of your things and have them delivered to the house."

"Okay, I want to be here when they do that…and I probably could…" I stopped talking. What was I going to do with Jessica's things? Everything came crashing down around me at the thought of the finality of giving her things away, and actually leaving the place we had shared together.

"Nat, what is it?" Mac asked.

"Jessica," was all I could say. Mac pulled me into his arms, holding me tight.

"We don't have to change a thing until you're ready. I'll just have someone pack up the rest of your personal belongings to bring to the house."

We stood there for a long time, Mac embracing me—doing what he did best—loving me. After some time, I was ready.

Arriving at Mac's home, I was a little overwhelmed by the fact I was going to live in this fabulous place with the man of my dreams. I felt like Cinderella the day after marrying Prince Charming. This was *my* happily ever after, I thought, looking at Mac.

Mac gave me a tour of the rest of his house. I had only been there once, and we had stayed in the great room. The master suite was practically the size of my condo. Besides a king-sized bed, it had a sofa, love seat, and fireplace. I could practically live in that room alone. Everything was serene, the color pallet being neutral. The sliding glass doors led out to a private terrace with hot tub and a view of the ocean as far as the eye could see.

"What do you think, Mrs. Carter?" Mac asked, coming up behind me, hugging me.

"Everything is beautiful and I feel like the luckiest woman alive to be here with you."

"I'm the lucky one," he said, turning me toward him. "You're the first woman I've ever been with that hasn't cared about my money. I know you're here because you want to be with me."

How was it that no woman had ever looked past the money to see the wonderful man who existed behind the façade? I hoped he never thinks I see him for his money. The man, himself, was worth far more than anything he could buy.

"I love you, Mac Carter," I said, standing on my tiptoes and kissing him.

"I could kiss you forever, but we have a party to get to on *our* yacht. We should get ready."

"I can't wait," I said, nuzzling my nose to his.

Mac showed me to my own walk-in closet. It was decked out with drawers, hooks, shelves, trays to pull out, and a bench in the middle to sit on. It was jaw-dropping. Some things were already hanging in the closet.

"I took the liberty of getting a few things for you to wear tonight, since I didn't tell you about the party in advance. He unzipped the garment bag and pulled out four dresses. He had matching shoes and handbags to go with each dress. I must have had a quizzical look on my face because he answered my question before I asked.

"Personal shopper at Nordstrom."

"You had Elise choose these things for me?"

"Yes, I swore her to secrecy. She's had to keep secrets before," he said, tilting his head slightly and smiling.

"I saw her when I was in the women's department and she asked my opinion on a couple of things, but I had no idea they were for me."

"Good. Then you already like a couple of them at least."

I took the gorgeous bright blue dress from his hands. "The earrings you gave me for Christmas will be perfect with this one. Thank you, Mac. So much."

"Yes, they will, and you, my beautiful bride, are worth it." Mac looked at his watch. "We have about an hour before we need to be there. I have a couple of things to do in my office, so I'll let you get ready."

I began unpacking my clothes into the closet, and then took my toiletries to the bathroom. Taking a quick shower, I felt pure joy as I washed my stomach, knowing that soon Mac and I would have a child. It was almost too good to be true, yet there I was, living my new reality. *Surreal.*

I was practically ready when Mac came in to shower and shave. All I needed to do was put on my shoes. I watched him undress and felt shivers looking at his masculine frame. When he turned to get in the shower I wanted to reach out and squeeze his tight ass. I knew if I did we'd be late for our own party, so I contained my urge. I watched my man shower and shave, making more than the bathroom steam up. I was looking forward to the party, but I really wanted to get to the after party with just the two of us.

When we pulled up to the dock, Mac took my hand, kissed it, and said, "I hope you will enjoy this night."

"I'm sure I will," I said, searching his eyes. Something was going on and I wasn't in on it. "Have you kept a secret from me, Mr. Carter?"

"You'll see, Mrs. Carter."

Approaching the yacht, it was suddenly very clear what was going on. I saw twinkling lights, floral arrangements, tables with white table cloths, lit candles and fine china. Beverly and Darren caught my eye, the Statton's, along with my coworkers, as did one of the ministers from my church. There were also people I didn't recognize, but I assumed Mac knew them. A beautiful cake was in one corner and a table of appetizers in another.

"Mac," I gasped. "How did you? I can't believe...this is incredible."

"Welcome to your wedding, baby," he said, drawing me in for a kiss. The love, radiating from the amazing people in my life, all gathered together in front of me on Mac's yacht, made my knees feel weak. My man did all of this for me? The love from my husband was more than I ever expected or hoped for.

Applause broke out when we came aboard the yacht. Kate and Charlie were the first to greet me. "Are you surprised?" they asked in unison.

"I'm more than surprised. I'm in a fairytale."

I met all the people I didn't know and hugged all the people I did. "How did you make all of this happen?" I asked Mac.

"There's no time to explain now. You have to go get ready."

"What do you mean, I am ready," I said scrunching up my face.

Kate took me by the arm. "We have a few things to do down below before we can get this shindig started."

I went down with Kate and Charlie straight to the master suite. I saw a bouquet of pink roses on the dresser and three extraordinary gowns laid out on the bed for me. On the chair were white lace bras and panties, and in front of the chair rested three shoe boxes.

I opened my mouth to speak several times, but nothing came out.

"Mac is amazing," said Charlie. "He put all of this together. We had no idea until Mitch and Neil filled us in after breakfast."

I felt like this was a "holy shit" moment, but I usually didn't cuss. Those, however, were the words that escaped my lips.

"Holy shit."

"I know, right? And I thought Neil was romantic. Mac has outdone him."

"You need to try on dresses and get ready. The ceremony will start the moment you slip on your shoes," Charlie said.

Kate and Charlie had me undressed faster than Mac had the previous night. Each gown was beautiful, but I knew the one that was for me. Mac had pointed it out when he took me dress shopping for the Statton's ball. I put on the undergarments meant for the dress. Stepping into the dress I truly felt like Cinderella, wondering if glass slippers were in one of the shoe boxes. Kate zipped me up and I turned to face her and Charlie.

"Natalie, you look so beautiful," Charlie squeaked out, her emotions getting away from her.

Tears formed in Kate's eyes. "You're the most beautiful bride I've ever seen."

I looked in the mirror. The halter portion of the dress had embroidered beading on it and the straps had tiny, intricately beaded flowers. The skirt portion was straight with a slit up the side. I checked myself from all angles and then noticed the box on the dresser next to the bouquet. It had a note on top of it.

I opened the envelope to read,

My Beautiful Natalie,

These diamonds sparkle, but nothing is as dazzling as you.
All My Love,
Mac

Opening the box felt like I was dreaming. Inside were earrings and a diamond necklace. They were beyond extraordinary and rendered me speechless.

"Wow Natalie, these are amazing," Charlie said, taking the box out of my hand to remove the necklace. Kate removed the earrings as Charlie placed the necklace on my neck. Once the earrings donned my ears, I turned to the shoe boxes. Kate was already heading toward the floor, lifting the lids of the boxes.

We all simultaneously said, "The ones in the middle." Then we laughed. In that moment, I knew the only thing that could top this day would be the day I gave birth to our son or daughter. I slipped on the shoes and was ready to meet my groom up on the deck.

Picking up the pale pink flowers I nodded at Kate and Charlie. "We'll be waiting for you upstairs," Kate said.

"When you hear the music, that's your cue," Charlie added. They departed and I said a silent prayer, thanking God for all He had done for me. The music began and I made my way up to the deck. Reaching the top, Daniel was there to give me away, a broad smile lighting up his face. He gave me a nod demonstrating his approval, then, led me to my husband. After kissing me on the cheek, he joined my hand to Mac's. The look on Mac's face was mesmerizing. He seemed in awe.

The minister began our wedding ceremony and before I knew it, Mac was beginning to say his vows.

"Natalie, before meeting you, I thought love at first sight was just a myth. But, then I saw you. From the moment I laid eyes on you, my heart was pierced in a way I had never experienced before. I knew you were special…unlike any other woman in this world. I know everything has happened quickly, and we've barely had time to catch our breath, but I want nothing more than to spend the rest of my life learning every nuance about you, building a life with you, fulfilling dreams with you, creating memories with you. I promise to make you feel loved and cherished every day of your life. You are my beautiful girl, and I love you with all my heart."

Mac lifted my hand and kissed it. I didn't know how I was going to say anything close to what he had just professed. So many things were swirling through my mind. Public speaking was not my thing, but with the amazing man before me, the words seemed to just flow. Taking a deep breath, I said, "Mac, until I met you, I had resigned myself to being alone. I was too afraid to open my heart to anyone. But the moment you held me on Thanksgiving, I was beholden to you, my heart felt bound to yours. Every single thing you have done to show me love has opened my heart to you. Now, I can't imagine my life without you. You have filled the part of me that has been missing for some time. I love you, am so thankful for you, and I promise to spend every day showing you just how much."

We stood there staring at each other, not able to tear our eyes away. The minister continued on with the rings and then the best part happened. "I now pronounce you husband and wife. You may kiss the bride." Mac slid his hands around my waist and kissed me in front of everyone we knew. It was sweet, passionate, perfect. I was completely his and he was completely mine. Now I was officially Mrs. Mac Carter.

Since the wedding was small, the receiving line was short, and being hugged by all those who loved me caused me to feel renewed somehow. I may have had loss, but all those faces were my gain, and they filled my life with joy. Although it was bittersweet that Jessica and my parents were not there to share the day, I could see I still had family surrounding me.

Dinner was served, and Mac had spared no expense from the salad, to the filet mignon, and lobster tail. Everyone was eating, drinking, having a wonderful time and I was finally able to ask Mac how it all came into being.

"How did you make this happen?" I asked my adoring husband. Before he could answer, the DJ announced it was time for our first dance as husband and wife.

Mac stood and held his hand out to me, "May I have this dance, Mrs. Carter?"

At Last began playing while he escorted me out to the dance floor, holding me close, whispering in my ear that he loved me.

"I love you so much, Mr. Carter. I can't believe you have done all of this for me," I said, doing my best not to get choked up.

"On Christmas, when I heard you and Kate talking about her

wedding, I wanted you to have the wedding of your dreams, too."

I looked into my husband's gorgeous crystal-blue eyes, that crinkled when he smiled at me, and said, "This is exactly what I wanted. You've given me the most perfect night I could ever imagine."

Mac kissed me. "You deserve this and more, baby. I plan on spending my life loving you, adoring you, worshipping you, spoiling you. You mean everything to me."

"Oh Mac, you're more than I could have ever hoped for. I didn't know what to make of you at first and I know I didn't let you in, but you found your way in regardless. You didn't give up on me."

"I'll never give up on you, baby. Never."

The song changed and some of our guests joined us on the dance floor, but my focus remained on my beautiful husband. "You put all of this together in less than a week. I'm impressed. And Kate and Charlie didn't even know. They couldn't help you."

"They were very helpful this afternoon, but I hired Sadie Phelps to pull this off."

"Come to think of it, Neil and Mitch accepted your invite very quickly. They didn't even give Kate or Charlie a chance to speak. What aren't you telling me?" I asked, one brow lifted and a smile spreading across my face.

"Okay. I'll confess. I told Neil and Mitch after we went golfing."

"They've known this whole time and kept your secret?"

"Yes. I've never been able to keep anything from Neil, he knows me too well, and Mitch threatened to beat me within an inch of my life if I hurt you." We both began chuckling.

"That sounds like Mitch. He's very protective, especially of me and Kate. Somehow, he became our big brother."

"I can respect that. And by looking at him, he could pretty much beat up anyone he wanted to." We both looked over at Charlie and Mitch dancing. He was by far more muscular than any other man on the yacht.

"You're not upset that I didn't keep our secret, are you?"

"No. How could I be upset? Look at the result of what's happened since Vegas. You tore down every defense I had, loving me in a way I never thought possible. I never thought a man as wonderful as you would come into my life." I felt my eyes become moist and I blinked a few times to hold back the tears...tears of pure delight for a change.

CHAPTER 30: MAC

All of our guests had gone and I was waiting in bed for Natalie to join me. She was in the bathroom doing what, I guess girls do...getting ready. I was more than ready just thinking about my gorgeous wife, the beautiful curves of her body, the sweet taste of her lips, and every sound she was going to utter from her exquisite mouth. Waiting to have her hot body wrapped around me was making all my blood rush to just the right place.

The door opened and Natalie stood there in her lace bra, panties, and silk robe that wasn't tied at the waist. I drank her in with my eyes, noticing how firm her breast were as her bra pushed them upward, her flat stomach that I wanted to run my tongue along, and the curve of her hips. Hips that I was going to connect to very soon.

Reaching out my hand, I said, "Come here, baby...let me love you."

Natalie came toward me, slipping her robe off, before taking my hand and joining me. She lay on her side pressing her body up against mine, one of her perfect breasts resting on my chest, the other against my side.

"I still can't believe this incredible day you've given me. I feel like I'm in a fairytale, only better. I get to know what happens after the prince marries his maiden and makes her a princess."

"Lots of things are going to happen, starting with this." I pulled her body on top of mine, her legs straddling my hips, making me even harder than before. I had been aching for my girl. I wanted everything from her, but to start with, I wanted to watch as I slid in and out of her, feeling her hot wet pussy gripping my cock. I sat forward and unhooked her bra, keeping my eyes locked on hers. I leaned back again to see my beautiful bride's body on top of mine. Then Natalie surprised me.

She leaned forward and began kissing below my ear, her tongue sliding down my neck, her breasts pressing against my chest. Feeling her body sliding down mine turned me from hard to stone, the anticipation...I wanted her so badly.

Natalie's kisses continued down to my nipples, the hot strokes of her tongue driving me wild. Within seconds, she glided her tongue down my abs and wrapped her hand around me. I made a low growling sound signaling my approval. Watching her mouth plunging toward me, I felt her lick me, starting at my shaft all the way to my head. I exhaled loudly as her mouth enveloped me, sucking, licking, and scraping with her teeth. She was so fucking hot sucking my cock like that, my hands found their way to her hair that draped over her shoulder and onto my hips. Wanting it to last, I had to concentrate, as her mouth continued in a rhythmic fashion.

"Come here," I said. "I don't want to come in your mouth right now."

She climbed back up my body and positioned herself right over my hips, her hand wrapped around my cock and she glided me back and forth over her wet, juicy pussy, spreading her hot stickiness all over. Slipping inside of her, she was a perfect, tight fit. I had the best view in the house, watching my girl moving up and down on my hardened shaft. Then Natalie leaned forward and I began pulling at her nipples, sucking on one as my fingers worked the other. No other woman had ever felt like that...like mine. The feel of her wrapped around my cock was so...

"Fuck, baby, you feel so damn good."

"I'm glad you like it, Mr. Carter."

"Love it...you grinding on me...watching your perfect breasts bouncing. Oh God..."

I wanted it to last, so I rolled us over, placing me on top. Hearing cries of pleasure was a necessity being with my girl. I licked both her nipples, bringing them into tight rosy buds, then made my way down her silky soft body. Inhaling deeply when I reached my target. I groaned. "You smell so good, baby. I need to taste you." Licking her clit, Natalie grabbed the sheets with her hands. She was squirming for a moment until I placed my forearms on her thighs, effectively securing them, although I could feel them quiver. Her moans from my tongue swirling around her clit, drove me on. "Give me what I want, baby," I commanded. I slipped two fingers inside of her and she began making the most erotic, beautiful sounds I've ever heard as her tight pussy squeezed my fingers. I shifted up into position and began moving in and out of her. With each slam against her body, she moaned loudly, her eyes staying on mine the entire time. Then my release came, like the end of a roller coaster ride slamming into a cool lake.

We were both exhausted from our love-making and drifted to sleep in each other's arms. I knew nothing in my life would ever be the same again.

Waking up with Natalie in my arms, reveling in the feel of her body close to mine, reality came crashing around me. Sunlight was peeking through a crack in the curtains and I knew we both had way too much to deal with that day. I wanted to whisk her away on an amazing honeymoon, but it was going to have to wait until I completed the merger and the trial was over. Damn, I wish I could be there for the trial. I hated that she would be going through such a horrid event without me.

I also still had Cassie to deal with, and the fact I hadn't told Natalie the truth. If she found out, it might cost me everything. Losing her would be losing everything.

Natalie began to awaken. "What time is it?" she asked groggily.

"It's almost seven. Time for us to get up."

Natalie groaned. "Can't we just stay here forever?"

"You have no idea how much that appeals to me, baby, but we both have work."

I moved her golden locks away from her face and kissed her on the lips. "Any idea where you would like to go on our honeymoon?"

"I'm not sure. It depends on how many vacation days I have left after Jessica's trial. I've taken off a week, but I don't know how long the trial will last."

"Nat, you know you can quit your job...do something else if you want. Prepare for the baby... take classes. I just want you to be happy."

Natalie seemed to mull that over for a moment while I began to get out of bed. "I love my job, but in a few months it's going to be hard standing on my feet all day, being pregnant."

I couldn't contain my smile when she said pregnant. Making my way to her side of the bed, I bent over and kissed her again on the lips. "You're going to be a wonderful mother."

Natalie sat up, the sheets pooling at her waist. Just seeing her that way made me want to get back into bed and do all sorts of things to her.

"Thanks, baby," she said, taking my hand. "I know you're going to make a great dad. You're so patient. Our child is going to be so fortunate to have you."

I kissed my girl on the top of her head for that compliment. "Trina should be making breakfast for us right now. Do you want to eat first or shower first? And by shower, I mean, together," I said, with lust evident in my eyes.

"In that case, I vote for shower first."

I turned on the water and Natalie dropped her robe. Seeing her standing there before me, the curves of her body on display, made my blood heat up. I let her get into the shower before me, following closely behind. Once inside, I wrapped my arms around her, cupping her breasts and kissing her in the spot on her neck that made her moan. Natalie wound her hands around me and started stroking me, sending me into overdrive. I turned her around, grabbed some body wash and began soaping her luscious body. Swirling the soap around her breasts made her nipples hard, and she looked so hot with soapy suds all over her. She managed to get some soap on her hands and slathered me all over as well. The hot water cascading between us, and beading up on her perfect body, was more than I could take…it was carnal, and I needed to be inside of her. I began rubbing her between her legs and could feel how wet she was with desire. I relished in the fact that I made her that way. I tilted her head and began kissing her, our tongues moving in unison. Clasping my hands around her exquisite heart-shaped ass, I lifted her up, wrapping her legs around my hips, leaning her back against the shower wall. As I slowly entered her hot core, I could feel her breast graze against my chest. It was pure ecstasy, making love to my beautiful girl…my wife.

After breakfast, I took Natalie back home so we could each dress for work, and then go to our perspective jobs. It sucked we couldn't take off for our honeymoon, but I would begin to plan something special for when I returned from London. We kissed goodbye and went our separate ways, Streeter following behind her.

I was walking on air until I reached the office and saw Cassie's car parked in my spot. Exhaling sharply, I mumbled to myself, "What the fuck is she doing here?" I obviously knew, but I didn't want to deal with her shit anymore. Walking through the doors, I braced myself for a nasty encounter.

Cassie sat in the waiting area across from Alice. Looking up at me, Alice's eyes were wide and she slightly shrugged.

"Good morning, Mr. Carter," Alice said.

"Good morning Alice. Please hold my calls." A smug look resided on Cassie's face when I glanced her direction. "Cassie," I said, motioning for her to enter my office.

I closed the door behind her and proceeded to my desk. She sat in a chair across from me.

"What do you want, Cassie?" I was tired of whatever game she was playing. It was going to end today.

"Mac, it's time for you to come to your senses and stop playing house with that…that…girl."

"I can assure you I am not playing house. Natalie and I are married." The words came out and I wanted to reel them back in, but it was too late. Neil's voice was in my head saying "Don't tell her anything."

Cassie glared at me. *How did I ever like this woman?* She must have been a really good actress.

She crossed her arms over her chest. "Excuse me? How have you married someone you barely know?"

"Call it fate…love at first sight. I don't know. I don't mean to hurt you, but we just weren't meant to be. Natalie is my wife and it's time for you to move on. I wish you all the best."

"What's best for me, is you, Mac Carter. You'll see."

With that melodramatic statement, she got up and left my office. I was relieved to see her go, but her statement was unsettling and I didn't know at what length she would go to get her way. I couldn't imagine her actually harming Natalie, but I wasn't certain. I called

Silverstone Security and gave them the 411, and asked for more security to protect my precious wife and child. If anything happened to them I would never forgive myself.

CHAPTER 31: NATALIE

The entire day seemed to go by in fast forward with customers exchanging their gifts and using their gift cards. Every spare moment we got, the girls and I talked about my husband and how incredibly romantic my surprise wedding was. I found out Mac had Beverly invite my friends from work to our wedding. He was so thoughtful, and I was basking in my own happiness.

Walking out of work, my mind had a chance to process where I was headed. Home. I started my car, feeling strange I was going to Mac's place, not mine. But his place was mine. The thought didn't seem real. None of it seemed real and I expected to wake up at any moment…alone.

I pulled into the driveway, but didn't have a garage opener, so I parked to the side so Mac could open the garage when he got home. Streeter did a sweep of the perimeter, and inside of the house, before I entered. Walking in the door, Mac texted me that he would be home in a couple of hours and would bring dinner with him. I sat on the sofa, sinking into it, wishing it could be wrapped around me and comfort me somehow. Two days until I had to look at the man responsible for the car crash that took Jessica away. Kate's suggestion of asking someone from work to go with me was a good one, but I didn't do it. Old habits die hard and even though Mac had cracked my armor, a huge part of me was just used to doing things alone. Maybe that was the way it was meant to be. Covering myself with the throw on the sofa I reclined, shutting my eyes, as exhaustion made any movement feel impossible. Inhaling deeply, I focused on the night before, the best night of my life.

"Baby, wake up," Mac said, gently caressing my arm.

Opening my eyes, my husband's handsome face came into focus. "You're home," I murmured. "I must have dozed off."

Mac put his hand on my face and I leaned into it. "I brought home some Chinese food. I wasn't sure what you would like, so I got two chicken dishes, a shrimp dish, and beef and broccoli."

I arched my back, stretching, and Mac slid his hands up my ribs. "I hope you can wait to eat, baby. I have something else in mind right now."

Before I could answer, Mac was kissing me, pressing me down into the sofa, making me forget there was anything else in the world that existed.

***

I was so glad Mac had brought home take-out since his fridge was pretty bare. He had managed to distract me from my hunger, but then I was ravenous. Everything looked tasty and when I sat at the table, I realized how much food I had taken. I stared at it absentmindedly…my mind drifting like I was floating in the ocean.

"Nat, you seem far away. What are you thinking about, baby?"

"Sorry, Mac. I do feel in a daze. Honestly, I've been thinking about dealing with the trial alone." He felt like the only person in the world who I could be open with. He was so good at loving me, I found myself desiring to tell him everything, not just the good things.

Mac took my hand. "Baby, I keep telling you that you're not alone. What about Charlie? Maybe she could go with you at least the first day."

"I don't want to impose. She'd have to take a sick day."

"Baby, I doubt she would see it as an imposition. Your friends love you and want to be there for you."

I gave a half-hearted nod, "You're right. I'll call her tonight and see if she can come with me. So, how was your day?" I asked, wanting to change the subject.

I listened intently as Mac described a day in the life of a CEO mogul. His expression was animated talking about the merger with Merrick Enterprises. It was a huge step in securing the global market for Carter Industries. Carrying on his father's legacy was very important to him, and he spoke with a gleam in his eye hoping one day to leave the company to our son or daughter.

After dinner, I took my cell to bathroom, drew a bath, and called Charlie.

"Hey, Charlie," I said.

"Hi, Mrs. Carter. I was just thinking about you. How's married life?"

"It's so good, Charlie, I can't even describe it. Mac is an amazing man and I can't believe all of this has happened to me."

"Sweetie, you deserve a man who is head over heels in love with you. I have to admit, the surprise wedding made me fall in love with him a little, too." We both started laughing.

"He is pretty romantic. But Mitch is romantic too, right?"

"Mitch…Mitch is the best. I couldn't ask for more. You, Kate, and I, are very lucky."

"Charlie, I have to tell you this all still feels like a dream. I keep thinking I'm going to wake up and it won't be real."

"Oh, Nat. It is real. Very real. Enjoy it and stop worrying that things are going to go wrong. Mac is your happily ever after."

"Thanks Charlie, I needed to hear that."

"Is something else on your mind? You seem a little down. Is it the trial?"

Charlie had a way of reading me, and I had worked so hard to conceal my feelings from her when I was hiding my marriage to Mac. "Well, I have to admit I'm not looking forward to dealing with this on my own. I'll have Streeter with me, but it's not the same as someone close to me. It's just Mac and Kate will be gone and everyone else is working."

"Well, I have some sick time stashed away. I can go with you on Monday."

"Are you sure? I don't want to put you out."

"Of course I'm sure. What time do we need to be there, eight?"

"It's going to start at eight."

"I'll pick you up, we can grab some Starbucks, and arrive there about a quarter till. I just need you to text me your new address."

I heard Mitch calling for Charlie in the background, so we decided she'd pick me up at seven and ended our call. About the same time, Mac came into the bathroom, gave me a salacious smile, disrobed, and got into the tub with me.

***

Before I knew it, time had evaporated like water in the hot sun. Mac was leaving for London and I was helping him pack the few remaining things he needed. We were married for what seemed like a second, and he had to go. Our time apart seemed like an eternity. All I wanted was to just be with him.

"Baby, I hate leaving you like this. I wish you could come with me," Mac said, holding me in his arms. I looked up into the eyes that had captured my soul, and wondered how I had lived without him all these years.

"Me too, baby. But, it's all out of our control." I rested my head against Mac's chest, so he wouldn't see my sorrow his leaving created. I didn't want him to feel bad. Uncharacteristically, he didn't notice. He had business on his mind and a mental list of what needed to be done.

Westin drove us to the airport. I wanted to spend every second possible with Mac before he left. Holding his hand in the back seat while Westin drove, had a sexy appeal to it. My mind wandered to him and me, our sweaty bodies mangled together in bed, how incredible it felt to have his mouth on me, his hands freely wandering my body. We had made love every day since New Year's Eve when I finally gave in to my feelings. It was going to be strange to sleep alone in our bed. It would be lonely without his body next to mine. He had changed things for me, and I was no longer used to being isolated like I had been before.

Mac had arranged for more security during his trip and one of the guards would be sleeping in the guest room, staying with me at all times. I knew I'd be safe, but it wouldn't be the same without him. I had become dependent on him, needing him more than I ever imagined possible.

Pulling up in front of the terminal, I told myself to be strong…no tears.

We both got out of the car and met at the trunk. Mac took out his suitcase and I handed him his carry on. Warmth spread over me thinking about the love letter I had slipped into his carry on when he wasn't looking.

He held me close, told me how much he loved me, and then made his way to the ticket counter. We had a plan of me joining him after the trial ended, since he was expecting to be in London for at least ten days. It would be amazing to spend a few days away with him, especially in a city I had always wanted to visit. Of course, Europe had many cities I wanted to become acquainted with.

Mac and I decided it would be better for either Westin or Streeter to drive me instead of following me. I wasn't sure about the idea at first, but after being chauffeured to the airport and back, I could see why people liked it. I could sit back, relax, and not deal with the stress of traffic. Yeah, a girl could get used to that kind of treatment.

CHAPTER 32: MAC

Leaving my girl for London seriously sucked. I couldn't get enough of her and I wanted to be with her...always. Ever since I could remember, I had wondered how guys let a woman become the center of their universe. Even with Neil and Kate, I sort of thought he was a sucker for her. Then Natalie came into my life, knocking me off my axis, and it's like nothing existed before her. We had been separated for five minutes and I already missed her fiercely.

My mind wandered through the events of Natalie becoming mine, until it was my turn to go through the security check point. The line had moved quickly and I made it to the terminal faster than anticipated. Sitting in the waiting area, I opened my carry on to do some work on my laptop. Pulling out the laptop, an envelope fell to the floor. My beautiful girl must have written me a note.

Dear Mac,

I know I have a hard time communicating verbally all that you mean to me, so I thought I would put it into words on paper. Since the moment we met, I have felt a special connection to you. At first I thought it was just your smoking good looks and hot body, but it's so much more than that. You have brought me back to life with your love and tenderness. I was drowning in a sea of despair, loss surrounding me like the blackness of night. You became the shining star that guided me to safe harbor, into your strong arms. No one, and nothing, can compare with you and what you mean to me. I'm yours. I was waiting for you and didn't even know it. I was desperate for you, but had no idea. Now my heart is filled, overflowing with all

you have given me, all that you are to me: my husband, my lover, my friend, my shelter in the storm of life. I love you more than any words can express and I'd surely be lost without you.
Your loving wife,
Natalie

Reading her letter I felt elated...knowing the depth of her feelings. I wanted to touch her beautiful face and tell her over and over how much I loved her, that nothing would ever separate my heart from hers. For a moment, I thought about blowing off the deal and going home to my Natalie, but I knew she wouldn't want me to have wasted all the time and effort I had put into it.

My wife was so precious to me and I knew just what I was going to do: find the best jeweler in London, and buy something for her that was as extraordinary as she was.

The plane began boarding, so I sent a text to my bride telling her I got the note and couldn't wait to be in her loving arms as soon as possible. When I hit the send button, the realization of how much this trip was going to suck, hit me like a tidal wave. A week, or longer, without my Natalie.

CHAPTER 33: NATALIE

Charlie arrived at the house right on time. Streeter was going to drive us to the courthouse, making the needed Starbucks pit stop along the way.

As soon as I opened the door, I grabbed onto Charlie and clung to her. She didn't say anything, she just held me. My body was shaking and I wasn't quite sure if it had more to do with going to court or being without Mac.

"Sweetie, it's going to be okay. I promise. You are strong enough to get through this. You're the strongest person I know."

I pulled back and looked into Charlie's loving eyes. "I've had to be strong for so long. It's a comfort to have someone to lean on."

"Oh, Nat. You should have leaned on me...on Kate...a long time ago. We'll always be here for you."

I smiled at my wonderful friend. I nodded slightly, too choked up to speak.

"Are you ready to go?" Charlie asked me, kindness emanating from her eyes.

"Yes. Streeter is going to drive us," I said, motioning toward him. He was standing behind me in the great room. I introduced them and we were off.

Arriving at the courthouse, we had about twenty minutes to spare. As we made our way toward the assigned courtroom, a familiar figure was moving toward me. I blinked a few times, thinking my eyes were playing tricks on me. But, I wasn't seeing things. It wasn't a mirage. This was actually happening. My eyes were seeing what my mind couldn't fathom, as we both stopped and stared at each other.

Neither of us spoke at first, and my feet seemed to be superglued to the floor. His gaze was intense, spellbinding, and I couldn't tear my eyes away from his.

"Natalie," he said, wrapping his arms around me, holding me so tight I thought I might break. But it was actually his reappearance in my life that threatened to break me.

"Ty...how...why... what are you doing here?" I asked, as he released me. I heard a gasp escape Charlie's mouth, her shock as evident as mine.

"I'm the new assistant district attorney. Your sister's case is the first one I am prosecuting in my new role. I'm so sorry...what happened to Jessica was terrible news. I know how much she meant to you."

Nodding my head, I felt faint, and nearly fell into Ty. He grabbed my arms as my knees buckled a little. "Natalie, are you okay? Do you need to sit down?"

I needed to disappear or become invisible—somehow escape this twisted dream I was having. Why now? Why would he come back now? "I'm fine, thanks." Ty was still holding onto me and I could feel the tension rising from Streeter, my protector. "I'm sorry...Charlie, Streeter, this is Ty, an old friend of mine."

Charlie put her hand out to shake Ty's and he released one of my arms to shake it. "It's nice to meet you, Ty," she said with reserve.

Streeter shook his hand too, but didn't say much. He was a man of few words. Ty was holding my left hand at this point, crushing my diamond ring into my fingers. Then he lifted my hand up and looked at my ring. "So, you're a misses now? Some lucky guy has snatched you up."

"Yes, this is Mrs. Mac Carter," Charlie said, going into hyper-protective mode. She and Mitch were a matched set in that department.

"Congratulations, Natalie," Ty said, his green eyes searing me. I had forgotten how devastatingly handsome he was. Even more so with age.

"Well, we better get a seat," Streeter said, no doubt feeling very uncomfortable.

"I guess I'll see you inside," I said to Ty. He released my hand and I began making my way into the courtroom with Charlie and Streeter. The minute we sat down, I knew I was in for it with Charlie.

"So…that's him? The guy who broke your heart?"

"Yeah, that's him. Tyler Latham."

"You said he was good looking, but you didn't mention he had Greek-god status. Natalie… he's beyond gorgeous."

I couldn't speak. I had been so attracted to Ty when I was a teenager. He was my first love… the one I thought I'd never get over. With his six-foot-two muscular frame, green eyes, and dark hair, I figured every woman who crossed his path wanted him. And obviously I was right—Charlie was practically drooling, even though her fiancé wasn't exactly hard on the eyes.

Court came to order, and the proceedings began. I watched every move Ty made and heard every word he spoke, but I wasn't truly listening. My mind had transported me back to the time when we were discussing me moving to the East coast to be together, before my mom had become ill. I couldn't concentrate on anything else, but he seemed completely unaffected by seeing me. Of course, he had been prepared, knowing I would be there. I was the one who had been blindsided, feeling like I was tumbling down a hill and couldn't stop.

I had no idea if anyone could tell that I was present physically, but my mind was somewhere else entirely…drifting on a sea of memories that should have long been forgotten. I could only hope that Streeter didn't notice. I would hate for him to tell Mac that it appeared I was still in love with my ex.

Without warning, the judge hit his gavel on the bench, and court was adjourned for lunch. I didn't move a muscle, because hours had gone by, and in my catatonic state I wasn't even certain of what had taken place.

"Natalie," Charlie said, placing her hand on mine. "Did you hear me?"

"No," I said, shaking my head.

"What do you want for lunch?"

"Oh, um, I guess we could see what the cafeteria has. It would just be easier to stay here."

"Are you doing okay?" she asked, searching my face.

"Um, I'm just a little overwhelmed. Lunch will probably help."

We began to rise from our seats. Much of the courtroom had emptied, and Justin, who I barely noticed, had been taken back to his cell.

As we entered the hallway, I heard Ty calling out my name. "Natalie."

I turned so see him rapidly approaching. "Can I talk to you for a minute...alone?"

I looked at Streeter and Charlie, both with furrowed brow. "It's alright. I'll meet you in the cafeteria."

"If you have an idea of what you would like, I can order it for you."

"Thanks, Charlie. A turkey sandwich or something like that. Or a chicken salad."

She nodded. She started walking away, but Streeter didn't. He stood firm, protecting me.

"Streeter, I'm perfectly safe. You can head down with Charlie."

"I'm on cell if you need anything, Mrs. Carter."

Streeter walked away and I turned to face Ty. "You have a body guard?" he asked incredulously. "What the hell's going on, Nat?"

"It's a long story. An ex of my husband's may be a threat to me, so Mac hired security until he gets everything straightened out."

"Wow, private security. Your husband must do well."

"He's CEO of Carter Industries...so he's wealthy."

"How long have you been together?"

"We got married last week."

Ty's jaw tightened. "Why isn't he here with you?"

"He had to go out of town on business. Is that what you want to talk to me about? Where my husband is?"

"No, I don't care about your husband at all."

"I see," I said, pressing my lips together. "What do you want, Ty?" I asked, all the blood draining from my face.

Ty stood there staring at me for a long moment. "Okay, here goes. I know I don't have any right to say this, but I want you back."

I thought I was hallucinating, like someone had injected me with some powerful drugs and everything in the room was going sideways. "What?" I said too loudly. "You have no rights at all Ty.

My heart belonged to you once, and you threw me away. Now, I'm with Mac. I'm married. Happily. What are you thinking?" I asked, grabbing onto the nearby wall to steady myself.

"Natalie, I know I fucked up. But I still love you and all I want is to be with you," he said, wrapping his arms around me, engulfing my body with his. "You can get an annulment," he whispered in my ear.

I pulled away, but he wouldn't let me go.

"I'm not getting an annulment."

"Nat, it's not like you've been married for years and have children. I'm back. What you've done can be undone," Ty said, with a hint of frustration in his voice.

He finally loosened his grip on me enough to look into my eyes. "I am pregnant with Mac's child and I'm not divorcing my husband," I hissed. "You're always used to getting exactly what you want, aren't you? I love my husband and I want to be with him. You and I are ancient history."

"You don't mean that. You and I are meant to be together. Nothing will ever change that," Ty said, as his mouth moved toward mine. He began kissing me and all of my feelings for him came rushing back. I tried with everything I had to push him away, my hands pressing against his chest. He got the message and let go of me, hurt radiating from his eyes.

"How dare you kiss me? What the hell are you thinking?"

"I already told you what I am thinking. You and me together, like it's supposed to be."

Talking to him was useless and I began to walk away, but he grabbed my hand.

"Natalie…please. Give me a chance. At least have dinner with me so we can talk."

The pleading in his voice made me feel unraveled. I hadn't heard it since he begged me to move to Boston with Jessica in tow. I wondered how different life would have been had I done that. Jessica would still be alive and I'd probably be Mrs. Latham. "Ty, I'm sorry, but there's nothing to talk about. I'm married, that's the end of the conversation," I said, pulling my hand away, and rapidly walking down the hall. To my relief, he didn't follow me. But he didn't have to. I was going to be his captive audience until the trial ended.

***

"Nat." I heard Charlie call out my name as I entered the busy cafeteria. Streeter was sitting at an adjacent table, no doubt feeling uncomfortable with my request to be left alone with Ty.

I sat at the table with Charlie and momentarily stared at the turkey sandwich she had bought me. I opened my purse and took out my wallet, removing a ten dollar bill to give to her.

"Nat, I don't want your money, but I do want an explanation. You look flush and your lipstick is smudged. What's going on? What did he want?"

I sighed loudly. "He wants me. He wants me back." Hearing myself saying the words seemed bizarre. If he had come back a month ago...I put my head in my hands.

"Well. What did you say?"

"I told him I have no intentions of leaving my husband and that things between us are over."

"How did he take it?" she asked, the sound of her voice rising.

"He grabbed me and kissed me, Charlie. He just kissed me."

Charlie opened her mouth to speak, but then closed it. I looked at her, slowly shaking my head. The entire morning seemed like I had entered a fun house, everything was distorted, misshapen, strange to my eyes.

"Nat, this is completely fucked up. Do you still have feelings for him after everything that's happened?"

I stared at my friend who always asked the tough questions. "He was my first love. I think I'll always have some feelings for him."

"Nat, you're going to have to search your heart on this one. I don't know what to tell you."

"I don't know what to tell me, either. I just... . I wish Mac was here and Ty wasn't." I hated feeling such confusion. It was madness. Mac was my everything.

The afternoon dragged on, and I had to see pictures of the accident site as Ty made his case against Justin. I pushed all thoughts of Ty out of my mind, concentrating on my sister and what had happened to her. Keeping the tears at bay was a monumental feat that I didn't accomplish. Charlie held my hand as tears rolled down my cheeks. I wasn't sure how much more of it I could endure.

But what did I want the outcome to be? Jessica's life was over and Justin had destroyed his with drugs. I looked over at Justin, who sat there contritely, staring at the same pictures that were going to haunt me. He was just a kid and this accident had happened out of stupidity, not malice. I wanted justice for my sister, but I didn't want Justin's head on a silver platter. It seemed however, that Ty did.

Adjourning for the day, I decided I needed to talk to Ty about the trial. I asked Charlie and Streeter to wait in the hall for me.

I approached Ty, who was sitting at his table, looking over some notes. "Ty."

"Natalie," he said, a hopeful look spreading over his face.

"I know you have a job to do, but I don't want this accident to ruin Justin's life. He needs help."

"Natalie, the guy is responsible for your sister's death. He needs to pay for his actions."

"Of course, but he didn't murder her. He's going to wake up every day for the rest of his life knowing she is dead because of him."

"What do you want me to do, let him off the hook?"

"No, but you don't have to go for the harshest sentence. I've already forgiven him and..." I trailed off, not finishing my thought. Ty's eyes were piercing a hole right through me.

"Natalie, you have the biggest heart of anyone I know. Only you would forgive the guy so quickly."

"I needed to. I'm going to be a mother soon and I don't want to have anger and bitterness in my heart. I want to be like my mom."

Ty's jaw tightened and he looked at me like I had just ripped his heart out. I just stood there staring back at him.

"I'll take what you are saying under advisement," he said, beginning to put his files into his briefcase.

"Thanks," I said. "Um...I'll see you tomorrow."

I made my way out of the courtroom, relieved the first day was over. Streeter drove us home, the silence making the air in the car thick somehow. I was too exhausted to talk and Charlie probably wasn't exactly sure what to say. It had been a long day.

When we got home, Charlie didn't come in. She offered to take another day off to go with me again the next day, but I told her it wasn't necessary. We hugged and I thanked her for being with me. Streeter checked everything out while we said our goodbyes.

CHAPTER 34: MAC

I had been worried about my girl all day, and hated that I was in London instead of being at home with her, comforting her after enduring such a horrible day. I couldn't imagine what she had been through, listening to the events of her sister's death.

Hearing her voice as she answered my call, made me want to get on the next plane. My girl sounded so sad, and so alone. I had promised her that she wouldn't feel that way again. *Damn.*

"Baby, I've been thinking about you all day. How are you holding up?"

"It was tough, but I managed with the help of Charlie and Streeter. He didn't say much, but he has a good way about him…it was comforting."

"I should be there for you, helping you through this. I wish I was there to hold you right now."

"Me too, baby. I miss you so much. How was your day?"

"It was hectic, but very productive. This merger is going to be a huge asset for the company and we accomplished a lot more than I expected."

"Oh good. I know you've been working on this for a while."

"That's why I couldn't exactly postpone it. It just pains me being away from my bride. I miss you, baby."

"Oh, Mac, I just want this to be over. I need you so much."

"I need you too, Nat. Is anything wrong besides the trial? You sound off to me."

"It's really nothing. I don't want you to worry."

"It doesn't sound like nothing. Nat, tell me what's bothering you?"

"Are you sitting down?"

"Natalie, tell me what's wrong."

"My old boyfriend, Ty, is the new ADA and he is prosecuting Jessica's case."

Son of a bitch. "I see. So, how did he react to seeing you?"

"He was polite, cordial. It was weird at first, but by the end of the day I was over feeling strange."

"Did you tell him that you're married?" I asked, trying not to sound insecure.

"Of course I did. Mac…I love you. I'm completely yours."

"I know. I just wasn't expecting you to say…I don't know. You just caught me off guard."

"I understand the feeling. I thought I was hallucinating when he was walking toward me this morning. But, the trial will be over quickly and I'll never have to see him again."

I hated that she was seeing him at all. "You're going through so much and then to have to deal with him on top of it. I'm sorry, Nat. Listen, I have to go. I have a meeting in a few minutes." *Shit. Not the best time to end a call.*

When I hung up I wanted to get on the next flight out and stake my claim to Natalie. Show the asshole he didn't stand a chance with her. That she was mine. My phone ringing brought me back to my reality.

"Hey, Mitch. What's up?"

"Man, you need to get back here like yesterday. Charlie just got home and she told me Natalie's ex Ty is the new ADA. He made a move on her. He wants her back. Natalie needs you now."

"Natalie just told me about Ty being back, but she didn't say anything happened. What did he do?"

"That bastard kissed her."

"What the fuck?"

"Natalie probably didn't want to upset you. She's so used to handling things on her own. But, I don't think she can handle Ty on her own. I'm worried about her, Mac."

"Okay, thanks man. I'll work on getting home."

"I don't want anything, or anyone, to hurt Natalie…just get home soon."

***

During my meeting, it was hard to concentrate. I just hoped my relationship could survive Ty's return. I didn't blame him for wanting her back. She was kind, loving, generous, submissive, classy, sexier than hell. I ached just thinking about her. I was a little worried Natalie hadn't told me herself about Ty's advances. Either she was afraid of my reaction or…God, I couldn't even fathom that…she wanted him, too.

I had never considered my love wouldn't be enough. I knew Nat loved me, but I also knew that at times, when someone is most vulnerable, like she was at that moment, it was easy to fall into the arms of someone with whom you've had history. She was willing to move across country for the man. *Fuck.* I didn't want to not trust her, but we have had a whirlwind romance. Would she consider leaving me? I willed myself to stop thinking about the worst-case scenario, and focus on what I needed to do to get the fuck out of here.

CHAPTER 35: NATALIE

Waking up to the sound of the alarm was so unwelcomed. I had tossed and turned all night, sleep eluding me. Two men occupied my mind and I was feeling guilty about not telling Mac everything. But how could I tell my husband that my old flame kissed me? That he wants me back? Mac would have flipped out.

Placing my hand on my stomach, I wondered. *Damn it.* I felt so confused. My emotions were running wild and I just wanted Mac to be there with me. I needed his strength, his love, his embrace. I didn't want to face Ty alone. I couldn't be alone with him. I didn't trust my own feelings, because part of me wanted to kiss him back yesterday. The voice in my head—the voice that had always guided my life, my mother—was telling me to flee temptation. Honoring my marriage was more important than my conflicted feelings. I knew that's what she would say to me if she were alive.

My phone lit up. It was Beverly. Thank God, the other voice in my head. Why hadn't I called her?

"Hi Beverly," I said, attempting to sound cheerful, but failing miserably.

"Hi sweetie, I moved some things around in my schedule so I can go to the courthouse with you the rest of the week if you'd like?"

That sounded almost too good to be true and tears streamed down my face. "I.... I would really like that," I choked out.

"Oh honey, it's going to be okay. I promise. Do you want me to pick you up or meet you there?"

"We can meet there. I know I didn't get to tell you this, but Mac hired security. Long story short, we've had a few challenges. His ex-girlfriend visited me at work and sent me dead flowers. She's been a little irrational, claiming she would do anything to get Mac back."

"What? That sounds insane. So you have a guard with you at all times?"

"Yes, so Streeter will drive me to the courthouse. I'll tell you more about it when I see you."

"Okay. I'm here for you, sweetie. Anything you need."

"There is one other thing you should know. Ty is back and he's the ADA trying Jessica's case."

"Holy shit. Are you kidding me? He's back? When did you find this out?"

"Yesterday, when he walked up to me before the trial started."

"Sounds like we have a lot to talk about. I'll meet you at the courthouse, and at lunch you can tell me everything."

"I'd like that. Thanks, Beverly. You had perfect timing, calling when you did. Thank you."

Our call ended and I felt relief. I couldn't have my mom, but I could have the next best thing.

Walking out of our master bedroom, I saw Streeter checking the interior of the house, making sure nothing was out of the ordinary. It was so strange to have another person in my house, there for the sole purpose of keeping me safe. How had my life become so complicated? A month ago I was a single girl. Now I was a married, pregnant woman, with security protecting me from Mac's ex. But who was going to protect me from mine? Ty had gotten to me a little yesterday, and I knew he wouldn't give up easily. But what I couldn't understand, nor truly forgive, was why had he let me go to begin with?

We parked at practically the same time as Beverly. She wrapped her arms around me and held me tight. "Thanks for being here."

"There's no place else I'd rather be."

I introduced her to Streeter and we made our way inside. Tunnel vision overtook me, and I didn't notice anything but the man standing at the end of the hall, looking at me, willing me to come to him.

"Ty, you remember Beverly, don't you?"

"Yes, of course," he said, extending his hand. "It's nice to see you again."

"You too," Beverly responded, shaking his hand.

"I see you still have your guard with you."

"Yes, I do." I had actually forgotten all about Streeter standing a few feet behind me.

"Well, we should make our way in," Beverly said, as she looked back and forth between Ty and me.

I nodded and began turning to enter the courtroom. Out of the corner of my eye I could see Ty still watching me.

During the proceedings, the defense called several witnesses to speak of the good character of Justin, and how much he had cared about Jessica.

When it was Ty's turn to cross-examine, he tore their testimonies apart citing Justin's prior run-ins with the law. I didn't know what to believe. Was he a misguided good guy or a bad boy? I decided I would accept the jury's verdict and not dwell on what was out of my control. It seemed like the trial was progressing much faster than I had anticipated, which was a relief. All I could do was hope for expediency, because watching Ty command the courtroom was, quite frankly, mesmerizing. He was such a good litigator, making points I would never have thought of in a million years.

Lunch was spent telling Beverly all about my interaction with Ty the day before. She didn't tell me what to do, instead she asked me what I was going to do. I loved the woman.

"I'm married to Mac and I plan on staying married to him."

"Let me ask you one other question. Do you have any feelings left for Ty?"

"Feelings left for Ty? Well, I wouldn't want to see anything bad happen to him, so I have friendly feelings for him, sure. I mean, feelings, what difference does it make, anyway? Just because he professed he wants me doesn't mean he gets to have me, or that I want him. So, of course, no feelings. None." I wasn't sure if I was trying to convince Beverly or myself by going on and on.

"I see. So, you didn't feel anything when he kissed you yesterday?"

"Well, I had a physical reaction, but that's only natural. I wasn't happy he kissed me, I wanted to be released, but he wouldn't let me go." I stopped talking, and Beverly and I sat there staring at each other.

"Sweetie, I'm not going to judge you if you felt something for the first man you ever loved. The intensity in his gaze said it all this morning."

"Oh, Beverly. Why did he have to come back? Two days ago, I was walking on air because I have an amazing husband. A man who has done everything in his power to make me happy. The wedding alone…the wedding was the most romantic experience of my life. He has showered love upon me and Ty has ripped me apart, confused me, made me so angry. How could I have any feelings for him?"

"But, you do."

"I know. I'm a horrible person."

Beverly put her hand on mine. "You're not a horrible person. You're a young woman with a difficult situation. But, after the trial is over, you wouldn't have to see Ty unless you wanted to."

"I know," I said in a small voice. Was that what I truly wanted?

We got up to go back to the courtroom. Beverly had given me questions, but no answers. She was helpful, though. She didn't just tell me what to do; she wanted me to come to my own conclusions. I hadn't told her one very important piece of information. I hadn't told her about a little bundle that would be arriving in the very near future.

"I'm going to stop at the ladies room. I'll meet you both inside," I said to Beverly and Streeter.

"Do you want me to stay out here, Mrs. Carter?"

"That won't be necessary. I think I'm pretty safe here in the courthouse."

He nodded.

When I walked out of the ladies room, Ty was standing there, waiting for me.

"Nat, have dinner with me tonight. I want us to talk."

"Ty, I can't have dinner with you. That would be completely inappropriate."

"I don't care about being appropriate, Natalie. I care about having you back in my life."

I rubbed my forehead with my fingers. He was so infuriating.

"So, how do you think this is going to go, Ty? Do you think I'm going to just dump my husband, who I love more than life, because you have decided you want me back? I'm not a teenager. I'm a woman with commitments. I made a promise to Mac, and to God, that I was going to love, honor, and cherish him until death. You're a great guy with a lot to offer, and I know there are a lot of women out there who would love to have you. You can find someone else. It can't be me."

Ty leaned in closer to me. I could smell the familiar aftershave he wore when we were together. "I've been with lots of someone's, but none of them were you. None of them tasted like you, smelled intoxicatingly good like you, felt like you. There's no one, but you."

I thought I was going to faint from Ty's words and proximity. "Um. Ty, you're too late."

"We're both still alive, so it's never too late."

With that statement, he turned and walked back into the courtroom. His words were echoing in my brain. If I meant that much to him, why did he leave me? I didn't think I would ever get the answer to my question. But, I hadn't even taken the time to ask. Would I be satisfied in getting his answer? Did I really want to know how he could just leave me?

The afternoon flew by, and it looked like the trial would be wrapped up sooner than anticipated. I was so grateful. I would be able to put the ordeal behind me, and get as far away from Ty as I could. I hated that he had left me breathless with his earlier proclamation.

Beverly brought me out of my reverie. "Do you want some company tonight? You could come to the house, or I could come over."

"Thanks, but I think I need to be alone. Plus, I didn't sleep well last night, so I want to get to bed early."

When I got home, I told Streeter I was going to lie down for a few minutes. I got into bed and the next thing I knew, it was five in the morning. I hadn't talked to Mac, and I began looking for my phone. I found it on the island, next to my purse. I had several texts from him and three messages. I hoped he had contacted Streeter when he couldn't reach me.

I didn't listen to his messages, I just texted him letting him know

I had fallen asleep and just woken up. Mac replied he was in a meeting, but he had called Streeter when he didn't hear back from me. I breathed a sigh of relief knowing everything was okay with my husband.

Beverly met me again at the courthouse. I managed to duck Ty before going in and taking a seat. I debated telling Streeter to keep Ty away from me, but I didn't want to cause a scene. My resolve when I woke up was very strong, and I wasn't going to let him get to me. If there was one thing I knew, God had brought Mac Carter into my life and given me the blessing of our baby. To give me strength, I kept glancing at the picture on my phone of Mac and myself on our wedding day. Looking at it kept me centered.

Before lunch, both Ty and the defense attorney gave their closing arguments. Now Justin's life was in the hands of the jury. Justin had kept his eyes downcast throughout the trial, showing his remorse over Jessica's death. The whole thing was a tragedy and I didn't know how years in prison would fix any of it. Justin's life would only become worse and I didn't think I would feel any better.

The time had come for the jury to deliberate and the judge dismissed everyone, saying we would be notified when the jury had reached a verdict. I think I was the first one to stand up when the bailiff said, "All rise." I just wanted to get the hell out of there and avoid Ty at all cost. But, Ty reached me as we were walking through the doors to enter the hallway.

"Natalie," he called.

I looked at him but didn't respond.

"I need to speak to you. It's important."

"Is it about the case?"

"No, something else."

"Ty, there's nothing left to say."

"Natalie, I found out some information you need to know. Please, hear me out."

"Ty, I'm done. I've gotta go. Goodbye." I walked away briskly and used Streeter as a wall between us.

"What do you think that was about?" Beverly asked as we walked to our cars.

"I have no idea and I don't care. He's my past and I need to focus on my future."

"Good, honey. You're making the right decision," Beverly said, as she hugged me goodbye.

"Thanks Beverly. I needed to hear that."

***

My things from the condo were delivered about an hour after I got home from court. It was everything but the furniture and Jessica's personal belongings. I had no idea when I would go through her things, but I knew I wanted to do it before the baby came. Having that hanging over my head wasn't the way I wanted to begin motherhood. The boxes had been labeled and put into the appropriate rooms. Unpacking was easy, as Mac had plenty of space for me to put things away. I had the most fun organizing my incredible closet, only filling about a third of the space. It was cathartic to have something to occupy my thoughts and take up some time.

I texted Mac to tell him what had transpired throughout the day. He didn't reply, but I wasn't surprised. He was busy working and I just wanted him to finish what he had to do so he could come home.

The doorbell rang and Streeter answered before I entered the living room. Hearing the voice on the other side of the door, I realized Ty had come to my home.

"Streeter, it's okay. You can let him in." I needed to put an end to this. Immediately.

"Natalie, I'm sorry to barge in like this, but I have to talk to you about your husband."

"What? Why do you want to talk about my husband?"

"Can we sit down? I think you're going to want to sit to hear this."

"Sure," I said, exhaling sharply. Ty followed me into the great room. I sat in a chair, while he took the sofa.

"How well do you know your husband?"

"I don't know how that's any of your business. Ty, just get to the point."

"Alright. The point is Mac had to get married as part of his trust."

I heard the words, but they didn't seem real. It was like everything had turned into slow motion and I sat there, staring at Ty.

"Natalie, did you hear me?"

"Yes. I can't believe you would come into my home and make up a story like that." The look in Ty's eyes told me he wasn't lying, though. I wasn't sure my heart could take it.

"Nat…"

"How did you find out about this?"

"The last couple of days, I had my assistant researching Mac. I know everything about him, including that he had to get married to keep control of his company."

Placing my head in my hands, I felt like I was having an out-of-body experience. Ty came to me and knelt before me. Looking up at him, I whispered, "Do you have any proof?"

He pulled an envelope out of his coat pocket and handed it to me. I looked at the copy of the document stating the perimeters of the trust. He had highlighted for me the area specifying the marriage clause.

I wanted to cry, scream, punch something. My jaw tightened and my heart began racing. The whole time I kept searching Mac's eyes for the truth, believing his sincerity, giving myself to him. I was pregnant with his child. Could I get past this and trust him again? Did he even love me? I had no idea.

"Nat, I'm sorry, but he doesn't love you. He tricked you into marrying him."

Ty managed to scoot me over and sit next to me in the oversized chair. He wrapped his arms around me, my body leaned into his, and there I was, in his arms—exactly where he wanted me to be.

"I love you, Natalie. I just want a chance to prove myself. I won't hurt you again. You have my word."

I didn't respond to Ty. My mind was overrun with thoughts, words, images, uncertainty. I didn't know how I was still breathing. The information on Mac hit me so hard.

CHAPTER 36: MAC

I had one of the other guards pick me up at the airport. I had just walked away from the merger, blown off a huge deal, to come home to be with Natalie. It's what I should have done to begin with. I told Jack Merrick I had a family emergency and I had to go. I didn't wait around to know if he understood or not. There would be other deals to be made in the future with other companies, but I could never replace Natalie if I lost her. I knew, all too well, that family is more important than business.

Opening my front door, I stood there for a minute, not believing my eyes. Was I too late? "Natalie? What's going on? Who is this guy and why the hell is he holding you?" I asked, dropping my bags to the ground. Natalie turned to look at me, despair etched over her face.

Getting up and walking over to me, she handed me a paper. "Mac, I think you need to explain to me what's going on."

I recognized it immediately. Bile rose to my throat and my gut tightened. She knew, and I wasn't the one to tell her, her old boyfriend was. I was so fucked. "Natalie, I can explain."

"Carter, what can you possibly say to explain this?" Ty, who was now standing, interjected.

"This is between me and my wife. I'd like you to leave," I said, as my fists balled up. I wanted to tear this guy apart limb by limb.

"I'm not leaving unless Natalie asks me to."

Natalie stood there quietly, her brow furrowed, deep in thought. I wanted to take her in my arms and make her understand, but I knew it was too soon for that. "Natalie, I didn't know about this until after we were married, I swear. I didn't trick you, I love you."

"When?"

"What do you mean?"

"When exactly did you find out? After Vegas, or after our wedding?"

I wanted to say after the wedding so I wouldn't seem like such an asshole, but I couldn't lie to her.

"I found out right after Vegas, the Monday we returned." I hated the way the words sounded as they came out of my mouth. The look of betrayal in her eyes scared the shit out of me. Why hadn't I told her? Everything was fucked up.

"I see," she said calmly. I wanted her to yell, throw something. Anything, but be calm.

"Natalie, why don't we pack a bag for you? You can come with me, I'll take care of you," Ty said.

If that man thought he was walking out of my house with my wife, he had another thing coming.

Natalie turned to Ty. "So, you want me to go with you? A man who devastated me within weeks of my parents dying? With no explanation or regard for what I was dealing with?"

Ty stood there staring at her, words apparently eluding him. He must have felt like a total ass, at that moment.

"Natalie, I'll explain everything, just come with me."

Staring at my beautiful wife, I noticed a red dot on her chest, coming in from the terrace.

"Natalie, watch out!" I yelled, as I lunged to get her out of the way, pushing her down as the bullet came racing toward her.

We both laid there, me partially on top of her. I then knew what searing pain felt like. I stopped the bullet with my body and my blood was spilling from me.

Streeter immediately returned fire and the shooter fled. He went out to the terrace, but couldn't see anyone.

"Oh my God, Mac, you've been shot," Natalie screamed. "Ty, call 911." Natalie managed to get out from under me and ran to the kitchen for some dish towels. Applying pressure to the wound in my back, tears were streaming from Natalie's eyes. "Baby, keep your eyes on me. Help is on the way."

Even though I was in more pain than I had ever experienced, hearing her call me baby made me feel a thousand times better.

Natalie looked over at Ty. "How long will they take?"

"They should be here in a few minutes. I'll get more towels."

"Mac, I love you so much. Everything is going to be okay," Natalie said, as she continued to apply pressure on my wound. "Please God, please let me keep my husband," Natalie pleaded as tears streamed down her face. "I can't live without him. Please," she sobbed.

I reached up to wipe her tears away. "Baby, no matter what happens, everything's going to be okay. Even if I don't make it you're still going to have a beautiful life. I promise."

"You're not going anywhere, Mac Carter. You're staying here with me, damn it."

Streeter approached. "Mrs. Carter, let me take a look at him." Streeter had brought in scissors from the kitchen and cut the back of my shirt right off. The grave look on his face told me everything I needed to know. I was shot in the back and I didn't know if I would survive, but I felt pretty confident that I may never walk again. But, I'd gladly give up everything to protect my Natalie.

"Streeter?" Natalie uttered. He looked at her but said nothing.

"The ambulance is here," Ty called out. He let them in and showed them the way.

Natalie kissed me lightly on the lips. As the paramedics tended to me, stabilizing me, she whispered over and over how much she loved me.

I began to lose consciousness when being moved to the gurney. Natalie was holding my hand as she walked out with the paramedics. Then, everything went dark.

CHAPTER 37: NATALIE

They got him onto the gurney and began wheeling him out to the ambulance. Holding his hand, I kept talking to him, but his eyes were closed and I had no idea if he could hear me.

"Nat, I'll follow behind," Ty told me. I didn't have the strength to respond to him. I just climbed into the ambulance with my husband, praying he would be okay. He had to be okay. "God, this isn't happening. I've lost everyone. Please don't take Mac, please," I sobbed. There was nothing else I could do.

My phone was in my pocket, so I texted Charlie and Beverly, telling them to come to the hospital. Then I realized Neil's parents were essentially Mac's parents. I didn't have their phone number, so I texted Kate. She replied with the number. I called Mrs. Statton.

"Mrs. Statton, this is Natalie."

"Hi Natalie, how are you?"

"I have bad news. Mac has been shot. We're on our way to the hospital, right now."

"Oh, my God. Which one?"

"Scripps in La Jolla."

"We'll be there, Natalie."

I ended the call. I couldn't say another word. Kate was texting me back, asking me what was going on. I responded with three words. Three words I never thought I would have to type. Mac's been shot.

My phone started ringing instantly. "Nat, we're at the airport right now getting on a plane."

"What?" I asked. The ambulance was pulling into the hospital.

"We'll be there as soon as we can."

"Okay, we're here. I gotta go." I ended the call and got out of the ambulance, following them as they rushed Mac in. The doctors were ready for Mac as the paramedics had called in a gunshot wound. I wanted to go where Mac was going, but they wouldn't let me.

A nurse named Michelle greeted me, and began taking down the information she needed. I didn't really know all of the details, and hoped Neil's parents might be able to fill in any of the missing information about Mac. Ty was the next person to come through the door, followed by Streeter. Neither of them said anything until Michelle stopped asking me questions.

"Mrs. Carter, why don't you take a seat in the waiting room. We'll let you know the minute we have any news."

Streeter extended his arm to me. "Mrs. Carter?" I took his arm and he led me to the waiting room. Ty followed behind.

We all sat down, Ty looking over at me. "Nat, I'm so sorry."

"What are you sorry about, Ty?"

"Everything." He put it that simply, but his devastated face spoke volumes. "Please forgive me for hurting you. I've been such an ass."

"Yes, you have," I said softly, looking into his gorgeous green eyes. "I forgive you, Ty. It's all in the past, anyway."

Ty picked up my hand and kissed it. At that moment, Charlie and Mitch came in. The glare on Mitch's face made me think Ty might soon need a hospital room, too. His teeth were gritted together, his nostrils flaring, his eyes slightly squinted.

"Charlie," I said, getting up to hug her. Then I hugged Mitch.

"What happened? Is Mac going to be okay?" Charlie asked.

"Someone was on the terrace with a gun. I think Mac saw them, and he pushed me down and got hit instead. He saved my life," I said, my voice trembling. I grabbed onto Mitch's arm for support.

"Come here, Nat," he said, giving me a bear hug. "Mac's strong. He's going to be okay."

With that, I lost it and sobbed uncontrollably in Mitch's arms. Charlie had her hand on my back.

"Nat, I'm so sorry, I can't believe this is happening," she said.

When they reached the hospital, Neil's family rushed into the emergency room asking about Mac.

"He's in surgery, right now. That's all I know," I told them, as they each hugged me. We all sat down to ready ourselves for the unbearable wait. While waiting, I explained to them what had happened. Well, as much as I could. It all happened so fast, and I was a little delirious from fatigue and worry.

"I can't lose him. This isn't happening. I should be the one in there. Not him. He saved my life. I can't lose him like I've..." I put my head in my hands and began sobbing again. My entire body was shaking.

I lifted my head and looked at Neil's mother. "Sophia, I'm so sorry. Please forgive me. This is all my fault. I know Mac is like a son to you and he could die because of me." It was like a dam burst and more tears streamed out of my swollen eyes.

"Sweetheart, you didn't shoot Mac, some lunatic did. I'm proud of him for protecting you. I would expect nothing less from him. He loves you more than his own life. You two are so lucky to have found each other," Sophia said, as she grabbed my hand. "We're all just going to have to have faith he's going to pull through this."

Mitch stood up. "I'm going to go to the cafeteria to get some coffee. Can I get anyone anything? Some water or coffee?"

"Water would be great," several people requested at once.

"Great," Mitch said. Then he turned toward Ty. "Ty, is it? Why don't you come along and help me carry the drinks back?" Ty got up, but didn't say anything.

Beverly and Daniel arrived. The moment I saw them, relief swept through me and I practically ran to them, hugging them like my life depended on it. When Beverly asked me what happened, I couldn't speak. I looked at Charlie and she filled them in on the details.

After a long while, Mitch and Ty returned with the drinks. Ty looked like he had been through the ringer during his time with Mitch. His mouth looked grim, held in a tight line, hiding anger perhaps? He wouldn't look at me. Instead, he looked at the ground. It was too much to try to understand what Mitch had said to him, but, I knew I loved Mitch just that much more for his effort to protect me.

"Natalie, can I talk to you in the hall for a minute?"

"Sure," I said, getting up to follow Ty.

"Mitch filled me in on some things, including that Mac didn't know about his trust when he married you in Vegas. I totally fucked up, again. I thought I was doing the right thing by telling you," he paused for a second. "No, no. That's not true. I thought when I told you about his secret you would dump him and come back to me."

I took in what he was saying and my heart broke a little. For so long I had wanted him back, had wanted to hear him say those words. "Ty, I don't know what to say. Until a few weeks ago, I would have done anything to have you in my life again. But, right now, I need you to leave. All I care about is Mac pulling through this, and everything else has to wait, including the fact he kept a secret from me."

Ty put his hand around the nape of my neck, his thumb caressed my face. "If anything changes, I'll be around. I'm not going anywhere. I love you, Natalie."

Kate and Neil walked up as Ty was professing his love for me. "Kate, Neil…why are you here and not in Maui?" I asked, breaking away from Ty, embracing them.

"I told you we were at the airport, Nat. We were coming home."

"I must have missed that. I'm so glad you are here, but why aren't you there?" My head hurt.

"It's a long story. Let's just say…Roger happened."

Before I could respond, two police officers walked up. "Are you Mrs. Carter?"

"Yes."

"I'm Officer Milano, and this is Officer Alvarez. We're going to need a statement about what happened."

"Officers, I'm Ty Latham, the new ADA. I was there when this happened. I'd like to give a statement and maybe you could talk to Mrs. Carter later? She needs to be with her family right now." Ty took out his business card and handed it to Milano.

"Okay, Mr. Latham. Mrs. Carter, here's my card and we'll be in touch if we need any further information."

"Thank you," I said, and Kate, Neil, and I, returned to the waiting room.

Hours had gone by and all we knew was that they had called in a specialist to operate on Mac. I sat there in my blood-stained clothing, just focusing on breathing. Was I losing someone else? Could it even be possible? It felt like a cruel joke, and I was being hit repeatedly in the face by the punch line. Charlie sat on my left and Kate on my right. Each of them held one of my hands. I hadn't said anything for a long time, thinking that if I spoke, everything in the world would come crashing down around me.

Charlie began to speak, but I interrupted her. "Don't say it's going to be okay. You don't know that. None of us know from one moment to the next what can happen."

The words no sooner left my mouth, as the doctor walked through the double doors. I rose to my feet along with Sophia and Magnus.

"I'm Dr. Rosenberg. You must be Mrs. Carter?"

"Yes."

"Your husband is in recovery. He's going to be fine. I don't want to get to technical on you, but the bullet ruptured his thecal sac which is connective tissue that protects the spinal cord."

"Is he going to be able to walk again, Doctor?" I asked, the blood draining from my face.

"He will have some paralysis until the swelling goes down, but he will be walking around in no time. Most likely a couple of days."

"Oh, thank you," I said, hugging the doctor. It probably was not protocol, but I didn't care. This was the man who helped save Mac's life.

Magnus pulled Sophia into his arms. "He's okay, he's okay," he choked out.

I let go of the doctor. "When can I see him?"

"He'll be moved into a room shortly. I'll make sure you see him soon. Hearing your voice will be good for him."

"Thank you so much." Dr. Rosenberg smiled, nodded, and walked away.

I turned to Charlie and Mitch who had stood up beside me. "You guys have been here for so long. Why don't you go home and I'll call you later? You too," I said toward Kate and Neil.

They all hugged me and made their way out of the waiting room. Daniel walked over to me, wrapping his arms around me. "I'm so glad Mac is going to be okay."

"Thanks," I murmured. "Why don't you and Beverly go home, too? I'm sure you're both exhausted."

"We can stay if you want us to," Daniel responded.

"No, I'll be okay. I'm going to stay here with Mac."

Beverly grabbed my hand and squeezed it. "Are you sure, honey?

We don't mind staying."

"I'm sure."

"Call us if you need anything."

"Yeah, go home and rest. We'll talk tomorrow."

The nurse came to tell me we could see Mac one at a time, and he was recovering in room 325. Streeter followed me up along with the Statton's. I went in first. I sat next to Mac, took his hand, brought it up to my lips and kissed it. "You gave us quite a scare, Mr. Carter, but the doctor assures me that you are going to be good as new in no time." Tears filled my eyes, even though I was trying to be strong. Seeing him lying there in that bed was overwhelming. I told him over and over how much he meant to me and I couldn't wait for him to open his gorgeous eyes.

Neil's parents were waiting to see him, too, so I went out to the hall. "I know you want to see him tonight. I'll be waiting out here," I said, squeezing Sophia's hand.

The Statton's went in to see Mac and I stood out in the hall with Streeter. "Streeter, we're going to need more security."

"I've already called it in and Westin should be here with a bag of things for you and Mr. Carter. We had a team go to your home to sweep the place, look for evidence, and pack your things. I've also booked a hotel room for you until we know who's behind this."

I stood there, stunned. I hadn't heard Streeter talk so much at one time. "Thank you, Streeter. How are we going to figure out who is after me?"

"You let us worry about that."

A few moments after the Statton's left, Westin showed up with two bags. I was so glad to have some essentials from home. Going through the bag, I found a pair of jeans, sweats, my long-sleeved gray-knit top, a toothbrush, and some clean underwear. I was kind of embarrassed Westin had gone through my underwear, but that was the least of my worries.

Getting ready for bed, my mind began to replay the events of the day. I lay on the sofa, covered myself with the blanket the nurse had provided, but couldn't fall asleep. It was all too much: the trial, Ty, Mac's secret, and the attempt on my life. My head felt like someone was using a jackhammer on it, and I had to keep telling myself that what had happened was real.

Suddenly, I was being awakened by someone touching my arm. Opening my eyes, Ty appeared with coffee and a bag in his hand.

"Ty, what time is it?"

"It's about seven. I'm on my way to work, but I thought I would stop by and check on you."

"You didn't have to do that," I said, sitting up. My eyes still felt heavy, and the last time I remembered it was two in the morning.

Ty sat next to me on the sofa and handed me the coffee and bag. I took a sip. "You remembered how I like it."

"I remember everything," he said with a look of intensity that would make any girl squirm.

I opened the bag to find an egg sandwich.

"Thank you. You're very thoughtful."

"Well, you continuously occupy my thoughts."

"Ty, you shouldn't say things like that."

He touched my hair, sadness clouding his eyes. "I better go. I'm assuming you won't be in court today, but I'll let you know the verdict when it's in."

"Thank you, and thanks for breakfast."

Drinking my coffee and eating my breakfast sandwich, I sat in silence, looking at Mac and thinking about all the wonderful things he had done to show me his love. Then my mind turned to the trust, and how he knew the day after we returned from Vegas about having to get married. "Oh, Mac. Why didn't you tell me?" I whispered, knowing he couldn't respond. Would I have married him if he had told me? Everything happened so fast and I was swept away by all of his romantic gestures. Then, there was Ty. He still had an effect on me. A heart-pounding, palm-sweating effect. Would I have given Ty another chance if I wasn't married to Mac? I put my hand on my stomach, thinking about the life growing inside me. Moving toward my husband, I sat beside him and took his hand, kissing it and holding it to my face. From the moment Mac put his arms around me on Thanksgiving, I had felt beholden to him, too. But not in an obligated way, more in a way that we were bound to each other, drawn together by a force greater than ourselves.

Dr. Rosenberg walked in and greeted me.

"Good morning, Mrs. Carter."

"Good morning, Dr. Rosenberg. Any idea when Mac will be

waking up."

"I gave him some pretty strong sedatives, but he should be waking up in the next few hours. Why don't you go home, rest for a while, and come back?"

As the doctor asked me to take a break, Neil came through the door.

"He's not awake yet?" Neil asked me.

"Not yet."

Neil and Dr. Rosenberg shook hands. "I'll be back later. You should consider going home for a while, Mrs. Carter."

"I agree with the doctor. Kate is waiting for you at the house. Why don't you head over there and relax for a little while?"

"Okay, thanks Neil," I said, hugging him before leaving.

"Natalie?"

I turned back to look at Neil.

"Mac is completely in love with you. When he found out about the trust, he was going to tell you, but I advised him against it." *Well, I hadn't seen that coming.*

"Why?"

"Because I didn't want you to get in your own way. I could see you two belonged together, but I knew you were scared, and I didn't want you to have a reason to run."

"I see."

"Do you see, Natalie? Mac took a bullet for you. He would give up his life to protect you."

"I know. Why are you telling me this?"

"Because of the man last night who couldn't take his eyes off you. Ty's in love with you, too. Kate filled me in after we left the hospital."

"Nothing has happened between Ty and me."

"But he wants something to happen. The question is, what do you want? You need to figure that out. That is, if you don't already know the answer."

I nodded and walked out the door. Neil had cut right through me and I didn't know what else to say. It wasn't as if those thoughts hadn't already been invading my mind. Did I honestly believe Ty was just in my past? Was that where I wanted him to stay? Was I certain Mac was my future?

CHAPTER 38: MAC

I opened my eyes to a most familiar face…Neil. "Hey man, how do feel?"

"Like I tried to use my body to stop a train."

"Yeah, you were in surgery for a long time, but the doc says you're going to be fine."

"What are you doing here? Why aren't you in Maui?"

"That's a long story. I'll fill you in later. Right now, I want to concentrate on you and why you're in this bed."

"All I care about is Natalie. She wasn't hurt was she?"

"No, she doesn't have a scratch on her. You saved her life."

"Where is she? I need to talk to her. She knows," I said in a panicky voice. Was she with Ty?

"She's with Kate. Before she left I told her I had advised you to withhold the truth."

"What did she say?"

"She asked me why and I told her you two belonged together, and I didn't want her to use the trust as an excuse to not give you a chance."

Fuck. "Did she say what she's going to do? Does she want to be with Ty?"

"No, man. All she told me was that nothing has happened between them."

"Well, I found out from Mitch that he kissed her. Wouldn't you say that's something?"

"Shit…yeah, I would."

"I walked from the merger and came back early because of Mitch's call. When I spoke to Natalie, she told me Ty was back, but she didn't tell me about the kiss."

Neil nodded his approval at my decision. "Okay, so she's guilty of withholding information too," he said, flipping into lawyer mode.

"I hope she sees it that way. I can't lose her."

"I know. I think Kate will get through to her."

A knock on the door interrupted us. "Come in."

"Mr. Statton, I've been able to dig up a lot since last week. Here's the file. Your wife told me where I could find you."

"Mac, this is Dean Evans, the investigator I hired to do some research on Cassie and the marriage clause in your trust."

"Glad to meet you. What did you find out?"

"Mr. Statton was right. It's a forgery. Your parents didn't have anything in the original trust about you being married. I had a handwriting expert compare the original document with the one Harold Brody gave you. There were discrepancies between the signatures."

"You mean this was some sort of scam? Did Cassie plant it or are she and Harold working together?" I asked.

"Cassie is Harold's daughter."

"What the fuck? So they are working together?"

"Yeah, they've done this before. Cassie Montgomery, aka Kimberly Montrose, married another rich man under the same circumstances, a Maxwell Ellington. After a few months, he was in an accident and died. She thought everything was going to her, but a week before he died, he had changed his will and she got nothing. The police didn't have enough evidence to arrest her, so she walked."

"How long has Harold worked for you?" Neil asked.

"A couple of years. I remember him being friends with my parents when I was a kid, so when he came to me for a job, I hired him. I met Cassie not long after."

"I have given a copy of the file to Detective Roberts. He should be coming here to talk to you soon," Dean said.

"So, their plan was to get rid of Natalie, coerce me into marrying Cassie, and then kill me off? This is unbelievable."

Neil sat there shaking his head. "It was just a hunch I had, that

Harold could have given you a forgery. None of it felt right to me."

"Obviously Harold didn't think I would take this to another lawyer. I guess he thought playing the victim card would distract me from having it authenticated, and it would have if you weren't my best friend. You've always had my back, Neil. Thanks, man."

Another knock at the door welcomed Detective Roberts into my hospital room. He filled us in on what had been happening since the shooting. My security team had found blood on the terrace, so they assumed Streeter had clipped the shooter. They also found the shell casing from the shooter's rifle. Cassie and Harold were already in custody, and Cassie had a wound on her arm and gunshot residue on her hands. Evidence confirmed. She was the shooter.

"They're both going away for a long time," said Detective Roberts.

"Do you think there was anyone else involved? I want my wife to be safe."

"Everything points directly to the two of them. We didn't find evidence of any other party involved."

A doctor cleared his throat at the door. "Gentlemen, Mr. Carter needs his rest, so unless you need him for any further police business, I'm going to ask you to leave."

Everyone cleared out except for Neil. "I'm Dr. Rosenberg. It's good to see you feeling up for visitors."

I extended my hand to shake his. "It's good to meet you Dr. Rosenberg. Things have been a little hectic in here since I woke up, but I am very concerned about something."

The doctor raised his eyebrows. "I can't feel my legs. Will I be able to walk again?"

"Oh, you haven't seen your wife yet. The immobility is temporary. Once the swelling goes down you will be able to feel your legs again. Probably a couple of days or so. The bullet ruptured the sac around your spine, but I repaired it. You won't have any problems."

"Thank you," I said. He checked all my vitals and my chart, then took his leave, no doubt going to see another patient.

CHAPTER 39: NATALIE

Kate had a fresh pot of coffee brewing when I arrived with Westin. She hugged me harder than I thought possible.

"How are you holding up, Nat?"

"I'm actually totally freaked out. Someone tried to kill me, I found out my husband had to marry me, or somebody, due to some trust, now he's lying in a hospital bed, my old flame wants me back, and the jury most likely will come back with a verdict today."

"Oh God, Nat. I can't imagine how you are keeping it all together. Go sit on the sofa. I'll bring coffee and we can talk."

I did as Kate told me. I had no energy for anything else. Sinking into her sofa felt cozy. I pulled the chenille throw over me and put my head back. Carrying a tray with coffee-filled mugs, sweetener, and her favorite hazelnut creamer, she placed it on the coffee table and sat next to me. As I began adding creamer to my coffee, Kate asked, "What are you going to do about Mac and Ty? Do you still love Ty?" Trust Kate to get straight to the heart of the matter. She and Neil were so well suited.

"I've been so messed up over this the last few days. I have feelings for both of them and no matter what I do, someone's going to be hurt."

"I think I have a way to help you decide." Kate got up to get her purse. She came back with it and taking out her wallet, she fished out a quarter. "Why don't we let fate intervene? I'll flip this coin and if it's heads, you stay with Mac, tails you go back to Ty."

"What? Are you crazy?" How could I let a quarter decide my future?

Kate didn't respond. She placed the quarter on her thumb, readying herself to flip it. Before she did she said, "Admit it. You want it to be one side more than the other."

"Heads," I said. "I want it to be heads."

"Now, you know," Kate said, placing the quarter on the table.

"Wow," I said, running my hand through my hair. No more second guessing myself. "That was a very dangerous game you were playing."

"But, it told you your true feelings, what you wanted deep down. The man you truly love is Mac."

"I really do. I can't imagine being without him."

"Good. I'm glad we got that settled." I nodded, grateful Kate was being assertive and decisive. That's what I needed.

"Now, as far as Mac having to get married. Nat, he would have married you regardless. He's in love with you. He's demonstrated it over and over. Your surprise wedding," Kate said, beginning to choke up, tears forming in her eyes, "was so incredible. He would do anything for you. Don't doubt his love."

Tears formed in my eyes, too, as I thought about that magical night, under the stars, saying I do to the man I was meant to spend the rest of my life with. "You're right," I whispered. Kate put her arms around me and held me tight, just like a sister, and it felt like things were being set right in my life.

"I need to get back to Mac. He needs to know I love him and want him."

"I'll text Neil and find out what's going on. I put clean clothes and a towel out for you in the guest bedroom if you want to take a shower and change."

"Yes, I could go for a quick shower. Thanks Kate." I made my way to the guest bedroom while Kate was texting.

When I returned, she told me Mac was awake, and Cassie and Harold had been arrested.

"Thanks Kate, for everything. I still want to know what happened in Maui, but…"

"Oh, it's okay. It can wait. Go see your husband."

I hugged Kate goodbye, and Westin drove me back to the

hospital.

Mac's room was empty when I arrived, so I went out to the nurses' station to find out where he was. Out of the corner of my eye, I saw Ty walking toward me. I looked over at him as he approached me.

"Hi, Nat."

"Hi."

"I wanted to come tell you in person, that the jury came back with a verdict this morning. Justin has been found guilty of manslaughter. He'll be serving three to five years depending on behavior. Just thought you'd want to know."

I closed my eyes for a moment, taking in the news. "Thanks for coming to tell me in person. I'm relieved to have the trial over with."

"I have to admit, I'm not. I won't be seeing you…unless… "

"You won't be seeing me, Ty. You'll always have a place in my heart as my first love, but that's it. Mac is who I've chosen."

Ty nodded. "Is it too much to ask for a hug goodbye?"

"Of course not," I said, looking into his sad green eyes. Ty wrapped his arms around me, pulled me close, and held me tight.

"Goodbye, Natalie," he said in a low voice.

"Goodbye," I said, as he released me. Ty turned and walked away. I didn't find out why he hadn't fought for me, but I didn't need to know anymore, because all that mattered was Mac. Mac's love somehow relieved my fear that I wasn't worth the effort.

I found an available nurse to locate my husband. "Dr. Rosenberg was running a few tests, but he should be back in his room by now."

"Oh, okay. I'll check again. Thanks."

I walked into Mac's room. He was lying in his bed with his eyes closed. Oh, how I loved that man.

CHAPTER 40: MAC

I opened my eyes when I felt Natalie's presence, but I didn't think I could conceal the hurt of watching Ty holding her. I thought we had a chance, but seeing them together told me how wrong I was.

Natalie rushed to my bedside, leaned down, and kissed me on the lips. At least I was getting a goodbye kiss. "Baby, I'm so glad you are okay. I was so scared."

"Nat, before you say anything else, I just want to tell you that I understand."

Natalie tilted her head. "I'm lost. Understand about what?"

I almost couldn't get the words out. "About Ty."

"Mac, what are you talking…"

"Let me get this out, Natalie. I know I said I'd never let you go, but I want you to be happy. I saw you two in the hall a few minutes ago. He was holding you, whispering in your ear. I understand if you want to go back to him. I love you too much to get in your way. We can work things out with custody when the baby comes."

"Mac, you are the kindest, most generous, loving man I have ever known. And if you think I am leaving you for one second, you are sadly mistaken." Natalie sat on the bed beside me, picked up my hand, and put it to her heart. "You are the love of my life, Mac Carter. You're the man I want to go to bed with every night and wake up with every morning."

"But I thought…"

"I was saying goodbye to him. That's all. Just a hug goodbye."

I grabbed her head and pulled her toward me, kissing my

beautiful girl. "A million things have been going through my mind. You didn't tell me on the phone that he kissed you at the courthouse. When I came home, he was there, informing you that I hadn't told you the truth… just now he was holding you in the hall. I thought we were over."

"No, Mac, if I have anything to say about it, we'll never be over."

EPILOGUE

The sun was rising as I stared out at the horizon, sipping on the vitamin-packed smoothie Trina had made for me, while Mac was behind me massaging my shoulders. We had been docked in Hawaii since the night before, and were enjoying the view of paradise. I leaned back and rested my head against Mac's chest. He was back to optimal health and the doctor had cleared us to take a long vacation. Mac had scoped out all of the adventures the islands had to offer, and zip-lining was one of them. I couldn't wait, as our zip-lining in Catalina had been the beginning for me in conquering my fears. It had helped me loosen the tight control I had been holding onto in my life.

It had been a several weeks since Mac had been released from the hospital, and another trial was on its way. Cassie and Harold's. They were facing charges of attempted murder and fraud. Mac had paid her a visit in jail, where she communicated her remorse for all she had done to him. He also got her to admit her father was responsible for the murder of Ellington, which made the DA happy, since Mac had been wired. They weren't going to get away with any of their crimes.

Both Mac and I would be testifying, but a different ADA would be prosecuting the case. Ty had recused himself since he knew us, and, as I was a conflict of interest. I wondered if he still had feelings for me, but the answer really didn't matter.

It was interesting that Mac had felt I was going to leave him. I guess, deep down, we both had similar fears of abandonment. We both had felt abandoned by our parents, even though it had been completely out of their control. I had been thinking perhaps we needed to see a grief counselor to resolve those fears, because it was possible it could harm our relationship. Mac had been willing to let me go. Would I have felt the same if the situation were reversed? Those were things we should work on. I knew we would, and I was certain we would be stronger as a result.

In the meantime, the power of Mac's love had completely overwhelmed, and in many ways, transformed me. His attentiveness, his kindness and selflessness, had amazed me constantly. I still grieved the loss of Jessica, but the more I learned to open myself up to my friends, the more I realized wasn't alone, without support, but rather, surrounded by family. A family who loved me very much. Neil's parents embraced me as their own, and I couldn't feel more blessed and welcomed. Watching Mac with Neil's niece, Olivia, had been incredible. At times, funny. But, I know he will be wonderful as a father to our child. We would soon be welcoming our first child. Victoria, if it was a girl, and Aiden, if it was a boy.

Kate and Neil were doing well considering everything Roger had put them through. She continued school, and in her free time, worked with Neil's mom helping the children's charity.

We were all busily preparing for Charlie and Mitch's wedding.

All was well in everyone's lives, so much so, I had to suppress the feeling something would go wrong. Obviously, old habits die hard.

"Mrs. Carter," Mac said, turning my body toward him. "Have I told you today just how much I love you?"

I looked into the eyes of the man who meant everything to me. "Yes, Mr. Carter, but I never grow tired of hearing it." I knew being beholden to Mac was something I would forever be thankful for, and I looked forward to our life together. I was no longer alone.

The End

ABOUT THE AUTHOR

Carlie Sexton has had a passion for reading her entire life. She loves it so that she dedicated her life to educating children. As a teacher, she has had the profound pleasure of teaching children to read and explore their imaginations through a good book. Just recently she decided to write a story that had been on her mind. Now she has several that she wants to turn into additional books. Writing has become a passion that she dearly loves.

Carlie lives with her handsome husband in Southern California. They enjoy the relaxed lifestyle that California provides. They have two dogs, but no children.

You can connect with Carlie on Facebook via her author page at facebook.com/carliesextonauthor, email her at CarlieSexton@ymail.com, or visit her blog at CarlieSextonRomance.com to see what is next on her horizon. If you enjoyed Beholden to You then you will also love to read Kate and Neil's story in The Killer Next Door series~

Fallen for You: http://myBook.to/ffyamazon
Taken by You: http://myBook.to/tbyamazon
Given to You: http://myBook.to/gtyamazon

Please leave a review for Beholden to You on Amazon! Thank you for reading my book!

Carlie